Unkept Promises

THE BEGINNING OF FRIENDSHIP

By Pamela Edge

Published by **Pamela Edge 2019**
Victoria, TX

ISBN: 978-1-7329621-1-8

Dedication

This book is dedicated to my mother who valiantly fought to beat ovarian cancer and my daughter, Jenica, who was killed in a car accident.

Mom, I am so proud of you. Your efforts to fight cancer through your positive attitude and give back to the community grew me as a woman and mother. It also prepared me for my personal fight to stay positive after my daughter, at only 22 years, was killed in a car accident.

My sweet daughter - it still takes my breath away to know I will never hold you in the physical world. But, *I can* still feel your energy and love. I will try each day to find laughter and joy. Because I know, I will see you again.

Unkept Promises is to help others remember to laugh and to find joy in their sister-friendships. As you read my book, dedicate your moment with my words to feeling the joy and laughter I poured into the story. You are so loved. Blessings! Pam

Unkept Promises
The Beginning of Friendship

And Other Secrets of Hormonally Challenged Women-Young and Getting Ripe

By Pamela Edge

Author's Note

In order to understand a friendship's depth, it must be viewed at its conception. Scientists define conception as the moment sperm enters an egg. However, with friendship, there is no sperm or egg doing the mambo Hokey Pokey. A friendship's conception results from some sort of supernatural charge that penetrates emotional barriers. Though this barrier is akin to a rubber, the charge can pierce it with life altering results. Friendship takes on a new life - one that transcends time, pimples, cellulite, and varicose veins.

TABLE OF CONTENTS

Chapter One

Withering Fruit

Dear Granny's Wisdom,

I never realized a man's back hair could make my inner sexual fruit jiggle on my withering vine. Yet, here I am ogling a man's graying full hair jacket as he climbs out of the pool. Why my body has a primal response to Sasquatch is beyond me. When I was in my twenties this never happened. Body hair made me nauseous. But now, I am not able to shake my eyes from his gray fur lined back, and all I can think is —can I braid it into cornrows? I think I am in love. So you might be asking, what advice do I really need? Well, here's my question: Is fifty too late to fall in love at first sight?

Thank you for your advice,
Flat lined inner fruit

I leaned back in my chair and gazed out of my office window, allowing the letter to float to the desk. Who would have thought that a small town's advice column would garnish international attention? The column started with the locals requesting advice from Granny's Wisdom column for things like getting rings off the furniture. Then people, from all over the world, became fascinated with small town logic and also sent requests for advice. Unfortunately, these letters grew weirder and weirder. And now, aging men were making inner fruit jiggle. What next?

I sat up quickly and said, "Wait a minute."

Looking at the letter again, I realized there was only one person who would seek advice about jiggling fruit and primal responses – Julie!

I tapped in her phone number and listened to the ring, she answered, "Hello."

I asked, "So, how's your love connection with Sasquatch?"

Laughter erupted. "Well, Raine, I guess you got my letter. Thank you for asking about my dog! He is doing just fine."

"Ya know, Julie. I almost took your letter seriously."

She responded, "Almost? What gave me away?"

"Basically, you used your dog's name and related fruit to your female anatomy. Only someone who knows Granny could connect human body parts with fruits and vegetables."

Julie asked, "Just curious, what advice would Granny's Wisdom have given me about my withered fruit resurrection after viewing a man's hairy back?"

I paused and let my mind think about Granny advice. "Well, I would have started the column with something about you being too old to go into heat. Then I might have given you the name and number for a good hair waxing salon."

"Very funny, Raine!"

"So Julie, I've got everything ready for your visit. The yearbooks, some wine, and bladder protections in case we laugh too hard."

Julie answered, "Ha, ha. I'm ready. I can't wait to visit about old times and of course talk to Granny."

At forty-five something, my sister-friendship with Julie is stronger than ever. Even though we have aged considerably, we still feel like teens.

My mother named me Raine because it rained the day I was born. Julie was named after her paternal grandmother. Physically, we are exact opposites of each other. I'm about five foot eight, and Julie is five foot even. My hair is brown and frizzy. Julie's hair is blond and straight. I am shaped like a pear, and Julie is shaped like cherry tomato with green bean legs. As teens, we were not knock-down gorgeous. However, with a vat of makeup, our typical appearance vamped into girl next door meets hussy Barbie.

We spent our teenage friendship growing closer through interesting experiences. Strange things always seemed to happen to one or both of us. I am not sure why…but I believe God's sense of humor needed to be sharpened and exercised. Later, when God used humor again, it could be funnier than the first time around. That was not to say Julie and I didn't mind being guinea pigs, but why didn't God use other people for a good chuckle.

As adults we don't live in the same city, but we talk quite often and get together at least once a year. Growing up in a small town has its perks, but excitement is not one of them. Unless you grow up with Granny. Good ol'Granny. Smiling, I wondered what she was doing at home. Hopefully, she was not trying to find a dating app that would accept a woman of her distinction. Shaking my head, I grabbed another letter.

Dear Granny's Wisdom,

I'm writing to you from a small town in Texas. We bought a small amount of acreage so my husband and I could raise our children in the country air. We make a habit of eating on our back porch to enjoy the trees and small creek that meanders through our property. Sounds beautiful, right? Well, we think so too. We have one problem. Flies. Big, fat Texas sized flies that never seem to appear until we bring out dinner. We can't enjoy one meal without flapping our arms to remove the pests. HELP! Any suggestions?

Fly Bombed

I thought about an answer. What would Granny say? It shouldn't not be too hard to channel my inner Granny. Heck, she raised me in Runge, pronounced Rung–eee where the town only has one set of blinking traffic lights. One set blinks red from north to south and the other from east to west. This way a traveler would be forced to stop and look each way at the great town of Runge. To make the town more exciting, our town mayor altered the red light blinking pattern. One week the pattern was blink, blink, pause; blink, blink, pause. Other weeks the pattern was shuffled to blink, blink, blinkity, blink. The mayor liked this particular pattern because it reminded him of country and western dancing, and it added a bit of culture to our small Texas town.

I chuckled, remembering Granny and I dancing to the light. Such a sad day for boredom. For whatever reason, the memory of dancing outside allowed advice to surface, so I typed.

Dear Fly Bombed,

Girl, I feel you. There is nothing worse than sitting down to a nice picnic meal and swatting at flies. I remember one time I drank a swimming fly out of my soda can. Texas is known for lots of things - including flies. You are right about big. You must also live near some livestock. The poop output will compound the problem. Here are some suggestions (although a fly swatter is the quickest way for relief).

1. *Hang bags of water in plastic bags - for some reason the light reflecting through the bag helps discourage the flies.*

2. *Screen in your porch - you are in Texas and bugs happen.*

3. *Take turns eating - one person waves her arms to remove the flies until everyone eats, and then the next person waves his arms.*

Granny

One more Granny's Wisdom response should complete the column. I grabbed the top letter and read:

Dear Granny's Wisdom,
In much of your advice, you reference fruits and/or vegetables. Sometimes it's weird. Why?
Corn-fused

Laughing, I slid my fingers over the keyboard and answered. This question had been asked in so many ways that it was second nature to answer it.

Dear Corn-fused,

I'm not actually Granny. I am her granddaughter. From the age of four, I have lived with Granny. Her unique perception of life influences, actually clouds, the way I handle everyday situations. You see, Granny believes God has a heavenly workshop filled with every type of fruit and vegetable. He uses the fruits and vegetables to serve as models for body types. Some people have lemon heads, carrot bodies, and watermelon butts. Others have squash bodies...just squash...no cherries, lemons, or even cumquats. Granny believes the ideal person has a celery body with a peach bottom-- kind of round and firm, but without the fuzz. The vegetable comparison thing makes sense to me because I compare Granny's brain to a cantaloupe with a few soft spots. So now, I naturally add fruit and vegetable references to life--it just makes sense.

Granny

Chapter Two

Conception of Friendship

Julie arrived in Runge early. She announced her entrance by honking each time she drove by my office window – ten times. The first three times were amusing, but by honk eight, I was not amused nor was Officer Matey. I moved quickly from inside the refurbished 1800's building to the area slightly south of the blinking light. From my point of view, I could see Julie, an approaching officer, and everything else within a mile radius.

The officer flipped on his brightest cherry lights and loudest sirens to garner the attention of the Runge residents. Julie stopped shy of me. I could see her smile in the rear view mirror. I, on the other hand, leaned against the brick wall, folded my arms, and waited for the show.

With the seriousness reserved for escaped felons, the fifty something Officer Matey exited his vehicle. As he passed me, I asked, "Slow day?"

"Raine, don't go sassing the law. You know people can't be driving recklessly."

"Maybe you better draw your gun too."

"You need to remember you are talking to a duly appointed officer representing the legislative system. I will go find your Granny and write her a ticket. She's probably done about five violations of the law in the last hour."

Sighing, I responded, "Aw, Matey, don't get your underwear in a twist. You know I'm just kidding."

"Raine, you are always just kidding. That's what makes you a

11

violation to life itself."

I placed my hand over my heart like he wounded me.

Officer Matey chuckled and said, "I can't continue jawing with you. I have a matter of a nuisance driver."

He swaggered to the car window, peered in and smiled. "Well, Miss Julie. Nice to see you. What are you doing back in Runge?"

Julie must have said something because Officer Matey continued his baseball-like officiating commentary. "Visiting with Raine? Bad to start a visit with a ticket. No, no, I can't let you go with a warning. Remember the last time you were here? You don't? *Well*, I sure do. It's hard for me to forget when you told my mom I searched your lady parts for contraband."

He scratched out a ticket and handed it to her through the window. As he walked past me he said, "Good day, Miss Raine."

"Real nice, Officer Matey. Real nice."

He answered, "I thought so."

He left in a blaze of glory, lights flashing and sirens going.

Julie parked and left her car. She hugged me.

"Well you don't seem upset," I said to her.

"Nah, I'm with you."

"Didn't you just get a ticket?"

"Oh, this paper? No, it's his phone number just in case I want to be searched for contraband. I should let his momma know he's at it again."

"No, Julie, that would not be nice. You know the last time that woman bruised him up pretty good with her flip flops. She may not be able to run fast now, but I think her aim is spot on."

I walked into the office and grabbed my purse. Julie asked, "So you like being a journalist?"

"Please, I'm not a journalist. I'm an advice columnist. Big difference."

"Not the way I see it. People give you news, and you journal. POOF! Journalist."

I shook my head, "Julie, you see things from a weird perspective."

"Hey, you still live with Granny. That's more than slanted. That's more like slanted all ground up, refried with a dash of crazy."

I answered, "Alright, it is odd. At least in your job you get to save the world one student at a time."

"Sure," she said in a trembling tone.

I gave her a sideways glance, and I realized her emotional side was already making its debut.

Julie nodded her head toward the front door of The Runge News.

Taking her hint, we left the building.

Her voice trembled and as she continued talking, "I didn't mean to say 'sure' in a negative way, but the job called to me because of our experiences with Unkept Promises. I never chose the occupation. It's just. Well, after what happened, and what we went through. Teaching chose me. I don't know why I'm telling you this. You already know."

Grabbing her hand, I pulled her into a hug. I said, "I know. Coming back to Runge makes you remember."

It was at that moment the supernatural bond of sister-friendship tightened, causing me to choke on my tears. No matter how long life separated us, our friendship remained constant.

And then we giggled for no reason. Julie broke away and announced, "Let's go to Regina's Grocery to see Sarge."

We laughed again and walked one block to the grocery store.

Officer Matey drove past us, sirens still blaring. He gave us a courtesy nod and continued down the road.

"Where do you think he is going?" asked Julie.

"No clue. He is probably driving to blow out the engine or to let you get a look at him. Ya know he's not that much older than we are. He was a rookie cop back when we were in high school."

Julie laughed. "Is he still scared to check on Granny when her thinking goes sideways?"

"Only when she tells Matey to put his cucumber in the screen door so she can slam it."

"Sounds like Granny."

Julie stood near a Regina's Grocery sign and reminisced, "I remember when I worked here. Hmmm. Seems like yesterday, and it also seems like yesterday when you worked here too. And that's how we met – when you nearly killed me by over misting the produce."

I snorted, "So the water landed on the floor. You should have been more careful when you walked. It was hilarious when you slid on your butt from the cantaloupes to the watermelon section."

"Hilari*ass* my cracked tail bone, but it did bring us together."

"And made me lose my job! I really hated it when Sarge made me hang up my Regina's Grocery apron."

The doors swished opened, and Sarge barreled out wearing the store issued manager's shirt and blue tight knit pants. She grabbed Julie and twirled her in circles. I realized Granny's assessment of Sarge's backside was correct. It did deviate from God's original vegetable inspiration to one with an overabundance of gravity. Her rear measured at least 64 inches across with the middle section sagging causing mashed potato lumps to be showcased like a bad movie. I couldn't keep my eyes off the divine masterpiece. Until Sarge spoke.

"Well, Raine. Thank you! You noticed I lost weight. It's that meat and cheese diet."

Stunned, I batted around comments, appropriate and inappropriate, until I mustarded up, "Yes, you are really looking - -"

Sarge completed the sentence, "good! And I feel good. The twins and I are able to go so many places because I have more energy. Let's go to my inner sanctum of sanity and talk."

I'm sure my right eyebrow moved high enough to swing my hair to the other side of my face. "You mean your office?"

Sarge shrugged her shoulders and turned slightly to issue a creative smile, "You say office, but I say 'temple of clear thinking' or whatever else I can think of."

She opened the metal door and ushered us inside. Not much had changed since we were teens. Julie plopped herself down and started looking at the pictures taped to the walls. I listened to Sarge and Julie as they caught up on lost time. Their close relationship made me feel like a person at a party that was not allowed to eat the refreshments.

A rapid knock interrupted the conversation cadence. A teenage boy announced from behind the closed door, "Ms. Hanks. Ms. Hanks, you are wanted in the refrigerated section. Granny is complaining about the Swiss cheese not having enough holes!"

Sarge smiled and hollered, "Don't make me come out to count the holes!"

"Yes, Ms. Hanks!" he squeaked.

Julie commented, "You know that's why Raine and I call you Sarge. You sound like a drill sergeant."

I added, "No way, Julie. We named her Sarge for two reasons. One, she used to work at a youth camp for the discipline challenged, and two, she was raised as a German shepherd."

The three of us looked at each other and giggled.

A knock at the door stopped our laughter. Once again the teenage worker spewed an update, "I don't mean to interrupt, but Granny is really getting angry. Now she says there are bats in my belfry. What's a belfry?"

"Means nothing. Just leave her alone," answered Sarge.

I asked Sarge, "So your employees call you Ms. Hanks?"

"Only you and Julie call me Sarge. My employees call me Ms. Hanks. You would know that if you did your grocery shopping in Runge instead of going all the way to San Antonio."

"I know, but I have too many memories of the past. I still have a hard time being in the store."

Sarge inhaled. "I get it. But sometimes, the past should not stop us from the future."

Another clanking knock sounded, and Sarge bounded from her rolling chair and swung the door open to Granny's smiling face.

"Well, hello!" announced a smiling Granny. She wrapped Julie in a warm hug. "I missed you so much. Raine told me you were coming. I've washed your sheets. I'm sure you two will be talking all night like you did when you were girls. Don't worry, I won't listen. Maybe. Julie, I saw your mom the other day."

Julie shrank and pulled away from Granny's arms.

Granny asked, "Still too soon for me to mention her? You know that woman pays every day for what she done. Heck, I myself go by her house at least once a month to remind her."

Julie closed her eyes and stated, "Um, thank you. But I wish you would stay away from her. You are more a mom to me than her."

Granny took in her comments and seemed to tuck Julie's words into her heart. With a quickness reserved for only a first string quarterback, Granny went deep and grabbed Julie around the waist lifting her into a spiraling hug. The two twirled twice before Granny released a faint *ffftat* which crescendoed into an indescribable low rumble.

"My eyes are burning!" squeaked the teenage boy.

Sarge's military training kicked in gear. She pushed the young man out of the danger zone. Then with the grace of a ballerina, she scooped Granny into her arms and placed her on the rolling chair. Julie and I watched as Sarge pushed Granny from the back of the store, past the refrigerated section, by the produce, and out of the store doors.

I turned to Julie and said, "Let's go home."

That evening we poured a glass of merlot and reminisced about how we met.

Julie tilted back her glass and licked the remaining fingers of wine. After pouring another glass, she smiled, tucking her hair behind her ear and fidgeting with her earring.

I looked at my friend and said softy, "I know that look. You thought about something. Was it legal or illegal?"

"Legal."

"Well- -."

16

Julie laughed and snorted. "Do you remember how Old Miss Sue Ellen Dawson rolled her grocery cart away so fast she broadsided it into Old Farmer Abner's cucumber?"

"I forgot about that! I remember how he clutched his garden until he nearly made a cucumber salad."

From outside the door, Granny hollered, "That was when Old Miss Sue Ellen Dawson used her power of touch, and she discovered Old Farmer Abner crumpled in a tightly curled ball!"

Julie opened the door to find Granny's ear at the base of the closed door. Julie asked, "Lose something?"

Smirking, Granny responded, "Nah, well, just my hearing. I was having a hard time following your conversation."

I called to Granny, "Come on in and…"

"Nah," she remarked. "I need to start my beauty routine."

After closing the door, Julie said, "Some things never change. So, did you know Miss Dawson tried to perform CPR on Abner? She pushed his head to the floor. Then she placed a lip-lock over his howling mouth. Her dentures shifted, dropped, and rested on Abner's chin."

Granny interrupted, "That's when fear caused Abner to become straight and rigid. When Sue Ellen began compressions, his howls shifted into a higher octave. As a side note, that man deserved that for not taking me to the prom in high school."

"That was a long time ago. Let it go!" I shouted.

We sat quietly for some time. Familiar sounds gathered around us. The tree outside my window rubbed the house as the wind blew. I knew what was coming, and it was the same each time we got together. We reminisced about how Unkept Promises changed our lives. Each reunion, we started by recounting how we met and going through our high school yearbook.

The conception of our friendship began when I lost my job at Regina's Grocery all because Julie slipped through the produce section.

17

Chapter Three

Two Trains Barreling Down One Track

It took me a week to tell Granny Perth about losing my job.

Granny squinted her eyes as she curtly stated, "I'm not surprised."

I must have stared at her wide-eyed and opened mouthed because she popped off and said, "You need to shut your mouth before you drool on yourself. Besides, if you can't clean your room, how can you take care of vegetables? You know this is a small town. You can't burn a roast without the whole town knowing about it. Old Farmer Abner told me about his bruised cucumber at the doctor's office four days ago. You should have seen the bag of ice he held over his garden. Between you and me, that was probably the most excitement that he felt in years. Whole accident probably did him some good."

"Granny!"

"Granny, nothing! Any man who asked Gina Gibson to the prom thirty years ago instead of me deserves to have his cucumber made into a tossed salad."

Then her voice dipped down into an almost guttural tone, and she walked out of the room with her shoulders rounded and legs bowed out like John Wayne. She forgot she was even talking to me. From the kitchen, I heard the dishes banging and clanging. All the while, I heard the constant low rumbling of her voice with intermittent words like 'Abner,' 'prom dress,' and 'slice up his cucumber.'

Granny's mind flipped a switch and a new train of thinking

barreled down her one-tracked mind. Over the years, the town of Runge learned to appreciate Granny for her colorful humor. Sometimes when the world became too cumbersome for her, she stepped into another place where she sifted through her concerns and problems. While sifting, she floured the townspeople with verbal ramblings, which may or may not have had anything to do with the current events. It took a few minutes or days for her to return to the 80's, but when she did, the folks in Runge, all 7,500 of them, breathed a sigh of relief.

I decided to let Granny sift. Since she often forgot what she said or did, it was left to me to explain why the furniture was rearranged, or the kitchen walls were a shocking shade of fuchsia. Often, it was easier to leave and avoid knowing what happened.

I pressed the front door closed and walked away. With no official destination, I played a familiar game: Follow the Leader. In this case, the leader was the biggest crack in the sidewalk. As long as there was a crack, I was safe; the moment the concrete was crack-less, I would have to find and jump to the nearest crack.

My eyes scanned the concrete and fixated on an oversized root which pulled a portion of the sidewalk from the soil. I didn't see another crack for about two feet, so I jumped. I would hate to lose so early in the game. As dumb as it sounded, the task kept my mind focused strictly on the game.

"Raine! Raine!" I heard my name yelled from the corner house. Through squinted eyes, I saw bruised tail boned Julie sitting and rocking on her front porch. With all the large ferns lining her porch, I almost missed her. My body cringed. I felt she was the number one reason I was fired.

Maybe I could walk away and pretend I never heard her. Then I reconsidered the situation. In a small town, someone was bound to be peering out between the Priscilla curtains spying on the neighbors. If I walked away from her, the neighbors would dial up their friends to tell them something like this:

"That rude girl, Raine, you know, Granny Perth's

granddaughter, has gone and ignored poor, sweet Julie. Raine just threw her head up and walked away from her like Julie had developed leprosy."

But if I talked with her they would call and say:

"Sweet Raine, Granny Perth's granddaughter, did the kindest thing. She visited Julie…"

The phone lines would buzz no matter what I did, but at least, if I visited Julie, the conversation will start out on a positive note. Of course, the blabbermouths would become bored with the sweet talk so they would eventually revert to more interesting gossip.

Hesitantly, I walked to Julie, having to concentrate on lifting each leg because they didn't want to go remotely close to her. As I approached, half my mind concentrated on making my mouth smile as if I was actually glad to see her, and the other half pondered what I should say to clumsy Julie.

"Hi Julie," I fumbled my words between my clinched teeth.

"Hi," Julie responded.

I slowly placed my foot on the first step of the porch and asked her, "How are you doing?"

"Well, I'm still quite sore, and it hurts to sit without my donut."

"A what?"

"Donut. It's a blow up cushion with a hole in the center. I sit on it to protect my crack."

"Your what?" I asked.

"You know, my bruised tail bone."

I paused. I needed to clear my mind of an unwanted picture of a crack between her crack, "Oh yeah," I answered.

Julie gripped the chair's arms and lifted. Her face contorted out of reverence for her pain. She lifted one hand off the arm and pulled out a miniature swimming float. It looked so strange I took another step up to get a better look and tripped on a potted plant. My body jerked right and then to the left. As I struggled to regain my balance, I toppled into the ferns. Relief washed over me realizing I was falling into a soft place, but the next second my rear end landed on something hard.

"Ouch!" I screamed.

Julie's mother rushed out, the porch door slamming behind her. "Julie, are you okay?"

"It's not me. It's Raine. She tripped on the plant and fell into the ferns."

Mrs. Twain asked, "Are you alright?"

As I sucked air in and out to keep from crying, I squeaked, "No, not really. My butt's bruised." Reaching down, I gripped a hard mass and lifted out a partially filled bottle of Jim Beam whiskey.

"Daddy, James!" Julie and Mrs. Twain said in unison.

Mrs. Twain quickly grabbed the bottle, opened it, and poured the entire contents into the fern bush. Then she set the empty bottle down on the porch and helped me out of the bushes.

Trying to make a little joke, I asked, "Is that your secret to growing such lush ferns?"

Mrs. Twain forced a polite laugh. While brushing off the fern and ground debris hitchhiking on my pants, she asked, "What hurts?"

By this time, my bottom throbbed as if I had been poked with a branding iron. Rubbing my backside, Mrs. Twain smiled a sad, sweet smile and answered, "I know just the thing to help." She picked up the empty bottle and walked inside, slamming the screen door. From the porch, I heard the bottle hit the side of a metal garbage pail and the creaking of the wooden floor planks as she returned with another donut.

"Here, sweetie," stated Mrs. Twain, as she placed it on a rocker next to Julie.

"Mom, this is Raine," said Julie.

"Yes, I have never officially met Raine, but I have had several interesting encounters with your Granny Perth. How is she doing?"

"Fine…except she's having one of her spells today."

Julie's mom shook her head and replied, "I guess I won't call her to let her know about your mishap. Maybe, after some rest, you will feel well enough to walk home."

Nodding my head, I sat down on the donut. It took me a little while to lift up and down to shift the donut to a comfortable spot. I heard Julie snicker and then cough to cover it up.

At first, Julie and I listened to the crickets chirping their nightly greetings. As the minutes ticked by, I decided even though we really hadn't said a word to each other, maybe Julie was not so bad after all. I didn't know it then, but falling into the bottle minefield was the best thing that could have ever happened to Julie, and me.

Our superficial conversation continued even as the lightning bugs started firing up their backsides, beckoning to the other bugs to come out and play.

"Do you think the lightning bugs need to sit on donuts after a night of butt-beeping?" asked Julie.

"Only if they slip, fall, and slide from the front yard to the backyard," I replied.

"Ha, ha," Julie responded with a tone that could melt cheese in a freezer.

We ended up giggling so hard we entered the 'wet crotch panty zone.' No matter what we said, laughter erupted and out seeped a trickle of tinkle.

"Enough," Julie said, squeezing her lower cheeks together to stop the flow of wetness.

I, on the other hand, had a different plan to dry my cotton panties. I pumped my legs back and forth to allow the evening air to squeeze in and dry my underwear. We sat in silence for quite some time, Julie squeezing and me pumping my legs.

Granny Perth has always said that a new friendship must be treated like a new fruit tree. Pruning, watering, and listening to its needs created healthy growth and mature fruit. In this friendship, I had already watered her, causing her to fall. Now we needed to prune our friendship to make it grow. This could only be done by swapping stories about past experiences. Julie would either think I was weird, or she would share an experience herself. By listening and pruning our past, our friendship would grow. I took a deep breath and began:

"Did you ever have Mr. Schmitt for seventh grade science?" I asked.

"No, we hadn't moved to Runge yet."

I responded, "That's right. I forgot. Well, Mr. Schmitt was famous for reacting to what he thought he heard."

"Huh?"

"His hearing aid was never adjusted properly so he used his eyes to track the things he heard. When a sound from the back of the room finally made it to his ears, his would track it and react to what he thought he heard, which made for interesting lessons."

"Ahh, I understand."

"One day, when we were dissecting frogs, the formaldehyde made my nose trickle. Not to be too graphic, but it was like water draining out of a faucet. I had no way of stopping it because I was wrist deep in frog guts, so I sniffed it to avoid dripage. Every time I sniffed, my lab partner Rudy McGarza echoed a sniff. As the class mimicked the "sniff" it reminded me of a new rendition of *Old McDonald had a Farm.*

Mr. Schmitt cocked his head from left to right listening to the sniff, sniff here and the sniff, sniff there. When he bellowed 'God Bless You,' the class answered him with laughter, which ricocheted down the hall bouncing off the metal lockers. I think Old Schmitt realized his mistake because he folded his arms and announced:

"Whoever lost their manners needs to be ashamed. If you must, please go to the bathroom. And shame, shame on the rest of you for trying to smell the rudeness."

Laughter poured out of Julie. In between the hee hee's and ho ho's, she grimaced.

"What's wrong?" I asked.

"All this laughing is making my tail bone hurt. Please stop…I need to rest," sighed Julie trying to regain control.

I stopped speaking and allowed the night noises to hug us. I glanced down the street and saw the blue glare of the television sets radiate from the windows like night-lights.

"I guess I better check on Granny. Maybe her mind is focused again."

Julie nodded, "I hope I see you at school tomorrow."

I nodded in agreement and waved goodbye.

I walked home. For a few minutes, I waited outside my house. The moon allowed just enough light to illuminate the area. The house looked haunted. Moon beams accented the years of junk scattered on each side of the garage. The junk, meant for recycling, was a reminder of forgotten good intentions.

With a deep sigh, I mentally put on my big girl panties and entered the house. "Granny, I'm home!"

Not hearing a response, I traipsed to the living room. Peeking from the doorframe, I saw Granny in her La-Z-Boy recliner. She had settled down into her "normal" evening routine. A shower curtain covered her body, leaving only her head exposed. She had smeared smashed avocado on her face and covered it with the avocado peel. This was to seal the vegetable's natural oils into her skin. She believed this nightly practice reduced wrinkles. In my opinion, it was a miserable failure and a total waste of what could have been guacamole. AND, Granny still had enough wrinkles to pull above her head and make green-tinted bunny ears.

With the television blaring, *Gunsmoke* could be heard from Dewitt County to the other side of the Rio Grande. I always liked watching Granny when she stared at the old western series. Beneath the shower curtain, I watched her hands pop up and down during the fight scenes likes she was going to help Marshal Dillon and Festus fight the bank robbers or whatever scoundrel entered Dodge City.

When Granny saw me, she carefully got up and turned the television down. Then she returned to her recliner. I knew I was in for a lengthy conversation because nothing ever came between her and Dodge City.

"Sit Julie, I mean Raine."

You didn't have to be a rocket scientist to know someone lip-locking the gossip brigade had telephoned Granny.

"Who told you I was at Julie's?"

"You know you can't fart without someone wanting to light candles at St. Phillips Catholic Church. Besides, that doesn't matter. The fact is you were at their home. You really need to be careful."

"What do you mean?"

"Mr. Twain can be a mean drunk..."

"Ya, I figured that one out when I fell on it."

"What? You fell on Mr. Twain? Did he hurt you?"

"No, I really fell on Mr. Jim Beam."

I gave Granny a quick summary of Mr. Beam, the bruise, and the donut. Granny smiled and tried not to laugh, but the amusement of the situation caused her face to break into a marathon of smiles. The avocado mask cracked into rivers of lines that made green chunks plop on the shower curtain. Granny declared, "Now you have done it. My face will not be soft for Dr. Pooley."

"Granny, that's a baby doctor. You are not..."

"No baby here," Granny stated, rubbing her rolls of fat. "I have my celebration of womanhood. You know, the yearly scraping of my inner fruit."

"Granny, stop. I don't want to know anymore."

"All right dear, but that's the only way to check for bad spots—always remember, bad spots develop into rotten fruit."

"Ewww. Stop Granny!"

Chapter Four

Slackers

The next school day was uneventful until the P.E. class. Twenty-five girls entered the locker room to begin dressing out for an hour of exercise and an introduction to basketball. It always amazed me the way the girls stripped down to their underclothes and then pranced around the locker room asking the other girls for deodorant or feminine hygiene products. Why anyone would share roll-on deodorant always bothered me. Just thinking about using it after someone else rubbed it on their pits made my stomach turn.

The girls with the oversized cantaloupes paraded around the open areas of the locker room while I, with my lemons, remained in the shadows of the back lockers not wanting my fruit to receive too much air time. Finally, the coach popped the door open a few inches and boomed, "I want everyone out here in two minutes!"

That was when the girls rushed around looking for their blue pin-striped uniforms. When we scrambled out of the locker room, we looked like female prisoners. The only logical reason behind the barbaric uniforms was tactical; the coaches could spot us in seconds if a student tried to skip class.

Old Coach Kernel Corn began class with a tweet of his whistle. The second tweet meant for us to get in our regular spots and begin exercises. The routine started the same way: stretches, jumping jacks, followed by crunches. Coach Kernel Corn, whose real name was Coach Whipley, stood in the front of the rows directing exercises by blowing his whistle. In the middle of the second set of windmills, I noticed Julie sitting on her donut in the bleachers. I

26

hadn't realized until that point that she was in the same physical education class. I pretended to have a pulled muscle and limped to her.

"Hey," I said. "I guess I didn't notice you in this class before."

"Not many people do," Julie stated. "Speaking of noticing...have you ever noticed how the girls with large ta tas are in the front of the class?"

I looked at the class and realized she was right. The P.E. class was arranged with watermelons in the front, and then cantaloupes, with cherry tomatoes rounding out the back. I responded in a whisper, "My how Coach Kernel Corn loves his fruit."

"Excuse me?" she whispered back.

I explained Granny Perth's belief in the fundamentals of fruits and vegetables in the creation of man. Julie listened and glanced at my lemons and her pears.

Julie said in a thoughtful voice, "Kernel Corn sure likes to watch those large fruits bounce."

Our sudden burst of laughter rebounded off the gym walls. A rapid fire of whistles followed our laughter. Coach Kernel Corn ambled over to us with his oversized belly swaying right and left. His voice roared, "Just what do you girls think you are doing?"

As if we couldn't hear him, he repeated himself, but this time he got in our face. As he grumbled, his coffee breath bathed our skin, "Just what do you girls think you are doing?"

For some reason my eyes never left his overlapping teeth which caused a yellow tooth to stick out like a corn kernel, so I responded, "Huh?

That one word landed Julie and I in the principal's office. We read our referral as we walked side-by-side to Principal Dander's office. It stated we had no regard for authority and interrupted the learning process. That part made us laugh.

At this point Julie began snickering and asked, "What did he mean by learning process? If we went back to ask, I don't think I could keep a straight face as his lips slid over his corn kernel."

I whispered back, "Me neither. I'm sure he was just peeved that he couldn't continue his active monitoring of fruit cups."

Even though we tried to remain upbeat about the impending doom, Julie's body reflected her fear. Her shoulders tightened in unison with her fists. She reminded me of a virgin as she walked towards a ritual sacrifice.

Who was to say what her parents would do to her. Granny would probably do a little verbal tap dance all over my head. That would be the worst of it, but with Julie's father…

We arrived at the office and sat down to await the school's version of the criminal justice system. My eyes scanned the room and noticed several pictures of Principal Dander. In the first picture, he looked about twenty-five. He stood frozen, tall, and proud as if he could conquer the world. There was a close up of his face, showcasing his dramatic cleft chin, and one of his nostrils was bigger than the other. His later pictures projected a dramatic change. His stomach went from flat to the size of a giant squash while also losing 98.5% of his hair. The remaining 1.5% stuck out of his head as a tragic reminder of his youth. The secretary cleared her throat and announced, "Principal Dander is ready to see you." Entering the office, we heard the secretary telecom Principal Dander.

"Sir, your wife is on line 1."

He mouthed the word *crap*.

Even though the word never left his mouth, it wasn't difficult understand his French. He began to write. I sat a little taller and watched him script a laundry list of items.

1. hair spray…max hold
2. toothpaste…gel, not paste
3. vinegar
4. enema
5. shredded cheddar cheese.

He added a few more items to his grocery list and read it back to his wife. As he read the list, he pawed his balding head like a

28

security blanket. His voice sounded beaten and sad.

He clamped the phone on the receiver and looked out of the window.

His head swiveled to face me. The cloud of doom erased, and a light flickered across his face.

In an almost sing-song voice he asked, "How are you doing?"

"Fine."

"How's your mom?"

"Fine."

"Granny doing okay?"

"She's fine."

Our conversational ping-pong unnerved me, so I coughed. His eyes never left me. I coughed again and ended with a grand faux sneeze. Julie giggled at my lame attempt to divert his attention, but concern riddled his face. He grabbed a tissue and extended it.

A bit of guilt hit me. I took the tissue and blew. Air filled the tissue, but I surprised myself when an unexpected plug of snot plastered the tissue. It pleased me to find my acting job appeared real.

Principal Dander turned his attention to Julie. He asked, "How's your family?"

She answered, "Fine."

Shifting his attention to the discipline referral, he read silently. This left me with time to look around the room. More pictures lined the wall. Most were of his wife and two children. It made me nauseous to think Mr. and Mrs. Dander made two Dander children. I wondered about the combination of the giant squash and string bean to make little Danderlings. In the most recent pictures, he stood in direct contrast to his wife. Her green bean shaped body seemed hidden by his squash. Next to the veggie portrait were two children, Marian and Kimmi. The oldest, Marian, was my age. Her definition of fun was verbally fighting and smacking others. I had only had one run in with her – and that ended with her ramming a pickle between my eyebrows. My eyes still stung from the salt. However, Kimmi made me smile. She seemed happy and wanting to please others. This must be a thorn in Marian's side.

Principal Dander cleared his throat and brought me out of my visualizing. He shuffled a pile of papers and looked at us. Reverting to his normal deep authoritative voice, he spouted a memorized speech about the importance of learning. In fact he continued his monologue even while signing papers and shuffling through other paperwork.

Finally, he paused and announced, "You girls have a week of detention. Report to Ms. Prine's room at 3:30."

So from 3:30 to 4:30 each day, we sat with a group of "slackers," which was what Ms. Prine called us during the hour of torture. Julie and I learned a lot in detention, but it had nothing to do with following the rules.

Ms. Prine started detention with roll call. Peering over her half glasses, she said, "Jess, Jess Montez, say here if you are here."

From the back of the room Jess said, "Here."

Ms. Prine continued, "Rudy McGarza?"

"Yo."

Ms. Prine grimaced. She slicked back her stray hair and cleared her throat. "Mr. Slacker, you will say *here* not *yo*. Until you address me with respect, I will not be able to respect you."

Rudy forced back his smile and responded, "Yes, ma'am."

There were only six of us in detention so why she had to take roll in a military fashion was beyond me.

Ms. Prine continued, "Julie Twain? Julie? Julie Twain?"

Why wasn't she answering? I looked at Julie. Her eyes were locked with Jess Montez's eyes. To break the bond, I pushed her arm.

Julie gazed forward answering, "Oh, Miss I'm here."

Once again, Ms. Prine grimaced and reminded the group, "Students, you will address me with respect. So please use Ma'am or Ms. Prine."

This was going to be a long hour. The rest of us "slackers" answered "here" as commanded by the detention master. Despite the rough beginning, the rest of detention was more revealing than irritating. We learned several things attending detention, and it wasn't what was intended.

The first thing Julie and I learned was Ms. Prine fell asleep after ten minutes of lecturing us on the basics of overcoming our "slacker" disposition. For the next fifty minutes, we spent detention exploring how far we could push our luck.

The second revelation was Ms. Prine's hair could hold about 17 miniature spitballs before she flipped her hand like she was swatting at a mosquito.

Third, Rudy McGarza's last name was a reflection of his parents' strong belief in their heritage. Mc was directly from his mother's Irish ancestry, but Garza was from his father's Mexican American ancestry. Of course, my big mouth had to ask what he would do if he married an Italian woman with the last name of Rossini—use the last name-- McGarzini?

Fourth, Julie and Jess Montez fell in love at first detention. By the second day of detention, they were an item. On the last day, right after Ms. Prine broke into a solo of ZZZZZ's, they had picked a date for marriage.

I learned one last thing. Not all monumental events occurred like at a romantic movie. I've always dreamed of my first kiss. Soft music would play. He would brush his hand across my cheek. As our lips would touch, a tingle would shimmy from my nose to my toes. The soft movement and delicate lip pressure would ignite emotional fireworks.

When the moment actually happened, it was not glorious. I looked at Rudy. He looked at me. Rudy asked in a deep voice that produced a squeak at the word kiss, "You want to kiss?"

I tried to appear nonchalant when I replied, "Sure."

We ducked beneath a desk – and it happened. My first kiss was like a Great Dane licking my face. When I pulled away from his lips, spit strings clung from his lips to mine like hot mozzarella cheese.

Apparently, this was Rudy's first kiss, too.

He wiped his mouth and whispered, "That was interesting."

My mind whirled. THAT'S *how* he described it? I paused to see if he produced string cheese without a partner.

"Interesting, for sure," I answered, while trying to keep from barfing.

It was a mutual decision to keep the spit swapping experience a secret. My life lesson: virgin kissers yielded uncomfortable results and large amounts of spit.

Chapter Five

RSD – Sex in the Hall

A week later, it was Runge High School's turn to host the quarterly RSD – Rural School Dance. In a rural community, the school population ranges from 50 to several hundred. With several rural schools coming together, each dance had a nice crowd.

Julie and I decided to attend the RSD. Right after school, we met at my house. We prepared for the dance by leafing through "Good Housekeeping" and "Seventeen" magazines. They were the only magazines we had in the house, so we maximized every advertisement using female models. I tore out the ads, and Julie taped them to the bathroom mirror. Of course, she left just enough room to see ourselves. Then we puzzled our dance faces together. One ad would be our muse for eye makeup while another for lip color. Rip, tape, piece - and Voila! Our personal primping began.

Julie said, "Mascara."

I handed it to her and said, "Eye liner."

She handed it to me.

We ping ponged our makeup requests like a surgeon requesting instruments. Finally we stopped and stared at the results in the bathroom mirror.

Julie wrapped an arm around my shoulder and said, "We look like Playboy Bunnies without the boobs."

"More like Dodge City saloon girls trying to get an edge on the competition," came Granny's comment from the doorway. "Now girls, let me show you how to apply makeup."

Granny wiped off our facial canvases. Then, she taught us the finer rules of makeup application. From beneath the bathroom sink,

33

Granny pulled out a leather bag and rummaged through it. Metal clinked against metal and paper rattled and crinkled. Her hidden treasure? Tweezers. Holding them like a trophy, she said, "They're a girl's best friend."

"…more like an instrument of torture," I said as Granny plucked and plucked and plucked.

Each yank made me grimace, especially when the tweezers tweezered skin. I yipped and said, "How is this going to make me look good for the dance?"

Smiling Granny said, "Raine, by removing the excessive hair it will make your eyes appear bigger and brighter. No one wants to see eyes masked by a bush."

Julie snickered.

Granny turned and announced, "You're next."

"Yikes."

An hour later, our hair and makeup looked great.

"Granny, how do you know so much about hair and makeup?" Julie asked.

"Girls, I was young once. There was a time when I was the best looking girl in Runge. Unfortunately, Abner was blinded by Gina Gibson's looks - that slut in pumps."

Once again, Granny started rambling about the high school prom. She left the room, slamming the bathroom door. I shrugged my shoulders and slid a finger through my hair.

Julie smoothed her hair again before suggesting, "Hey, Raine, let's see who can dance with the most guys. The loser does the winner's homework for a week."

"Don't you think Jess would be upset?"

Julie smiled, "Nah, he'd think it was funny. And if I won, you would be doing my homework, so I would have more time with him."

I thought about it and wondered, "Sounds okay, but do pity dances count?"

Julie asked, "What are pity dances?"

34

I explained, "Girls dancing with ugly boys, and good looking boys dancing with us."

"Are you saying we're ugly?"

"Nah, just not attractive to stupid good-looking guys."

An hour later, we arrived at the Runge gym. Wanting to win, I scanned the crowd for guys. My eyes caught a boy staring at me. Then he winked. Cool, I thought. I walked towards him, and he winked again. This guy must really like me I thought. A song hit the airwave about girls just wanting to have fun. The triple tap of the music made me just want to dance, so I grabbed his hand and headed towards the dance floor. He pulled back hard enough to make me feel like I was pulling a wagon. I thought he was shy, so I pulled harder. On the dance floor, I turned towards him and started to dance. He winked at me and danced too.

The song ended, and we walked back to where I first spotted him. Along the way, big, hulky looking boys kept greeting him with, "Hey, Winkie."

Smiling, I walked away from him. He winked and turned to his friends. That's one dance for me, I thought.

"How did you know Winkie Johnson?"

I turned towards the questioning voice and saw Marsha Greeves. I asked, "Huh?"

"How did you meet Winkie Johnson? He's Yorktown High School's best football player."

"We just met. When I walked in the gym, he winked at me so I thought he wanted to dance with me."

Marsha laughed so hard her mule-like teeth protruded, and her braying squeal exploded, causing heads to turn our way. Finally she said, "He wasn't winking at you. He has a twitch that makes him look like he is winking. That's why he's called Winkie."

At that moment, I realized I was his pity dance. I'm sure my face turned red, and I decided the dance contest was not in the best interest of my self-confidence.

I looked around to find Julie. I saw her dancing with a guy almost three times her height. Her short stature made his height look even taller. Despite the visual oddity, the guy could dance. In a way, he was the best part of the evening because his movement showed that he cared about the music's beat.

Finding an empty chair, I sat and waited for Julie. She went from dancing with Mr. Too Tall to Jess Montez's arms. "Lady," by Kenny Rogers filled the gym. Jess wrapped his arms around Julie in an embrace fitting for a romantic movie. Mrs. Watts, a dance chaperone, spotted the body contact. Her lipstick sat perched on her lips like a fish nibbling bread from the water's surface. Scary! I was not sure whether she was going to speak, bite, or spit. Mrs. Watt tapped them on the shoulder, and the two parted about six inches, but as Mrs. Watt, aka fish-lips, left the two closed the distance to zero.

I didn't want to stay at the dance. The pity dance had sucked out the fun. It also frustrated me to see Jess and Julie falling deeper in love. I watched as Jess brushed away Julie's hair from her face and went in for a kiss. Julie dodged his lips playfully, but Jess placed a hand on the side of her face and calmed her playful movements. Their lips touched. I looked above their heads to see if fireworks erupted, but only dust motes shot through the DJ's colorful dance lights.

Why not me? Why couldn't I find a boyfriend? Am I that bad a person that I can only have pity dances? For that matter, would kissing always be so disgusting? I felt like screaming, so I went to the restroom. It was not a great place to hide from the world, but it worked in a temper tantrum.

The second stall was always my favorite. Most people want the last or first. I have always felt there would be fewer germs or cooties in this stall. I did not need to pee but wanted to sit, so I added a double layer of toilet paper on the seat and sat.

To pass the time, I looked around the stall. I spotted four screws in the upper right corner but only three on the bottom corner. Several portions of the metal walls areas contained scratched messages. I ran my fingers over the scratches. I thought, what did they say? How long ago were the scratches made? I used my fingernail and scraped away the remaining coats of paint. The first word was Phyllis. With a bit more peeling, I unearthed the word loves. My pointer nail dulled, so I used my thumbnail as a paint scraper. The last word was not really a word but the initials of PD. I laughed to myself. Who would name their child Phyllis? Then it hit me. Granny named mom, Phyllis. I mentally hit myself on the forehead and called myself a putz.

I continued looking and spotted several wayward mop strings caught in the bottom stall screws. The strings had about an inch of dust, so much for the second stall being the cleanest…

The door to the restroom opened, and two girls entered. A girl with a high babyish voice said, "Can you believe it?"

"I know," answered the nasally voice.

The babyish voice giggled and replied, "I don't think they even knew we were watching."

"I know," answered the nasally voice.

Baby voice continued, "Wrong, just wrong. No one should be rolling around the hallway like animals doing the nasty."

This was getting to be interesting, so I leaned forward. I peered through the crack between the door and the hinge, but between being nosy and my desire to be comfortable, the toilet paper shifted and one cheek dangled from the seat. I lifted and settled my butt fat back on the throne.

The slight gap of time caused me to miss a portion of the conversation, and who was speaking. I thought, who was doing the nasty? Curious and tired of playing toilet stall Peeping Tom, I left my refuge and reentered the main section of the gym. Only a small number of students and chaperones remained. Most of these people were sweeping, wiping tables, or taking down decorations. I scanned the gym for Julie's blue flowered dress but scored a zero. I popped my head out of the gym doors, but Julie wasn't outside.

After giving the gym a perfunctory glance, I decided to check the main section of the school building. I'm not sure *why*, but I had checked everywhere else. As my heels tapped the hall flooring, echoes bounced off the lockers. I felt like I was in a haunted movie. The silence between taps increased my stress level by four thousand percent. I turned quickly to see if a shadowy ghoul was about to rip me a new one. Heightened by fear, my hearing edged towards supersonic. I could probably hear a rat fart through a pillow at about 100 yards.

That's when I heard it…a metallic clank followed by another and another. Curiosity overpowered my fears, so I traced the sound and worked my way deeper into the school. With each step, my mind whirred with a possible reason for the noise. Not for a moment did I believe I would find flowers – blue flowers with a boy who looked like he was sniffing the bouquet. Even with her dress over her head, I could see a sprout of Julie's hair smacking the metal locker. My mind replayed the words "...rolling around the hallway like animals doing the nasty."

With the sound puzzle solved, I tried to understand *who, what, where, when, how* and *why* this was happening. Okay, so I knew *the who, what, where, when, and the how...but WHY*? **Why** were Julie and Jess doing the nasty in the school hallway?

The clanking stopped and the flowers shifted. Julie said, "Hey, Raine."

"Hey is all you can say to me? I have been looking everywhere for you and all you can say is hey? My gosh, I find you getting a concussion and all you can say is hey? Would you have said that to Principal Dander or a dance chaperone if they had found you? Oh yeah, I can hear it now. Hey Principal Dander, I want to audition for the marching band using my skills as a head banger."

"Raine, stop."

"Stop? Now there's a word you should have used earlier. I'll tell you what. The minute you stop using one or two words to speak to me, let me know. I'm leaving. Ya know. There were two girls talking about someone doing the nasty. I'm guessing they were talking about you, so did you charge for the show?"

Julie sighed, "Raine, stop!"

I shook my head and said, "Again with the two words…Here's my last two words: See you."

As I walked away, I turned to look at Julie and Jess. Her face reminded me of someone caught picking boogers, and Jess' face just flat out looked goofy. He was about as attractive as a Great Dane itching his balls with a toilet plunger.

Chapter Six

Yahtzee

It had been several weeks since the dance. I saw Julie and Jess around school, but I kept away. Rumors about the "nasty" traveled on the gossip vine until there was not much to tell anymore.

After school, I walked home the long way. Not that there is a lot of distance to go the long way in Runge, but it allowed me some think time. Julie consumed my thoughts. At school, I caught Julie watching me. It seemed to me she wanted to talk…maybe even say she was sorry for… That's when it hit me. SHE was the one who made a bad decision, and it had nothing to do with me. Maybe I was being overly sensitive about it. But why did I feel so upset? I knew doing the nasty was wrong, especially with an audience. Why did I feel angry? At that point, I decided to let it ride. I needed to move on. I had to…otherwise I might turn out like Granny or worse yet, my mom.

Deep in thought and gazing off in the distance, I didn't realize I was staring at Shelton Ramsey, Runge's very own professional mower. Most folks called him Scooter because he scooted from one lawn to another. Scooter was a unique person. He graduated valedictorian, but after one year at the University of Texas, he believed he was smarter than every professor in Austin. Scooter's strange appearance reflected his perspective of life – free and easy. His curly brown hair was held back in a ponytail. The tail danced across the midsection of his back every time he made a mowing pass. He wore aviator glasses no matter the time of day. Scooter sensed me watching him. He gave me a quick wave and continued his up - down mowing pattern.

After several passes, his mower edged close to me. Scooter shut off the mower and asked, "You okay?"

"Yeah."

"You seemed pretty deep in thought. Can I help you?"

"No, I just have something on my mind. I better go. Granny needs me to get the mail. I always have to get the mail on Thursday because Granny works at the food bank."

Okay, I was rambling now, I talk too much when I am nervous. At least it was a good excuse to leave him. For some reason, Scooter has always given me the heebie-jeebies. That strange feeling that doesn't transition anywhere…to fear…to happiness… It was just the heebie-jeebies.

Scooter's mower revved to life again, and I walked to the mailbox. I laughed to myself thinking about Granny and the food bank. She volunteered once a week and loved her position. Her job was training the new volunteers. She had her initial speech to the volunteer-victims memorized. Granny Perth even warmed up her "long running" spiel after Walter Cronkite did the news. The speech went something like this:

"You are here for one of several reasons: 1. You are required to have volunteer hours. 2. You believe you're helping the people beneath you. 3. You're bored. 4. You are a certified do-gooder. No matter why you are here, you must realize that the people entering through that door… (This is when she would make a dramatic gesture towards the front door.) …are people with feelings just like you and me. They deserve the same respect you would give anyone else. Now, keeping that in mind, I want you to fill the paper bag like this: two cans of pink salmon, one bag of rice, one bag of noodles, two cans of green beans, one can of corn, one pudding pack, and a container of cookies. Make sure you stack the cans on the bottom of the bag because no one wants smashed cookies while watching television."

Smiling about the visual, I opened the mailbox and grabbed

the mail. The second I touched the letter, I knew it was from Mom. It reeked of my mother's perfume, stale smoke, and lost dreams. I walked inside the house, poured a glass of water, and sat at the kitchen table. The envelope remained unopened for several minutes, and then I slid my finger under the seal and pulled out the letter.

From the backdoor I heard, "Hello. Raine, we need to talk. Don't ignore me. Raine? Is anyone here?"

I recognized Julie's voice. Timing. This was the worst time for her to talk about the situation. Before I had a chance to read the letter, Julie entered the kitchen and plopped down in the chair next to me.

She sighed and said, "I wanted to apologize for my beha...."

When she saw the look on my face, she stopped. "What do you have?"

With one swift movement, she grasped the letter and began reading:

Dear Raine,

I hope Granny has been treating you well. You will never guess my good news. I'm married. I met him at the Bingo Parlor in Carson City, Nevada. He was passing out the bingo cards when our eyes met. We were married two days later. This is real love. I know what you are thinking. He's not like the others. I'll bring him home to meet you sometime. Please, tell Granny the good news. Make sure you tell her on Thursday afternoon when she is in a good mood after teaching the volunteers how to sack the food.
Love,
Mom

Julie looked up and said, "Oops. I guess I shouldn't have read that. I'm sorry. I only came over to talk about ...you know..."

I didn't say anything for a few moments, but then I laughed.

Not the laugh which normally happens after a good joke, but the kind of laughter which represents nervousness bordering on hysteria. Julie moved away about four inches, carefully folded the letter, and inserted it back into the envelope. "I guess I should be going now."

That's when tears slid and splattered on the table. Now that Julie knew something of my past, I felt almost relieved. I wanted her to know, but I had no clue how someone with a "normal" family would understand my situation.

Julie slowly slid near me and placed her arm around my shoulder. Her touch flipped a switch launching my tear drops into a tear waterfall. The more I tried to stop crying, the more the tears flowed from my eyes. Julie began to slowly rock back and forth as if she were trying to sooth a small child. Perhaps, at that moment I actually felt like a small child because as she rocked, I rocked with her. As the rocking continued, my inner hysteria seemed to settle. Julie slowed down her motherly rocking and reached for the tissue box. Finding it empty, she strolled out of the kitchen and returned with a long stream of toilet paper trailing behind her. She rolled it back and forth until it looked like a short stack of pancakes.

Julie said, "Since it's one ply paper, I thought you might need quite a bit to wipe off your face."

I nodded. Julie sat quietly as she watched me pull strips of paper off the paper flapjacks. I blew my nose, but it seemed that once the faucet turned on…it didn't want to stop. I ended up twirling two pieces of the toilet paper into a point and shoving one up each nostril.

Julie laughed, "Nice job there Raine, the plumber."

When her eyes caught my glare, she shifted back into her concerned friend mode.

I took a deep breath and retorted in a stuffed up nose voice, "Alright. Let me tell you about Mom."

"Mom is a drifter. She has done everything from being a circus clown to raising ducks for a wildlife preserve. She loves to love, but forgets the love when a new love comes along. Her love can last anywhere from one hour to four years. You're looking at four years. She left town right after my fourth birthday and returned only when she felt the whim to love on me or needed money."

I paused to allow Julie time to process this introduction to my mom. It seemed weird to speak about Mom. Granny and I didn't really discuss it. It was just part of our life, like breathing.

I continued, "I've never met my dad. Even Granny doesn't know who he is. Mom just turned up pregnant and then left four years after my birth. The only thing Mom ever said was that I was the best thing out of the relationship. As far as marriages…she has been married three times, now four. The first love of her life was an elephant trainer from the circus. James had a thing for peanuts. He collected peanuts shaped like objects. He had one he believed looked like President Carter and another deformed peanut that resembled Mount Rushmore. Mom said she loved him because his creativity could make even normal things seem great. Then there was Ramon, the mariachi player. This time the music filled her soul. Of course, that lasted only until Ramon discovered peanuts in his bed."

Julie interrupted, "Peanuts?"

"Yes, peanuts. James came back to see if he could patch things up with Mom."

"Mmm, Raine? By the way, how do you know all of these details?"

"Mom, like Granny Perth, has no problem letting the truth tumble out. They are like a walking soap opera. I laugh because when Mom and Granny get together, each tries to swap stories larger and grander than the other."

"How did you turn out normal?"

"I guess I turned out like my dad; whoever he was… is. In a way I feel abandoned. My real mom doesn't want me, and my real dad doesn't know about me. I'm just glad Granny adopted me. She's my real parent."

There was a moment of silence, and Julie appeared stunned. She blinked a few times and then stated, "Now, tell me about step-dad number three."

"Father Nature. Actually, his name was Bernie, but I called him Father Nature. His long flowing beard and deep voice reminded me of a masculine Mother Nature. Mom said she loved him because he was going to help her settle down and become one with nature. This was when she raised orphaned ducks for a wildlife preserve."

"How did she know they were orphans?"

"I'm not sure. When she came across a nest with no adult duck, she claimed the ducks were orphaned."

Julie chuckled and commented, "Maybe the parent ducks left for a little while to get food."

"I guess, she never thought of that. Mom is smart when it comes to creative thinking until it gets down to common sense."

I pulled the snot plugs out of my nose. The brief interruption in the story flow allowed me to wonder about Julie's visit. "So, Julie, why did you come over?"

She laughed. "Well, I wanted to apologize and ask if you wanted to spend the night at my house."

"I'm not sure Granny will let me go."

"Why?"

"Mmmm…" I paused for second. I didn't know how to tell her that Granny was afraid of the liquid devil.

I stared a bit too long while I was trying to gather my thoughts and find magic words to coat my next sentence.

"Oh," flatly answered Julie. "I didn't think you knew."

"Granny was concerned, so she…"

Julie lowered her eyes and whispered, "I guess we both have a secret."

That same night Julie spent the night with me. Granny Perth didn't want me at Julie's house, so she suggested we reverse the sleeping arrangements. Julie's mom only requested that we stay in the house and no visitations with any boys by phone or otherwise. Granny was only delighted to oblige. She knew two girls plus one Granny equaled Championship Yahtzee.

45

After supper, Granny shouted, "It's time for the game of Yahtzee!"

All three of us dashed upstairs and put on our pajamas. There was nothing better than laughing and eating in an outfit that would not bind or split. Once back at the kitchen table, Granny started her Yahtzee ritual, which never ceased to amaze me. She ripped off the score cards with a flip of her wrist. Then she announced that she would go first, as always. Grabbing the five dice, she rolled them around in her hand to feel all of the edges, blew on them, and then spewed out some sort of sacred Yahtzee mumbo jumbo. This game was just like all of the other games – full of lying, cheating, and bit of stealing points. And that was Granny's side of the Yahtzee table.

Granny grabbed the dice and rolled them around in her hands. Then she puffed her hands full of her hot air and bellied out, "Mama wants to have a six!"

With Granny's south Texas accent, her six sounded a lot like the word sex. I'm sure Granny didn't know how bad that sounded. However, she must have wanted some sixes pretty badly because with the force she used on the dice, they moved from the table to the kitchen floor. She popped out of her chair and yelled, "Don't touch them!"

Granny's joints snapped and crackled until she finally made it to the floor. After gathering her dice, she announced, "I have two fours and three sixes. I got myself a full house, but I sure wish I could have had another six."

"Now that's what I'm talking about! I wouldn't mind having some myself. Only I'd rather have something a bit younger," declared a strange man as he slid his eyes up and down Granny's body.

Granny bounded away from the table and quickly grabbed her Smith and Wesson from the pan cabinet. She leveled the gun at the stranger. Her eyes took in every visual nuance starting with his six foot, skinny boned body up to his greasy, haphazardly parted blond hair. The longer the two stood in a Mexican standoff, the more a rotting odor covered with sweet smelling cologne permeated the room. Tears welled in my eyes. Even Granny blinked rapidly to keep her eyes clear and focused on her target. I glanced over at Julie. Her mouth was frozen in an "O" shape while her breath adhered to her lungs.

Granny blurted, "Mr. Wesson wants to know why you are here."

"Is that a way to treat your family?

"The only thing I see standin' in front of me is a piece of rotten stinkin' fruit. AND BOY, let me tell you something. God gives us choices, but the only choices I see before me is a person who allowed fruit flies to feast on your flesh."

"Excuse me? Phyllis told me you were a ding bat, but she didn't mention you had mean a streak wider than a sumo wrestler's butt crack."

"How do you know Phyllis? What did you do to her? Where is she?"

"Granny, Phyllis is my wife."

Suddenly an explosion split reality, causing my ears to ring until I heard static. When I finally opened my eyes, Granny was flat on her back, gun in hand. Unfortunately, the sunflower wallpaper peeled away from the gaping bullet hole in the wall. Gravity pulled on the wallpaper causing Grandpa Perth's picture to shatter to the kitchen floor.

For a few moments, wall plaster rained to the floor.

"Just what is going on in here!" screamed my mother. At least that's what her lips seemed to be saying. The gun's blast seemed to mute her voice, not to mention every other sound in the room. Everyone, except my mother, had a frozen look of horror similar to stepping in a warm pile of dog poo.

My mom continued talking. When she realized the gun blast had temporarily deafened us, she acted out what she meant to say. She pointed to her ring and then to Rotting Fruit man. Granny just shook her head in slow back and forth movements. I'm not sure if

Granny was upset about the marriage, or if the stench from Rotting Fruit man backed into her brain like constipation.

I looked up at the clock and the hands blurred into a handshake. My tears continued draining, attempting to wash away the odor. Finally, I could not stand it anymore. I stood, tapped my mom on the shoulder, and yelled, "What stinks?"

Mom laughed and started acting out the cause of the odor. She began with driving the car and doing the pee pee wiggle. I watched as she acted out stopping the car, getting out, and sprinkling urine along the side of the road. Changing characters, she got on her hands and knees. Extending one arm, she centered it on her backside like a tail. She only had to lift her tail once for me to realize that a skunk blasted Rotting Fruit man. Personally I thought the skunk had great taste.

Once again, Granny leveled Mr. Wesson at Mr. Rotting Fruit. Granny yelled loud, "Get out!"

It took less than three seconds for him to scramble out of the house. My mother grabbed the gun away from Granny and tucked it into the pan cabinet. That was when the street lights illuminated the police car as it drove into the driveway. My mom pulled the kitchen curtain to the side revealing the new guests. We watched two uniformed officers exit the patrol car. They didn't seem too frightened considering they were called for the shooting. I guess they figured it was Granny Perth's house, and the weird and strange were part of the norm.

Rotting Fruit man must have been on the back porch because when officers spotted him, they went into defense mode. The two officers pulled their guns and aimed at Rotting Fruit man. When the skunk smell hit the officers, they backed up and then re-aimed. Poor Rotting Fruit man knew the officers were yelling, but he couldn't hear well enough to decide if he should put up his hands, standstill, or lay down on the ground. Finally, he stood and held up his hands. By this time, mom ran outside and explained the situation. Mom has a way with words and body language. She can persuade a homeless man to give up his last blanket and make him feel good about it.

The officers nodded their heads and laughed. She must have known them because she gave each one a hug. Even from the window, I could see the officers visually ogling my mom's chest. As she bent down to straighten her sandal straps, her top billowed open allowing her melons to dangle. She began to sway her shoulders making her fruit swing in a small, circular pattern. It was the dance of hypnotic melons.

By this time, Julie and Granny were watching too. I didn't know that a fruit orchard could be used to blind men from rational reasoning into a drooling state. The melon thing peeved Granny. She pushed us away from the window and rushed to the patrol car. The officers saw her coming. It took less than thirty seconds for them to get into the car, back down the driveway, and head away from the house, dirt flying into the air. Granny grabbed the water hose and sprayed my mom from head to toe.

"This will cool you off, hussy!" bellowed Granny.

Then Granny turned the hose on Rotten Fruit man. Granny gave some sort of command, and Mom came sloshing into the house, hair dripping, and melons perky. I realized my hearing had come back to some extent when I heard Mom muttering under her breath, 'I'd like to cool her off!'

Mom collected every tomato-based product from ketchup to spaghetti sauce. Then she grabbed the dishwashing detergent. Julie and I followed her to the front yard.

Granny Perth ordered, "Girls, pour the whole arsenal of tomato products on Mr. Stinky Pants and rub it into his skin. This will help take away most of the skunk smell. Don't look at me like that! Just do it!"

"Girls, keep the soap out of Gordon's eyes," commanded my mom.

This was the first time I had heard the man's name. The name did not fit him. He seemed more like Rover, Spot, or Mr. Stinky. As I poured the tomato products on him, I noticed the deep creases and wrinkles around his eyes and mouth. Above his eye an amoeba shaped mole sat like a begging dog. His cheek held a jagged scar that zigzagged to his decaying teeth.

The three of us lathered him from head to toe with tomato sauce and dish washing detergent. The bubbling red made him look like a used tampon.

"Is this necessary?" groaned Gordon as he blew tomato bubbles out of his mouth.

Granny's hearing must have improved. She answered his question with another question.   "Would you like to enter my house?"

Under his breath he muttered, "Old bat."

"Stinky Pants," Granny retorted.

"Gray Haired Psycho."

"Fruit Fly Flicker."

Chapter Seven

Fiery Gossip

It was decided Julie should not spend the night. Given the recent guests, we thought it safer for her to go home. Besides, she might need therapy for years if Granny flipped a mental switch about Mom's new marriage.

Granny burned Gordon's clothes and gave him some of Grandpa Perth's old clothing. Aside from the clothing age warp, Gordon almost looked human. Mom and Gordon slept in Granny's room while Granny and I slept in my room. I hate sleeping with Granny. Every morning there was an avocado chunk, green tinted outline of Granny Perth's head. It reminded me of the chalk outlining a dead body. Thank goodness there was a small drool pool on the flattened pillow that let me know Granny was alive.

I slept with my back to Granny, mostly to avoid her slobber spots. I watched the second hand on the alarm clock spin around the numbers, and by six, I was determined to leave the house to avoid my mom, the man, and the Runge Grapevine. Our neighbor, Mrs. Lapp, lip locked the vine on a daily basis. I figured she was drooling to pump me for information about Mom and the gunshot. I stepped away from our house. Typically, it took Mrs. Lapp only about 15 seconds to be out of her house and ready to feed the vine.

One, two, three, four I counted. Five, six, seven,...I waited. Eight, nine, ten, eleven and, "Raine, Raine, I saw your mom come in last night. Is everything alright? I heard a gunshot."

Dang! She was quicker than usual. Sighing, I answered, "Everything is fine, and yes, Mom is here."

"Well, then who was that man? I saw four women washing him in the front yard. Were they having some sort of sexual orgy?

51

We don't stand for none of that here in Runge. We have our morals."

"Mrs. Lapp, that man is my mother's new husband. *And* there was no sexual orgy. He was sprayed by a skunk so we washed him with tomato sauce."

"It looked immoral."

She closed her front door. I smiled to myself thinking about her lips puckering against the town's sacred grapevine.

When I entered the halls of Runge High, Julie met me.

"Are you okay? What happened? Is your mom really married to that man? Does the house smell any better?"

"Ya know, if you stop asking questions I'll tell you."

By the time I caught her up on the drama, I was almost tardy to my first period class. English was boring as usual. Mrs. Whiner droned on and on about verbs. Halfway through the class, Jess Montez poked me in the back with a folded note. Carefully I unfolded it, trying to open a piece of paper in a quiet place. Every crinkle of the note drew attention to me. Soon eighteen pairs of eyes were glued on me to figure out the note's contents. I waited until Mrs. Whiner sharpened her pencils. For some reason she sharpened pencils to mask the sound of her flatulence predicament. However, since she was such a good teacher, the majority of us overlooked the indiscretion. Mrs. Whiner's students have passed a joke down from year to year which was actually hitting its fourth generation. There have always been slight deviations of the joke, but it went something like this: What do you learn in Mrs. Whiner's class besides English? Mouth breathing!

During the daily pencil sharpening ritual, I read the note. *Dear Raine, tell Julie to meet me after school in the park. My mom is checking me out of school early for a dentist appointment. I heard you had a rough Friday night. Be careful. Something doesn't sound right. Jess.*

Hmmmm…Something does not sound right. What does that mean? Nothing ever sounded right with my family. As I reread the note, my fingers traced the outline of the paper. My haphazard movement triggered Mrs. Whiner's sixth-sense. Suddenly, a corn chippish smell triggered my gagging reflex. I looked into Mrs. Whiner's brown eyes and spotted a slightly sinister expression behind her mascara-covered eyelashes. Before I knew it, she ripped the paper out of my hands.

"Alright missy, what do *we* have here?"

Why do teachers use the pronoun we? Mrs. Whiner had nothing to do with the note. She was popping her smell into my business, and it was beginning to chap my hide.

"It's personal," I answered.

"It must not be too personal if you read it in my class. CLASS, pay attention! What do we do when we find a note?"

The class answered in a monotone voice, "We read it."

As Mrs. Whiner traveled to the front of the class, the students broke free from the day's drudgery. Their body posture became alive and aware of the fresh, raw gossip about to be unleashed. Eyes flashed from me to the back of the paper, like a tennis match. She read.

Dear Raine,

Tell Julie to meet me after school in the park. My mom is checking me out of school early for a dentist appointment. I heard you had a rough Friday night. Be careful. Something doesn't sound right. Jess.

Whispers started on the downbeat of the last word. Mrs. Whiner glanced at me with raised eyebrows. "I agree with Jess. Old Miss Sue Ellen Dawson filled me in about your mom and something doesn't seem right. How long did your mother know this man? What does he really want?"

I rolled my eyes inwardly. This couldn't be happening. The Runge grapevine was definitely moving at record speed. My head throbbed trying to think of an appropriate answer. Within the inner chambers of my mind, an alarm rang. It seemed to grow louder and louder until Jess Montez grabbed the sides of my face and yelled, "Fire Alarm! Don't you hear it? We have to get out!"

That explained the mind alarm. I grabbed my books and headed out of the door. The halls seemed slightly smoky, so maybe this wasn't just a fire drill. About the time I figured this out so did the entire Runge High student population. The fight or flight reflex went into overdrive, and the students forgot all the years of fire drills. They forgot to walk in a line and remain calm. The students turned into a herd of crazed animals, running and leaping for safety like gazelles fleeing a predator. Several students fell as the herd's defense mechanism moved into a full stampede. Screaming, yelling, and chaos crescendoed into an unbearable sound. That's when the sound stopped as I slid to the floor, and feet pounded my body.

****

"Ah, geeze"

I heard the voice say. I felt man-sized hands grip my body, lift me, and begin walking down the stairs. The huff and puff of his breath plus the way my body rested on his oversized belly indicated that Coach Kernel Corn rescued me. I opened my eyes and saw the landscape teeter-totter from left to right. I felt like a damsel in distress carried by Godzilla.

Emergency personnel littered the school grounds. Students, parents, and rubber-neckers craned their necks to see the latest victim of Runge's first school fire. Paramedics placed me on a gurney and rolled me to a newly created triage area behind the school sign which proudly proclaimed the Runge High School's motto: *Education and Safety First.*

The first wave of pain hit just as the second wave revved forward. On the gurney, I curled up and moaned. No matter how I turned, twisted, or positioned myself, the pain continued.

"Help me!" I screamed between a moan and a shriek. I tried to close my eyes and focus on something else other than the pain.

What had happened? Where did the fire begin? I was mid-thought when I felt someone touch my arm.

Opening my eyes, I spotted Gordon. "How are you, sweetheart?" he asked.

"Are you her father?" asked a paramedic.

"Yes," he answered.

I shook my head no as the pain doubled and riveted through the back part of my ribs. The paramedic must have misunderstood my behavior for a daughter requiring the comfort of her father.

"Honey, Daddy won't leave you," the paramedic stated soothingly. Then he gave Gordon an ice pack and told him to put it on my ribs.

"Where's Mom?" I grunted.

"She is on her way," he answered.

"Why are you here?"

Gordon said in a fake, honey voice, "There, there you have just been in a fire. Why don't you rest?"

I stared at him trying to burn a hole in his forehead. Pain stopped my focus, and I resumed whimpering with a healthy portion of groaning. Gordon brushed his hand across my face to move my hair. The mere touch of his hand combined with a hint of skunk cologne scared me, so I bit him.

Gordon threw the ice bag at my head at the precise time Granny and Mom arrived.

Granny yelled, "What are you doing?"

Gordon spun and stomped away. Mom looked from me to Gordon. She kissed my forehead and went after him, but Granny stayed with me, like always.

In a rapid succession, Granny asked me, "Raine, are you okay? How did you get out of school? How did the fire start?"

At that moment, I heard Coach Kernel Corn ask the paramedics, "How's Raine?"

"If you hadn't picked her up and brought her out when you did, well..." the paramedic's voice trailed off into a mix of silence and reflection.

As Granny listened, tears filled the wrinkled pockets of her face. Overcome with emotion, she hugged Coach Kernel Corn. Her nose fit perfectly in his bellybutton. With his oversized body dwarfing hers, they looked like a Saint Bernard and a scrawny Chihuahua trying to do the Tango.

The coach and paramedics left to assist others. Granny sat on the gurney and stroked my hair. Suddenly, firemen poured out of the school. The fire men and women shouted, "Bomb! Move back!"

A fireman tried to diffuse the news by restating the information in a calm voice, "Move back! We believe there might be a bomb in the building."

The paramedics tossed patients into the ambulances. Granny rode in the ambulance with me which was a tight squeeze, but having her with me made the experience almost bearable.

With lights full steam, the emergency crews raced to the hospital. Since Runge was so small, the ambulances travelled to San Antonio. The lengthy trip allowed Granny and me to hear the events, blow-by-blow, on the paramedics' emergency radio. The bomb squad was called, and the area was evacuated. Bomb squad arrived. Smoking firecrackers were found throughout the building which explained the fire alarm and evacuation.

Later, the radio announced a metal box of unknown origin was found inside Principal Dander's office. Bomb squad was analyzing it. Moments later, there was an all-clear announced.

****

While in the hospital bed, I mulled over a few thoughts. First, I reflected on my bruised ribs, and the number of ribs Granny served. It nauseated me to think about the beef ribs, pork ribs and Granny's mystery meat ribs that slid over my lips. Never would I have eaten them if I had known bruised ribs hurt so much.

My second thought was about Gordon's sudden presence.

How did he get to the fire so quickly? Why was he without mom? What was the connection?

A quick rap at the door interrupted my deep mental thinking. "Hello, Raine."

Julie entered my room with her mother. The two visually scoured the hospital room and me. I felt a bit like an animal in a zoo exhibit.

"GRRRRR," I growled in response to my mental picture of being caged.

"Are you in pain?" asked Mrs. Twain.

I did a mental head slap and answered by shaking my head, no.

We chitchatted a while, and Mrs. Twain left the room to visit with other hospital fire patients. Julie remained.

"What happened?" asked Julie.

"What do you mean?"

"First, you were behind me, and then you were gone. I couldn't find you. When I turned around to get back into the school to find you, Coach Kernel Corn wouldn't let me back in the building. That's when he ran back into the school, so he is a hero."

I explained what I remembered from my perspective. It hit me that perhaps Julie had seen Gordon or my mom.

"Julie, after you got out of the building, did you see my mom or Gordon?"

"Actually, now that you mention it, I did see your mom talking to Principal Dander. They seemed to be arguing about something, but that was after I was in the school courtyard. I just figured it was about you getting hurt, but I didn't realize she hadn't seen you."

Julie's observations needed to be recorded before I took my next pain pill. One pain pill usually washed my memory for a few hours. I grabbed several napkins from my breakfast tray and started writing notes.

Fire – Kernel Corn – Gordon – Mom – Dander – Granny.

After looking at my notes, I realized I knew one thing. Four of the five vowels in the words were used leaving only the letter U...symbolically it seemed to refer to me. I really didn't think that was a clue, but it did explain who was going to need to do most of the searching for clues.

Julie leaned over me and read the list. Pushing the hospital's rolling table out of the way, she sat on the bed. Normally, she didn't get in my personal space, so I knew what she was about to do or say was important.

Carefully she wrapped her arms around me and whispered, "I'm so glad you are alive."

"Me, too," I answered.

"And..." she paused. "I love you...like a sister."

Emotions overwhelmed me. Taking a deep breath, I answered, "Me too, you."

It was at that point it dawned on me to get Julie to do a little investigating. Perhaps she could volunteer at the crime scene. She could serve donuts and coffee to the investigators rummaging through possible evidence.

"Julie, we need to find out who started the fire."

"We? You got to be kidding."

"Seriously, Julie." I paused and looked at her with as much strength as possible. "I can't explain it, but I think Gordon started it. I just hope Mom is not involved too. Sometimes she's one poop shy of constipation."

"Gross!!!! Do you always have to make comparisons to nasty things?"

I rolled my eyes and said, "I had to make sure you were listening. Obviously I can't snoop, so you will need to look around."

Julie responded, "Perhaps the fire started in the cafeteria – or there was a short in the electrical wiring."

"No, Julie. I can't explain it, but I really think Gordon is somehow involved."

"Why?"

"He must have been at the school when the fire started. How else could he have been there so quickly?"

Julie's mouth opened slightly as she thought about it. Quietly, she said, "Okay."

"What do you mean okay?" I responded.

"Well – I'm not sure what I can do, but I will try."

The next morning, Granny Perth took me home. I figured mom and Gordon had left, but when I got home, Mom was sunbathing in the front yard. That would have been all right, except she was wearing nothing but two hills and an elaborate design of cellulite. In the meantime, Gordon was taking Polaroid pictures at various angles. I could see about twenty photos drying on the front porch.

"Figures," I said under my breath.

About that time, Granny spotted her daughter's exposed garden. Granny got out of the car like a cowboy dismounting his horse. With her best John Wayne swagger, she sidled up to mom. Gordon threw down the camera and rushed to hide the water hose. He spouted, "These pictures just happen to be a glorious piece of art. We are going to sell them to Playboy!"

However, Granny had other ideas. She grabbed Mom's ear, jerked her up, and pulled her to the back of the house. The whole scene was so funny I started to laugh. My ribs screamed in protest. As Mom's legs sloshed cellulite, I held my breath to keep from laughing.

At that point, I realized Granny's mind flipped a switch. Her voice deepened into a guttural ancient language. It was as if the Holy Spirit came down and caused her to speak in tongues that could have left God scratching His head in wonder. The language may have been foreign, but the message was the same. Mom was in deep doo.

Once Granny and Mom reached the back of the house, curiosity got the best of me, so I inched my way to the back of the garage through Granny's clutter. With my bummed ribs, my movements had to be calculated. The mountains of milk bottles, tires, and cans were still waiting for Granny's good intentions to recycle. Even a rusted washing machine and refrigerator added to the hazardous battlefield. It took a bit of time, but I finally gained access to The Granny – Mom showdown.

Just as I squatted behind a pile of mufflers, I heard someone whisper in an irritated voice, "Sweet mother of crap on a stick!"

I turned and spotted Gordon's foot sporting a dented urinal. Why Granny thought she could recycle a bedpan was beyond me, but there it was lying in wait for an unsuspecting foot. Gordon jerked his leg several times, but it remained secure. Gordon pushed aside several old lard cans and sat on the dirt. With a bit of twisting and turning he removed the extra appendage.

Sheepishly smiling, he edged closer to the show. As we squatted, side-by-side, we watched the verbal duel of the crusty ladies. I realized this was the first thing my newest step-dad and I did together…and probably the last.

Granny's eyebrows narrowed, nearly touching her cheek. She growled, "Girl, I'm going to beat your butt just like I did when you were younger!"

"You will have to catch me first, Old Bat!"

"No problem." That's when Granny stuck out her orthopedic shoe and Mom ate dirt. Then Granny sat on my mom's back and began whacking her rump. The first whack left a hand print. The second whack caused the red print to jiggle. By the time Granny's hand readied for another whack, Mom flipped Granny and sat on her. Pinning Granny's arms to the ground, Mom positioned her face above Granny's nose.

"Old woman, let the torture begin."

At that moment, a glob of spit slid out of Mom's mouth and seemed to hover mystically in the air. Just when it seemed the spit would split and fall, Mom sucked it into her mouth. Granny swiveled her head to avoid any saliva droplets. As a side note, it was interesting the way Granny's neck jiggled in the opposite direction as her head.

The humorous visual overpowered Mom's anger because she started laughing. Granny echoed her laugh, and the two stopped wrestling. Mom rolled off Granny and the two stood, walking hand in hand into the house. It was weird to watch an old woman and a naked woman walk together. My teachers at school would have called this a teachable moment because they physically looked like antonyms – exact opposites of each other in a variety of ways. How could they go from anger to laughter in such a short time? Go figure...family.

Chapter Eight

Unkept Promises Must be Punished

There is an oak tree growing outside my bedroom. The tree limbs extend in every direction, including near my room. This afforded my friends an opportunity climb their way to my room without disturbing Granny. So, it did not surprise me to see Julie knocking on my window the next morning. Stiff from the night, I grunted my way to the window. With some effort, I pushed open the window and asked, "What?"

She rolled her eyes and replied, "An investigation team is meeting at sunrise. I wanted to be there, so I stopped by early to see if you had any advice." She reached forward and wiped the corner of my mouth. She wiped again, and again.

"What is it?" I yelled.

"Umm…dried toothpaste."

I gave her my best dirty look. I mentally jogged from my personal hygiene back to the team's investigation.

Wiping my face with the back of my hand I began, "So, what are you taking to the school?"

Julie opened her backpack and began an inventory.

"Pencil and paper for notes."

"Good."

"Donuts…."

"Good. Food provides an excuse for everything."

A protectiveness I've really only felt for Granny swallowed me. I added, "Julie, please be careful."

She tossed me an air kiss and crawled through the window.

I must have slept about three hours or more because the sun

was mid-sky. Julie knocked on the window frame and crawled into my room. My stomach knotted, waiting for the report.

Julie sat on the bed's edge and began, "Okay, you are not going to believe this! The investigation is focused in Dander's office. Apparently, they found letters in the metal container. Whoever left them really wanted someone to read them. They sure went to a lot of trouble to capture the community's attention."

"I'm surprised they let you into the office."

"The workers didn't know I was there," Julie smiled and continued. "I was kneeling behind the secretary's desk to look and listen."

"Smart thinking," I answered.

"Here's the strange part. Someone wrote *Unkept Promises must be punished* on Dander's office wall."

"What promises?"

"How would I know? By the way, did you know the letters were not just plain letters...they were love letters."

"How do you know?"

"That's the interesting part."

"What? Julie, you have got to stop with the drama. TELL me about the letters."

"They were written to Dander."

"LOVE LETTERS?"

"I heard the investigation team reading some of the letters, laughing their butts off."

"What was so funny?"

"The letter proclaimed love to Principal Dander and how the two of them were going to have babies after she graduated."

"Surely the letters were from his wife while they dated in college."

"Nope, when the letters referred to Mr. Dander...the letter actually used the words Mr. Dander. Part of the letter talked about their private time during math tutoring, but the last part described his ding dong."

We screamed *EWWWW* and laughed so hard we entered the wet crotch panty zone.

Granny and Mom rushed into my bedroom. Granny shouted, "What happened?"

Julie tried to explain, but all she could utter between giggles was bomb...love letters...Dander...student. The hilarious moment made my body react primitively. Threads of pain rippled through my rib cage. I pulled in air and held it, wrapped my arms around my chest and tried to regain control of my agony. I failed to block the images of a balding man playing kissy face with a failing math student, so laughter leaked, causing more pain. Again I held my breath.

"She's not breathing," Granny announced after assessing the situation.

Who is not breathing? I looked at Julie. She tilted her head back and a snort bordering on a donkey bray hit the airwaves - definitely breathing. The only person left was me. Was I breathing?

I took stock of my lungs. No in out movement, so I tried to pull in air.

"She's turning blue!" Mom yelled. "Do something!"

Granny grabbed my cheeks and blew in my face. The jolt of air made me take a deep breath. My stomach turned. It didn't take a rocket scientist to figure out that Granny's last meal had been liver and onions. I held my breath again. Bad move...She blew, again.

I guess the smell shocked my body into taking in enough air to satisfy Granny that I was once again breathing. She smiled and stepped back as if inspecting her work.

My mom leaned over me, her necklaces clinking like cheap wine glasses. She asked, "You okay?"

I nodded.

Mom asked Julie, "What about Principal Dander?"

I told her about Julie's investigation and the description of Mr. Dander's man part. I wanted to punctuate the story with excitement, so I announced, "Julie found out that the bomb was not a bomb. It was a box full of love letters."

Mom looked horrified. She asked, "What else did Julie find out?"

I answered with a dramatic flair, "Dander had an affair with a high school student."

Mom took in a sharp breath of air. She stepped back and seemed transported to another world. Suddenly she stood straight and tall. Her gazed shifted to me.

"I love you."

"I love you too, Mom."

Mom kissed the top of my head, cheek, and nose. Her affection seemed slow and methodical....the kiss soft and tender. Granny's right eyebrow nearly rose to her widow's peak. I could tell her mind grasped the nuances of Mom's actions.

"Why, Mom?"

She looked at me as if she wanted to memorize my face.

I asked again, "Why Mom?"

Silence.

Mom hugged Granny and patted Julie on the shoulder...and she left my room.

I could hear her packing. Gordon and Mom talked in hushed tones. At times it became loud, but I was never able to really understand anything. Thank goodness Granny placed her ear to the wall.

"Okay, Gordon wanted to know why they were leaving in such a rush. Phyllis answered that it was time to go. Why? Gordon wanted to know..."

Granny's face looked confused and she added, "Gordon's saying something about French fries. Or maybe, he said pinched smiles. Shheesh, this just isn't making sense."

It didn't take long before the front door slammed with a finality that made me shiver. The El Camino's engine clanked and chugged to life. I listened for clues which would allow me to mentally map their way out of town. The car travelled and turned on Main Street and skidded off. Where they were going was unknown to me and probably them. By now I should be immune to the skid marks across my heart, but it hurt, really hurt. I inhaled and held my breath hoping to hear the El Camino return but except for the sound of our house settling, silence punctuated the air waves.

"Okay," said Granny.

I answered, "Okay."

After a brief pause, Julie asked, "What's okay? What just happened?"

I grabbed my stuffed rabbit, Feeffers, and squeezed. Slowly, I answered, "Mom's leaving...again."

"Oh."

The next morning Granny brought me the newspaper. She stated, "Thought you might like to read something interesting."

The headline splashed on the front page:

Letters Found at Runge High School

Important Notice: Due to the damage, school will close early for summer vacation.

Runge High School's fire alarms rang. The students fled causing many injuries. A fireman discovered what looked like a bomb. With the bomb squad in route, the area surrounding the school was evacuated. Coach Whipley was instrumental in saving many students. Freshman Jessica Jones said, "Coach Whipley helped me get out of the hallway. Without him, I'm sure I would have been trampled." Junior Mike Baynes said, "It was smoky in the halls. He used his coaching voice to guide us to the staircase."

Fifteen students were taken to the hospital for injuries ranging from bruised ribs to cuts. Investigation officials have indicated foul play. A type of firework that releases smoke was found in the main area of the school. A small fire contained to the office area resulted in fire, water, and smoke damage to the first floor of Runge High School. The most interesting find was a fire proof box and a message painted on Principal Dander's wall. It read: "Unkept Promises *were not kept.*" ...see more on A6

I flipped to A6 and saw a full spread of pictures from the school to the infamous box. Questions mounted, but answers were nowhere. I spent the remainder of the day resting and by next morning, I felt somewhat better so I decided to fix myself breakfast.

I went downstairs, feeling empty and abandoned. I poured myself a bowl of Cheerios and covered it with chocolate syrup. ...a lot of chocolate syrup.

I turned on the television to watch the Price is Right show. Mouthful after mouthful, I shoveled the cereal into my pie hole. I was glad I had decided to use the serving spoon.

The show's host, Bob Barker, called a new contestant to the stage. That's when the door bell rang.

I guess I didn't answer the door quick enough because it rang again and again.

Must be an emergency, I thought. I walked my Cheerio filled chipmunk cheeks to the door and opened it. A woman...not just any woman – but it was Principal Dander's green bean bodied wife standing in my doorway. I stepped from the house and looked towards the driveway. Principal Dander sat in the driver's seat of a 1976 Gray Buick Skylark. His sad face brightened slightly but returned to its downward position when Mrs. Dander yelled, "Don't you dare smile you piece of horse slop."

I heard Mrs. Dander grunt, "Where is she?"

"Who?" I uttered with a few Cheerios spilling out my mouth. Okay, let me be honest... a lot of Cheerios.

"Phyllis!"

"Gone."

"Where?"

"Dunno."

"Didn't she tell you?"

"Tell me what?"

"I'm your step-mom."

I stepped back and barfed. Cheerios and chocolate syrup exploded from my cramping stomach.

Mrs. Dander stepped in the opposite direction and yelled, "Good Lord!"

Granny walked in the room and replied, "Yes, He is."

Looking at my explosion Granny added, "MERCY! What is going on here?"

"Other than vomit?" asked Mrs. Dander as she rolled her eyes.

Tears streamed down my face as I tattled, "She told me she was my step-mom."

Granny asked, "What is the meaning of this Grace?"

"It's true. My husband had an affair with Phyllis."

Granny stumbled backwards and folded into her armchair. She took a deep breath. "But…" started Granny. She paused to do a quick calculation and added, "Phyllis was in high school when…"

"It seems my husband was taken with Phyllis. That was the way Rob put it. The event started innocently with math tutoring, but as time passed, my husband must have given her a real education."

Mrs. Dander yelled, "Rob, get in here!"

The car door slammed. His sad, tired feet shuffled to the door. Sweat glistened on his forehead causing several strands of his hair to stick to his forehead.

He looked at me and then his shoes.

"Sit."

He sat.

Mrs. Dander proceeded to take on the role of newscaster. She announced, "Apparently, Phyllis has been blackmailing Rob for years – 15 years to be exact."

Principal Dander's head hung lower, almost resting on his squash-shaped belly. He seemed a shell of a man. His wife continued, "I couldn't figure out why money kept disappearing from our bank account. At first, the amounts were small, but over the years, the amount increased. Rob kept telling me he was paying bills. That didn't make sense because I always paid the bills. However, when I found letters in a shoe box from Phyllis to Rob – that's when I put it together."

Her monologue was getting on my nerves, so I said, "Prove it!"

Mrs. Dander's eyes sharpened, and she handed me a piece of paper.

"What's this?"

"Read it."

I decided to play tough and said, "Make me."

"Do it anyway."

Something about her authoritative tone caused fear to bulldoze through my nerves. My head lowered slightly which was just enough for me to glance at the note. It was in Mom's handwriting.

My dearest Robby,

Thanks for the necklace. I love it. I have some good news. We are going to have a baby. It's time to leave your wife and start our family. I'm so happy.

Love,

Phyllis XXXOOO

I yelled, "What do you want from me?"

He stood beside me. Pointing to his wife, "She has been pretty vocal about the situation. I think you and I need to talk."

"Isn't it a bit late?"

"No, it's finally the right time."

I looked at Dander and closed my eyes…, my mind flipped to the family pictures in his office. If this is true...before long I might look like a squash. UGH!

I slept until 3 A.M. I awoke feeling my chin, nose, and forehead. Did I look like a member of the Dander family? I flipped on my lamp and pulled out my yearbook. I had to know. I looked for matching eyes, nose shape, and forehead. I saw nothing until my eyes landed on my chin – my cleft chin. Mom didn't have one, so I must have gotten it from him. I turned another few pages and found a close-up of Principal Dander…one nostril was bigger than the other. For me, that proved it. I am a Danderling. Sickening.

Groaning, I slammed the yearbook closed. I thought about the pictures in Dander's office. Would I lose 98% of my hair? Which vegetable would I resemble as an adult? I mentally scanned the Regina's Grocery produce section. I wove through the leafy vegetables to the potatoes. By the time I reached the Russet potatoes, my eyes grew heavy. I fell back to sleep and I began to dream.

A thick fog blanketed the cemetery…The Runge Cemetery. Slowly a headstone appeared. It read William "Billy" Perth – loving husband and father – June 2, 1910 – July 3, 1980.

I said, "Weird."

"What's weird?"

I swiveled my head towards the voice and saw my Gramps Perth. Somewhere deep within me I acknowledged this was most likely a dream. However, I couldn't help but give Gramps a visual ogling. He looked good for a dead person. Best part – he still wore skin.

He opened his mouth and sounded like he did before July 3. "Babe, come give your Gramps a kiss."

Loads of thoughts crashed into my mind. Would he smell? Is this a trick? How would his skin feel?

I waited too long because he grabbed me and planted a kiss on my cheek. He smelled just like Old Spice. I felt so comfortable that I snuggled into him. We sat on his headstone and hugged like the Prodigal son coming home.

"My, you have grown. You look like your mom when she was your age."

"Gramps, you look good too."

He smiled and asked, "How's school?"

"Fine – except we had smoking firecrackers and a

fake bomb."

Gramps shook his head and answered, "I heard about that."

His comment stunned me. "How would you know, Gramps?"

"What do you mean?"

"Gramps, not to be rude, but how would you have heard about the high school drama?"

He smiled. "I may be dead, but I have connections. Claire Fitzson likes to hang out in the high school library."

"So, it's true. The high school's first librarian is haunting the library."

"Around here we don't call it a haunting, but a walk on the live side."

He paused and continued, "At night the cemetery comes alive."

Gramps smiled and looked around the cemetery. A buzzing sound filled my ears. It became louder and louder until hundreds of cemetery residents appeared. A group of men played dominoes beneath an oak tree. Some women quilted. While others talked in small groups, often laughing.

I asked, "Gramps..."

Not finding Gramps near me, I scanned the area. Next to the Rest in Peace sign was a regulation basketball court. I'm not sure where it came from, but Michael Jordon would have been impressed.

I watched several men peeling off their suit coats and shirts. I knew the men were Gramp's age because they had grey hair on their chest and back. I felt movement by my side and saw my second grade teacher, Mrs. Swartz, sitting beside me.

"Bunch of silverbacks, they think they are ready for the NBA," she laughed.

"Silverbacks?"

In a Midwestern accent, she explained. "Old men lose the hair on their head and grow it on their backs. They remind me of the silverback gorillas. Watch Bill. He has a 25% success rate of hitting the basket."

At that moment, he shot the ball and missed. Mrs. Swartz elbowed me and uttered, "Ehhh, looky there."

A gentleman from the corner of the cemetery yelled, "Air ball."

Bill barked back sarcastically, "Well now, Chester. Aren't you Captain Obvious!"

Chester clutched his heart. He yelled back, "Bill, you're making my blood pressure go up. I think my heart is about to give out, again."

Bill shook his head, "Nah, you didn't die because of your heart. You died from a bad case of the uglies. I never could see how your wife kissed you."

Mrs. Swartz and I laughed and laughed at the players. Finally, the early morning light pierced the darkness. The men waved and disappeared. I looked around, and Mrs. Swartz was gone. My Gramps settled next to me and said, "You are who you are…two people may have made you but your destiny rests within you. The only thing that stops you is thinking you can't do something. I love you, Raine."

He hugged me, and I was alone. The bright morning light forced my eyes closed, but when I opened them again, I looked around my room. That was strange I thought. I reflected on my dream. Gramps looked great, and I could still feel the warmth of his hug.

The phone rang. I answered it with my grandfather's favorite phone greeting: Joe's Bar and Grill.

"Umm. May I speak with Raine?"

"Who is this?"

"Raine?" There was a pause. "It's me, Principal Dander. Um-, you know-" He hesitated and finished, "your dad."

"Um yeah, so I was told."

"I'd like to talk to you."

"…talk?"

"…in person."

"Nope, I owe you nothing."

Silence. A heavy sigh filled the phone line. "It's like this Raine. Your mom and I decided to keep this a secret to protect you. We did what we thought was best."

"So not telling me I had a fa..." I decided to leave the word unfinished. It was too difficult to say.

Once again, silence filled the phone line.

He added, "It's like this. With me being married, we thought the community would treat you poorly."

"Me, poorly? Or you poorly?"

"Listen. Just listen to me. I want to talk to you in person. It is too hard to talk about this on the phone. It's time you know the truth."

"Truth? That's an odd word to use. What truth can you possibly tell me that I really need to learn?"

He left the question unanswered and stated, "I'll pick you up in an hour. We'll go to Crampton Park and talk."

My mind calculated why he selected Crampton Park. With conviction I stated, "That's about as secluded as you can get."

I almost heard him shrug. I continued, "What about Granny? I want her with me. Or should I say, I need her with me."

An awkward silence slid into the conversation. The longer the silence the wider I smiled. I knew Dander probably had a big one hit the back of his pants knowing Granny was going to be my bodyguard.

Finally, Dander answered, "Ok."

"Granny and I'll see you in an hour."

Chapter Nine

Dander Truth

I looked at the clock – 10 minutes 'til Dander time. My stomach churned – and it wasn't the cereal talking.

I knew he was right. I needed to hear his version of the truth. If any of this had merit or even if it didn't, I was going to go through a heap full of crap. The kids in school will definitely go for my jugular with comments about my newest dad…real or otherwise.

He rang the doorbell and greeted me with, "Hi."

I gave a noncommittal grunt as a greeting.

"Rob," Granny acknowledged Dander.

"Granny."

"How's the wife?" Granny said smirking.

Principal Dander grimaced, but answered, "Fine."

I could tell this was going to be one abnormally strange meeting.

Granny slid into the back seat. I sat in the passenger's seat. Dander drove.

The smells in a car can say a lot about a person. If the car smelled of food, the person bought lots of fast food. Or…if the car smelled of strong perfume or cologne, the car owner was overcompensating for a personal hygiene issue. Principal Dander's car smelled like nothing…no food, perfume, fart, or dirty socks. The car smelled dry, sad, bland, nada – nothing. Not a good sign.

We arrived at Crampton Park and parked away from the prying eyes. He cleared his throat and inquired, "How are you feeling today?"

I rolled my eyes. "Are you asking about my health or the fact you didn't have the balls to tell me about this when I was younger."

I was uncertain if I could say *balls* to my principal. However, considering the situation, I used the word anyway.

Granny popped, "Good one, Raine."

He smiled slightly and replied, "Your mom used to say sarcastic things like that…made me laugh."

I made a mental note to avoid sarcasm.

He looked away and breathed deeply. "It's like this. I was a math teacher at the high school. Your mom needed math tutoring, so we met after school. At first, we worked on algebraic equations, but soon we spent more time talking. We discussed life, baseball, dreams, and living outside of Runge."

"This is rich," commented Granny. "You should get some sort of acting award."

Dander continued despite Granny's outburst. "Your mother and I enjoyed being together."

Granny added, "I'm sure *you* enjoyed it."

Dander turned and spoke to Granny in a tone somewhere between a roaring gorilla and a revving Mustang. "Woman, you are going to listen. You are here to support your granddaughter. I will say all of this once. My goal here is to validate Raine's existence – not hear your sidebar comments. Now, either you be quiet and listen **or** get out and walk home. Those are your two choices and your only two choices."

Granny slumped in her seat, folding her arms. Dander took another deep breath and turned to me.

"Anyway, your mother and I had soulful conversations and we fell in love."

I rolled my eyes.

"Yes, we fell in love." He paused, took a deep breath, and continued, "That's when you were made from love."

"Then, why didn't you tell me that I was your daughter."

"I was married. I had a kid."

75

"Two."

"Huh?" Dander looked confused.

I reminded him, "At that time you had two children."

"Oh ya, right. I was working at the school. If this ever came out, I would have lost my job and not been able to support you."

"Support? What support?"

"I gave your mother money. I did the best I could for you. Your mother made choices that were *my* fault. She needed me, but I was unable to help her. I will fix that now…Over the years, I have never stopped loving her."

Granny bellowed, "But you raped her!"

EEKS! That hung in the air.

I saw a bead of perspiration speed over Dander's cheek. He didn't look well. Taking a quick breath, he said, "I loved her then, and I love her now."

Granny antagonized him by adding; "Now you say you have always loved her. I would hate to see what you would do if you hated her!"

I looked at Granny. Her mind flipped into the danger zone. Her eyes narrowed, and she looked more and more like John Wayne. There was going to be trouble. Even Dander sensed the danger.

He said, "Settle down, Granny. Everything is going to be okay."

SMACK! Granny whacked him in the head. She yelled, "You hurt my girl. You took away her childhood. You are going to pay for all of this – one way or another."

Dander shook his head. He answered, "Granny, I have been paying - every hour of every day. Each time Phyllis remarried I knew it was because she wanted to find love like ours."

Granny wormed closer to Dander and continued hitting him. Dander swung open the car door and got out. Granny followed him. I watched as Granny belted him. She reminded me of a tiny wrestler trying to take down King Kong.

Dander stood there letting her release her anger. Finally,

Granny stopped, sat in the driver's seat, and slumped.

I shrieked, "Granny! Are you okay?"

"Yeah, I am fine. Take me home, I need a nap."

I looked at Dander and saw him clutching his left arm. He stumbled a bit and fell to the ground. At first, he seemed conscious, but it didn't last for long.

"Granny, I think Principal Dander is having a heart attack!"

She gathered her strength and scrambled from the Buick. By the time I made my way to Dander, Granny had assessed the medical situation.

Granny confirmed, "Yup, he's having a heart attack. Didn't you learn ESP in the Girl Scouts?"

"Don't you mean CPR?"

"Raine, just help him live. I'm going to drive to get help. No one will find us out here, and there is no way we can get him into the car."

Granny drove off as I checked his airway. No air. I checked for a heartbeat. No beat. I began CPR. In my mind, I prayed.

Dear Lord: Why do these things always happen to me?

Dear Lord: Help this man live.

Dear Lord: Help me have enough money for therapy.

Dear Lord: Let me have a chance to make Dander's life miserable.

Dear Lord: Please let him stay alive. Amen.

At the last syllable of amen, he coughed, sputtered, and opened his eyes.

"Thank you God! Principal Dander, I think you had a heart attack. Try not to move. Granny's getting help."

Dander coughed and his face turned a shade lighter than maroon. I should have avoided the words *Granny* and *help* in the same sentence. A few minutes passed which seemed longer than waiting naked on a doctor's examination table. Finally, the ambulance rounded the corner, cherries a-blazing. The driver stopped the vehicle fairly near their newest patient. Within seconds, two men grabbed their gear to stabilize Dander.

Kevin Longsly, the lead paramedic, started laughing as he rolled Principal Dander to the back of the ambulance.

Longsly quipped, "Well, well. It is somewhat interesting that now I'm in control. Good thing I'm a forgiving man. You made my high school days miserable, Principal Dander." He paused a second and added, "I don't understand why you always blamed me for the things missing from the teacher's lounge."

Principal Dander leaned forward and whispered, "Security cameras."

Longsly rolled his eyes, "Jeez! I was such a putz."

"For a putz, you turned out pretty well," Dander smiled slightly and fell asleep.

The ambulance drove away, cherries blazing once again. I did a 360 spin, and realized I was alone. I turned again, and I was still alone – definitely alone. When was Granny coming back?

I mentally recapped the last hour. First Dander told me about his love connection with Mom. Then he yelled at Granny. A heart attack and CPR followed this. I could only imagine what the town would say if Principal Dander died. The basic summary of this situation: the people would think I used CPR to make a DOA.

In the distance, I heard a car speeding my way. I knew instinctively it was Granny, aka Nascar Granny. I quickly moved to the side. I've seen her braking action…not pretty. Sure enough, Granny made her way around the corner and slid the car to a stop, gravel spraying.

"Hop in," she ordered.

"Do you want me to drive, Granny?"

"You know you don't have a driver's license."

I knew she was right, but with her driving record, she would not have one for too much longer.

Chapter Ten

Hospital Visitors

Granny and I walked into the San Antonio hospital waiting room. Everyone stopped talking and gawked. And let it begin, I thought. The room was divided into sections. First there was the Dander section. The Runge High teachers clustered in another area. Some of the high school students milled about in the hallway. The final area was Rejectland. Since Granny and I were honorary members, we sat in the back of the back of the back of the room. Did I mention we were all the way in the back?

Despite a lot of staring, no one really said anything to us. Suddenly a door opened and a nurse exited. She said, "Is the Dander family here?"

The family stood. The nurse smiled and said, "He is doing just fine."

Mrs. Dander sighed and asked, "May we see him?"

"The doctors only want one person to visit him at a time. Mr. Dander asked to see..."

Mrs. Dander got up to go back, but the nurse had not completed her sentence.

"Granny."

Stunned, Mrs. Dander stood, mouth gaping. After gathering her senses, she said, "I don't think so. I'm his wife. I'm going back, *first*!"

The nurse stood in front of the door and said, "No. Mr. Dander requested Granny Perth. Is she here?"

Granny began to walk from the back of the back of the back

of the room to the front. As Granny passed the Dander family, she nodded hello. Then Granny looked at Mrs. Dander and stated, "Grace."

"Granny."

With that, Granny disappeared.

I was left alone in the back of the back of the back of the room. Mrs. Dander swiveled around and joined me. She had the gait of a constipated raptor.

She leaned towards me and whispered between clenched teeth, "Just what would Rob want with Granny? Was she sleeping with him too?"

Stunned, I said nothing. The visual of Perth-Dander Mombo was too horrifying.

Mrs. Dander continued, "You're not now or ever going to be part of my family. Don't even think about it. You're just as trashy as your mother."

That did it.

I leaned closer to Mrs. Dander and whispered, "Don't you think we should discuss this in private? There are too many people around."

She leaned closer to my ear and announced loudly, "I don't care who hears!"

Anger swept through me and about snapped the back of my underwear in protest.

I announced in a thunderous yet calm voice, I said, "Mrs. Dander, or should I call you MOM…" I paused, waiting for her reaction. It's not like I had anything to lose so I added, "Thank you for inviting me to dinner, but I will have to ask my Granny."

Mrs. Dander's face contorted. I thought for a moment she was going to hit me, but she returned to her two children. She sat and stared at me. It didn't take a college degree to know her maternal feelings about me were null and void.

The door opened, and Granny returned to the waiting room. She walked to the back of the back of the back of the room. The entire waiting room watched Mrs. Dander, Granny, and me.

I asked Granny, "What did he want?"

"You'll see," she stated.

The nurse interrupted and announced, "Mr. Dander would like to see Raine Dander."

I looked around to see Raine Dander. Granny leaned over and said, "I think she means you."

Woof. This whole situation was going to the dogs. I walked from the back of the back of the back of the room to the open door. As I passed Mrs. Dander, I stuck out my tongue. Childish, maybe, satisfying…definitely.

While walking into Dander's room, I felt sorry for his kids. They didn't deserve this, but neither did I. A sheet covered everything but his head. I looked over his belly mound just to see his face had blended into the white sheets. He lifted his hand and beckoned.

"Raine, come here."

I walked to him. Fear almost paralyzed my movement. He grabbed my hand and pulled it to his lips. After kissing it, he looked at me and said, "It's time for me to be your dad."

"It's okay Principal Dander. I'm okay with the current set up."

"I'm not. Since the world will soon know about you and your mother, it's time I cut the ties. I'm going to divorce her."

"Divorce…What are you talking about?"

"Divorcing the Gila monster of a woman I've been with for too many years. Do you know how good that feels to say that? I hate my wife!"

"No, absolutely not. You need to stay married to the Gila monster."

"But you need a dad."

"I'm okay without a dad. Besides, what about your kids?"

"You mean *your* sisters?"

SHEEESH! My stomach rolled.

I mouthed the word *step*. I didn't want to say the word, but I couldn't hold it in my mind.

Dander read my lips and asked, "Raine, what did you *step* in?"

I thought. Should I tell him a pile of crap, or should I say the truth.

Not wanting him to have another heart attack, I said, "Nothing."

"Raine, tell Mrs. Dander to come in. I'm going to shed some major pounds by getting rid of that woman. She drove me to this heart attack. My other kids will be fine. I'll set up visitation. I just need to move on with my life. I can't believe how free I feel. I'm probably going to be jobless, but I'm extremely happy."

At that, he smiled a Mona Lisa smile, and I left the room. My feet moved me in the waiting room's direction, but my heart wanted to transport me to a safe location – under my bedcovers. When I entered the waiting room, all eyes met mine. I stated, "Mrs. Dander, he's ready for you."

"About time."

Her children watched their mother leave the room. Once gone, their eyes swiveled to me.

Sixteen year old Marian, Dander's oldest, looked at me and asked, "Is it true?"

"What?" I asked.

"Our dad is your dad."

"That's what I'm told."

"Our mom says your mom is a slut. I guess it's true."

Anger gripped my tits and gave me a Texas titty twister. I stepped forward to illustrate my sisterly love and tried to grab a fistful of hair, but I was pulled backwards just before I made first contact. I turned and saw Julie. Relief coursed through me.

Julie stepped in front of me and continued the conversation with Marian.

"Marian, Raine doesn't want to fight. We need to remain

UNKEPT PROMISES

calm for Principal Dander's sake."

Marian said, "My dad's heart attack still doesn't take away the fact your mom is a slut."

The youngest Danderling, Kimmi, added, "Yeah, slut."

Kimmi seemed pleased with her word repetition, and a mischievous smile slid across her plate shaped face.

I looked at Julie. Her attitude had always been- when life takes a dump on you, crawl out and step over IT.

Getting on eye level with Kimmi, Julie patted her head and said, "You are so beautiful. You sure do look like Raine's mom."

Kimmi smiled and said, "Yeah, Raine's mom."

Julie grabbed my arm and pulled me to the other side of the room. As we walked I whispered, "Good one. I wonder if Kimmi was smart enough to know that was a cut down."

Marian yelled, "She's smart enough!" She pulled her arm back about six inches and swung, smacking Julie with a geriatric thunk.

Julie smiled, "Was that supposed to hurt?"

Marian answered, "If that didn't hurt, maybe this will."

"Yeah, this will," added Kimmi.

Marian grabbed a wooden chair. Since the chair was heavier than Marian anticipated, she only lifted it a few inches before swinging. It was not the force that caused Julie and me to fall like dominoes, just the surprise knocking us off balance.

We hit the cold-waxed floor. I looked up, and Granny belted Marian.

Round-eyed Kimmi said, "Uh oh."

At that point, life took a dump and every Danderling, teacher, and friend began fighting. Suddenly a door slammed. The entire room of heavy weight and lightweight wrestlers froze and turned to see who slammed it. Grace Dander's eyes flamed, and her fists clenched with a power that nearly popped off her knuckles. She bellowed, "Where is that piece of trash?"

Kimmi mimicked, "Yeah, piece of trash!"

Instinctively, the fighting convention participants parted, exposing me. I did what any other person would do: RUN!

I heard her behind me. Her huffing and puffing sounded like a freight train with asthma. I knew she had no endurance, so I took the stairs. There was no way she could travel down even one flight – not to mention five. Finally, I hit the first floor landing. I ripped open the metal door, ran from the stairwell, and smacked into a beer bellied security guard.

"Let me go! Let me go! A wart faced baboon is after me!"

The security guard held me tighter. Behind the security guard, I heard Grace Dander utter, "Who are you calling a wart faced baboon?"

She struggled to get away from the tight-handed security guard.

How was it possible for the baboon to move her bean sprout legs downstairs so quickly?

Ding. A second elevator door opened, and a security guard carried Granny with her arms and legs flapping in the air. Another security guard carried Julie. Elevators are definitely faster than stairs…DUH.

Ding. The elevators opened again, and the Danderlings exited like ducklings. Marian had her own personal security escort, with her sister following.

The security guards escorted us out of the hospital. One guard said, "You fight here again…we will call the police."

Mrs. Dander yelled, "What about my husband?"

The security guard questioned, "Yeah, what about your husband?"

"He is in the hospital."

"You should have thought about that when you tried to drop kick the old woman!"

A little smile slithered across Mrs. Dander's face.

Chapter Eleven

New Residence

Three days later, the phone rang. Julie answered it.

"Perth residence."

A strange high-pitched voice asked, "May I speak with Raine?"

"Principal Dander, I know it's you. Disguising your voice won't help. She doesn't want to speak to you."

I watched Julie. She looked at me, blinking several times. Then she said, "Okay," and hung up the phone.

I asked, "What?"

"He needs your help."

"You have got to be kidding."

"Mrs. Dander won't take him home."

I laughed. "I don't want him either."

Julie laughed softly and added, "He says Granny's late."

"For what?"

Once again, Julie laughed softly, "…to pick him up. He said Granny would bring him home."

"Where?"

"Your house."

I yelled, "Granny!"

Granny walked in and flopped in her recliner. She popped her soda tab and said, "He caught me at a bad time. I was feeling soft and vulnerable - should I have said no?"

She took several deep pulls on the soda, burped, and added, "I'll pick him up in a bit. Let's make him worry."

85

I asked, "But Granny, why didn't you tell me about this?"

"I didn't want to worry you. I figured his wife would want him. Guess I was wrong."

Granny finished her drink and grabbed her purse. "I'll be back soon with you know who."

Julie patted my back and said, "It will be okay. I know that it will work out, but if it doesn't, you could come to my house."

"…and stay with your dad? I don't think so."

Julie looked down. "That wasn't nice. I know he has problems, but he's still my dad."

"Sorry."

"That's okay." Julie smiled and added, "…at least my dad isn't the principal."

I tossed a pillow at her head and yelled, "Butt wipe!"

Julie stayed a bit longer, and then went home.

About two hours later, Granny arrived home with the principal. From my bedroom window, I watched Dander get out of the car and slowly shuffle into the house. What now? I thought.

I decided to hide in my room for the rest of my life or until the old fart left. From downstairs, I heard Granny yelling for me. UGH! I thought. Slowly I made my way downstairs only to meet Dander.

"Hi," I mumbled.

He nodded and sat in Granny's recliner.

Granny said, "Go grab the rest of his things out of the car. Then take them to your mom's room."

"But that's next to my room."

"Right. And my room's down the hall. What's the problem?"

"It's next to my room is the problem."

"Get over it."

"You have got to be kidding. Get over it…That's all you can say? Get over it. Why do I have to get over it? I'm not the one who started this. It was him not me. Get over it? I don't think so."

With that, I went upstairs and packed my bags. I thought, I'll get over it when I get away from here.

It didn't take me long to stuff my bags with my clothes and toiletries. Then I thumped, thumped, thumped my suitcase down the stairs.

Granny asked, "Where are you going?"

As I walked out the front door, I said, "You told me to 'Get over it'. This is how I'm getting over it."

I slammed the door shut. From inside the house I heard Principal Dander call out, "Don't go. I just got here."

Granny added, "She'll be back."

After walking about two blocks, I decided to go to Julie's house. Maybe I could stay in her room. Julie didn't talk often about her dad, or his drinking problem. I just hoped this wouldn't push him over the edge and cause him to have a royal hissy fit.

After thumping my suitcase up her front porch stairs, I wondered how many Jim Beam bottles hid in the bushes, waiting for unsuspecting victims. Julie and her mom must have heard my thump, thump because they answered the door before I knocked.

"What happened?" Julie asked.

"Principal Dander happened."

I gave them the lowdown. Julie looked at her mom and asked, "Please, let her stay."

Mrs. Twain closed her eyes and mentally debated the pros and cons. She grimaced and asked, "What about Granny?"

"Granny – Smanny. She told me to 'Get over it.' So I did. That's why I am here."

Once again, Mrs. Twain closed her eyes to continue her mental debate.

Finally, she answered, "Yes. However, Raine, you will need to stay out of Mr. Twain's way. He can be rather grumpy. Sometimes he says and does things… well; he does not really mean to be like that."

Julie added, "Don't worry, Mom. It will be fine."

The smile on Julie's face made we feel at home. Her friendship seemed like the only thing in my life that felt normal.

We lugged my stuff to her room. After organizing my clothing in her closet and making a pallet on the floor, we made our way to the kitchen. Mrs. Twain stood over the sink, washing the same dish over and over.

"It's clean," Julie offered informatively.

"Yeah, I was just thinking," sighed Mrs. Twain.

"About what?"

"When life was easier."

"Mom, what do you mean?"

Mrs. Twain circled the dish again. "Oh baby. Never you mind; it will all be fine."

Julie and I went back to her room and flipped on the radio. The unfamiliar song's rhythmic bass called to Julie and me so we danced. My moves involved a lot of hip thrashing with a mixture of hair flipping, but Julie's moves reminded me of a Jack Russell terrier jumping up and down in a box.

We laughed and laughed, and my stomach muscles strained to the point I thought I was going rip my skin. It was one of those times that anything we did made us laugh harder. At one point, I decided to go try a very rarely heard of jump called the 'dresser to the bed air flip'. My goal was to jump from the dresser, hit the bed, and roll to the floor. Unfortunately, the door opened, and Julie's dad glared at us. He stomped into the bedroom and switched off the radio.

As he bellowed, his flaring nostrils and spit droplets articulated each word, "I need quiet!"

He walked out, slamming the door. I looked at Julie, and she shrugged her shoulders.

I asked, "Did he have a bad day?"

"Nah."

Sarcastically I asked, "Good day?"

"Maybe."

"What's a bad day?"

Julie shrugged again and said, "He didn't hit me."

From downstairs, I heard the news anchor, Walter Cronkite, drone on and on about the world news. Cronkite always sounded like Charlie Brown's teacher to me. Wa wa wah wah wahn...Then again, my third grade teacher sounded like Walter Cronkite.

The television's volume grew until the news update music made the floor vibrate. About this time, Julie and I decided to get a snack. At first we didn't hear her parents talking because of the television's volume, but with each step, it was evident the kitchen was a verbal battleground - over me.

Mr. Twain grumped, "You should have asked me. I am the head of this household, and you have overstepped your place."

There was a bit of silence. Then Mrs. Twain replied in a fragile voice, "Honey, I just wanted to help Raine."

"But now look what you have done. The whole town knows about Dander's horny fling that fathered a bastard child. The gray hairs of the town are watching every move. This is like Runge's own soap opera. With Raine here, they will be watching us, too."

That did it. I walked in the kitchen using Granny's John Wayne swagger. I flung my words, "What do you mean by calling me a bastard? I think you're the devil for even saying that! If people watch your house, it's because you abuse your family."

Mr. Twain's eyes bulged goldfish round. A reddish glow swam up his face. Spittle formed in the corners of his mouth, making a tiny bubble inflate and deflate as he breathed. His hand jetted towards me. I dodged the first blow, but the second blow hit my face and bounced me off the kitchen cabinet. Then he got eye level with me and yelled, his breath bathing me in alcohol.

"Little girl. Let me remind you that you are in my house. I am the law here, and I cannot tolerate your sass. Get home before I pop you so hard crap comes out your ear."

Huffing, Julie's dad stormed out of the house and started the car, revving the engine. He drove away with such a vengeance there was a wake in the darkness. In the kitchen, the three of us stood

89

motionless. What just happened, I thought. Mrs. Twain grabbed a sandwich bag and filled it with ice.

She laid it over my developing bruise and said, "Raine, he's not always like this. I should have asked him permission, so this was my fault."

Julie took over speaking. "Umm, Raine, I know this will be a lot to ask, but please don't say anything."

This must have happened before. Julie and her mom were too composed. Maybe that was why the Twain family moved so often. My silence must have made the two uncomfortable.

Mrs. Twain continued, "I know this is hard for you to believe, but he is a good man. He is actually doing a lot better. It is important for Julie and me to continue helping him. If you let others know, our family will be torn apart."

I remained quiet. The sting on my face did not hurt as badly as the stinger piercing my heart. Why did they think like this?

Julie added. "I never told you about this because Daddy is truly doing better. He's cut down on his drinking. It's been a long time since he lost his temper like that."

I shook my head. "You mean this *has* happened before?"

The Twain women looked at each other but didn't say a word.

"Great," I stated.

Pivoting on my heels, I left the kitchen and began to pack. I did not take time to fold my clothes. I just tossed them into the luggage, flipped the levers to close it, and left. Julie called after me, but I kept walking home. By the time I arrived home, I remembered Principal Dander was in my house. The hit must have knocked my memory loose.

Flinging open the front door, I entered the house, and thumped, thumped up the stairs. Then I walked down the stairs and out the front door. I grabbed Dander's luggage from the Buick and thump, thump, thumped it up the stairs. Mid stairs I heard Granny say, "See, I told you she would be back."

I didn't hear his reply. I didn't care, or so I thought, but a feeling located in the center of my body began to build. It was like worry or concern. Maybe I did care what Principal Dander was saying to Granny.

I crept down the stairs to listen. I heard nothing but another Gunsmoke episode. Peering around the corner I saw Granny's face covered in avocado and her body encapsulated in a shower curtain. Principal Dander had his bare feet propped on the coffee table. He wore dark, green elastic waistband jogging shorts and a clean and pressed white t-shirt. During the commercials, Granny asked Dander if he really liked Miss Kitty, the saloon girl.

He replied, "I always thought she was going to marry Doc."

"Nah, he was too old for her. Besides, I don't think he had the ticker for such a hotty."

A little smile appeared on Dander's face. He replied, "Never allow looks to taint your thinking."

Granny looked at him answering, "What the hell does that mean?"

Not waiting for a reply she continued, "I've been around the block a few times. There's one thing I do know. If a person is old on the outside, they are old on the inside. Your way of thinking is a load of rotting fruit."

Dander closed his eyes and smiled. "Ya know, Granny, it has been a long time since I've felt this relaxed. Thanks for letting me stay here."

Granny massaged a slice of avocado into the folds of her neck skin. She shifted her body beneath the shower curtain. Then she looked towards the stairs and said, "Raine, you can come out now."

Dander opened his eyes, turned towards me, and smiled. His smile was way too big for his face. Hesitantly, I walked towards them and sat on the couch.

Granny said, "Aren't we the happy little family? We should pose for a Norman Rockwell portrait."

Dander laughed, "Rockwell would call the painting 'The Real American Family.'"

I retaliated with my own title, "'Wishing Fathers were Boogers.'"

"Huh? What in the world does that mean?" questioned Granny.

Obviously, she had not heard the old booger-picking joke, so I helped her out.   "…boogers can be picked."

Dander added, "…at least fathers are not eaten."

Granny laughed, "Dander, you made a joke. Good job!"

Chapter Twelve

Bun in the Oven

I was getting ready for school when the phone rang. I heard Granny call, "Dander, it's for you."

"Hello," he said, answering the phone.

Wanting to hear, I tiptoed out of my room, down the stairs, and just out of his view. I watched as Dander listened. The color drained from his face, and he placed his left hand over his eyes and rubbed. Finally, Dander replied, "I understand."

He placed the phone in its cradle and released a long, meaty, sad sigh. I thought someone died. His reaction slugged my emotions from anger to watered-down compassion, so I placed my hand on his arm. Swiveling his bald head, he visually intercepted my touch. He placed his hand over mine and pulled me around for a hug. A creepy crawly feeling enveloped me, especially when I remembered he was my principal. I made a turtle back to avoid touching except for our arms. Strangely, the warmth of his arms momentarily drove away the feeling. Was this how a father's arms felt? Safe, warm, protective... I resented myself for allowing a tender morsel to tap on my heart. What happened? Get a grip I yelled within myself. I wiggled a bit to cue him for an immediate release.

I scrounged up the courage and asked, "What happened?"

He looked up and to the right, as if searching for the right words. "Well, kiddo, the school board gave me a vacation – a permanent vacation pending an investigation. Even though I'm on medical leave, the school board wants to have time to do a proper investigation. I guess, the school district did not take too kindly to me falling in love with your mom."

I grimaced at the words *love* and *mom* in the same sentence. A tsunami of nausea slapped against my stomach wall.

I suggested, "Just deny it. That way it will all go away. They can't prove it. How would they know I was your daughter? Words are words but proof would require something medical or lawyerish."

"Raine, the proof is the words. The fire inspectors discovered some proof at the fire scene."

Without thinking I responded, "I wonder who put the love letters outside your office."

Dander asked, "How did you know?"

"What?"

"The letters were love letters."

I gave him my best blank stare and responded, "You know how small the town is…I probably heard somewhere."

"Where?"

"I don't know. Maybe the beauty shop."

Dander shook his head, "Couldn't have been there. The only people who knew were the fire inspectors. Besides, the inspectors are men, and they only get a haircut at Larry's Chop and Go. Those men would cut off their right foot before going into a beauty salon for a haircut."

He stopped for a moment and pawed his balding head. This particular mannerism was his thinking pose. The more he pawed, the more he mentally processed.

He added, "They decided to withhold the information from the public for two reasons. First, the guys didn't want my history aired into the gossip airways. Second, withholding information gave the investigators ammunition to find the guilty party."

I thought about what he said. Should I tell him the truth? Did he think I started the fire?

I moved my hand through my hair, weaving my fingers through several curls. Taking a deep breath I said, "Okay, I sort of sent Julie to the high school to check things out."

Dander answered, "You did?"

Once again he pawed his head and added, "What did Julie tell you?"

"To be honest, she heard one of the investigators reading a letter. The people listening laughed their butts off."

Dander hung his head and said, "That's what I was afraid of. Sometimes Phyllis got a bit graphic. She was young and so was I. It's unfortunate I never burned them."

"Why didn't you burn 'em?"

"I guess I liked rereading them. It reminded me of my first real love. The letters reminded me of a love based on compatibility. I wish I would have left my wife when you were conceived."

My stomach turned at the word conceived. Disgusting word. Wait a minute. I recalled he said it was unfortunate he never burned the letters. That must mean he wished the whole leaving his wife thing never happened.

"Principal Dander?"

"You mean, Dad."

Not happening I thought. "Ahh. You said you wished you would have burned the letters. Doesn't that mean you never really wanted to leave your wife?"

He shook his head back and forth. Pawing his head he answered, "Before I answer that, my name is Dad – not Principal Dander, Dander, or Rob. And, I finally have a chance to change history with Phyllis."

I shook my head back and forth. Without knowing, I curled a few strands of hair on my finger and responded, "No, not Dad. I'm not sure what I will call you, but it won't be Dad. It's wrong. You owe your children a father. You can't just leave them."

"Why not call me Pop? And, they still have me."

"But it's wrong – not Pop, either."

"I don't understand. – If Pop is not good, call me Father."

"Father is a no go. And, I've never known my dad. But your kids, they have always known you. You can't just leave them or your wife. You married her…in a church."

"Raine, I didn't know you were religious. What about Pap?"

"How about not. Granny took me to vacation Bible school at that Lutheran church. I guess that makes me religious."

"Hmmm. Is that so? I thought being religious meant you believed in God - not just attended vacation Bible school."

I thought a second. What was going on? Was our discussion about religion, morals, or names?

I decided to give in just a little. "If you will stay with your wife, I'll call you P.D.D."

"P.D.D. What's that mean?"

"Principal Dander Dad."

He smiled and said, "I'll counter that offer. For now, you can call me PD^2. At least that doesn't sound like a venereal disease."

I laughed. "That sounds like the robot from Star Wars. How about DD?"

Principal Dander shook his head from side to side. "That's a sad excuse for a father's name. Let's make it simple. Just call me Dander. When you are ready, call me Dad."

I thought again and answered, "That's sounds okay."

With the name negotiations over, I figured it was time to ask the real question. "So, Dander, who wanted to expose your fling with Mom?"

He pawed his head again and responded, "Ooff. I just can't imagine who would want to hurt me. That's not to say I didn't piss off a few parents or students. What principal doesn't? But typically they yell, scream, belly ache, or key my car, not this. What really concerns me is the way it was done. There was too much drama trying to expose my indiscretion. There were so many injured students."

Subconsciously I rubbed my ribs, "I know."

He continued, "Maybe my wife found the letters and wanted to hurt me. She can be quite vindictive. One time she got mad at her best friend over an allegedly stolen recipe. Grace told me later she broke into her friend's house and farted on her pillow.

"Please. That wouldn't hurt anyone."

Principal Dander grimaced, "ACK! You've never smelled Grace's farts. There was many a morning my nose hairs curled and blocked my airflow."

Together, we laughed. Who would have thought a principal could be funny?

The next morning, I woke to Julie rapping at my window. Her wild eyes danced in her eye sockets. I opened the window and pushed away the screen. She crawled inside my room.

Julie said, "I waited as long as possible. I need to talk to you. It's very important."

"What's up?" I asked.

Words formed in her mouth but hugged her lips keeping her from speaking.

"What?" I asked.

She stammered a bit more like an old car trying to start.

"I'm pregnant," she uttered. Julie cradled her face with her hands and cried.

"Are you sure?" I questioned. It's not that I doubted her. Heck, I knew about her doing the nasty. But what did Julie really know about being pregnant. It wasn't like getting pregnant was going to Regina's Grocery and purchasing a baby.

Between snot snorting and wiping drainage on her sleeve, she added, "Jess is the father."

"Duh," I answered. Did she think I was that stupid?

Julie sputtered with a mixture of snot and tears.

I asked, "Does Jess know?"

Julie shook her head while looking at the floor.

Since I just learned I had a father…not just a thought of a dad, but a living breathing person that created me. Not telling Jess really ripped through my emotions.

"You're telling me Jess doesn't know…What about your parents?"

Julie pursed her lips, pulled a crumpled tissue from her

pocket, and trumpeted her snot into it.

"No, they don't know either."

"Who does know?

"You."

"Why just me?"

"Well, I've been thinking. If I don't say anything about the baby that gives me a couple of months to figure out what to do."

Something in the way she tilted her head or she pursed her lips, indicated I would not like what she was thinking.

Julie continued, "When my parents do know, I'm going to need to run. I can start bringing some stuff over. With all the recycled junk everywhere, no one will notice a couple of extra trash bags."

"Don't you think your parents will understand? Sure they will be mad about it, but things will settle down."

"Puh-leeeze. Dad will probably kill me."

"You don't know that."

I flashbacked to the day he popped me. I guess it could happen.

"So you're telling me when your parents find out – you're going to hide at my house?"

"Yes."

"Your parents will know where you went."

"Yeah, but mom won't do anything that dad doesn't tell her to do – he'll just…"

"Hit your mom," I added.

Julie's silence told me I was right.

"Bring your mom with you."

"Huh?"

"When he finds out, bring your mom to my house with you."

"So you're telling me that you want me, my mom, you, Granny, and Principal Dander to live together?"

"Yeah, I guess that's what I'm saying."

Tears trickled in two perfect parallel lines down Julie's face. She peered through the tears and said, "Really? I never thought someone would do that for me."

"That's stupid. Anyone would do that for you."

"Raine, not anyone…we have moved a lot, and I've learned one big lesson. Unless you are born into a family, most people don't have time for you. Sometimes I feel like I'm park trash. Not just any park trash, but the trash that's stuck to the bottom of a Do Not Litter Sign. Unless a person wants to pick up someone else's trash, it's left behind."

"Bull crap, girl…you are not trash. Besides, if I saw you, I'd pick you up and recycle you."

Julie answered, "Really? You would recycle me? That's the nicest thing anyone ever said to me."

"Julie, how do you know you're pregnant?"

Julie answered, "I feel it."

"You feel what?"

"A woman just knows if she's pregnant," responded Julie. She paused for a second and then asked, "What do I do about *it*?"

Julie referring to the baby as an *it* bothered me. "I'll answer your question with a question. Do you like me?"

"Yes, of course. That's a stupid question. You're my best friend."

"If my mom didn't have me, I wouldn't be your best friend. The *it* is a baby. A life…a best friend to someone."

At this point, Julie's tears battered an exit from her eyes. Wrapping my arms around her, I held her tightly. Then I grabbed Feeffers and tucked him between us. Julie smiled acknowledging the added childhood security,

I'm not sure how long Julie clung to me, and I clung to her, but at one point a green meadow flashed in my mind. Trails wove through the green. Bits of bread crumbs led from one path to another. I felt myself become relaxed and the landscape became sharper and crisper. Soon it jazzed into 3D. My body spiraled downward into the mix of trails, breadcrumbs, and landscape. Before me, Grandpa Perth sat.

Grandpa Perth asked, "So, you need me again?"

I looked at him.

I nodded without thinking and answered, "Ah, yeah. I'm guessing so since I'm in another dream talking to a dead person."

"You're at a crossroads again. You have an opportunity right now to start a life with your father, or you have the opportunity to turn another way. The choice is yours. But let me give you one piece of advice; family is family. It's not a dress you can wear one day and find it out of fashion the next. It covers you completely; it encapsulates your whole being."

"Grandpa, you know about my other situation, don't you?"

"Are you talking about Julie? OR are you talking about the fire?"

"I guess both. Grandpa, I feel like the fire has to do with me. I also feel like my situation with Dander has caused me to see things differently. Like the reason I am going through the Dander crap is to help Julie and her baby."

"Now Raine, don't you be so self-absorbed that everything has to be about you. The fire was a message. Someone's voice wants to be heard. And the path it traveled had you on it, but it wasn't about you. Look at the big picture. Who would stand to gain from a fire exposing the misconduct of Principal Dander? Once you do that, the answer will be revealed."

He paused a second and added, "Oh, and baby girl before I leave you again, life has only one opportunity to live, and after it is snuffed out, it's gone - except in dreams. I love you and want you to know…"

The wind picked up and tossed leaf litter from the trail to the air. The landscape disappeared.

"Raine, Raine…what's wrong with you?"

"Wha—what do you mean?"

"I thought you passed out, but I guess you were only asleep."

"Jeez Julie, you screwed up my dream. Grandpa Perth was about to tell me something about you."

Julie pushed me away from her hug and looked at me and said, "You're telling me you want to go back to dreaming."

"I guess that is weird, but Grandpa is usually right about everything. In the last dream, he was so wise."

Julie's face whitened, and she whispered, "Do you normally have dreams just to speak to dead people? This is something you have never told me about."

"Puh..leeze, this was only the second time it's happened. I'm not some sort of death whisperer."

"Oh. Raine, is it possible you are the wise one? Maybe the dream snaps awake a part of your brain that helps you make decisions, or maybe it predicts the future."

"Um, I think not. What you see is pretty much what you get."

Even though my door was closed, we could hear Granny coming upstairs singing her snooping song – loud and proud. When she wants to eavesdrop, she makes up strange songs.

"Gotta a song I wanna sing," said Granny. The song grew louder as Granny climbed the stairs. She softly hummed a portion of the song and then continued blasting, "The life I love is singing about my friends and their husbands."

Granny putzed about in the hallway. It sounded like she was dusting the hallway knickknacks. Julie grabbed an old spiral under my bed. She slid a pen out of the metal spiral loops and began to write. When finished, she slid the spiral to me.

It read: I'm afraid.

I wrote back: About what?

"Singing words about dirty houses and squishy bananas."

Julie wrote: Having a baby.

I wrote: Are you sure you are pregnant?

Julie wrote: My boobs hurt.

I wrote: Sometimes my boobs hurt.

Julie wrote: Are you pregnant?

"The life I love is blending fruit with my friends."

I wrote: Nope.

Julie wrote: How do you know?

I wrote: DUH!

"And I can't see the squirrel in the feeder."

A thud hit my bedroom door making Julie and I jump.

Granny yelled, "Poop on a stick!"

I asked, "You okay Granny?"

"ACK! I stubbed my toe and dropped my feather duster. It wasn't bad until the dust flew out of the duster and clouded the hallway. Now I've got to dust again."

Julie rolled her eyes and mouthed: Bull.

Then Julie added: She just wanted to listen to us.

I nodded my head in agreement.

She continued: If I am, what do I do?

I wrote: "?"

After a few seconds of mental brainstorming I wrote: Buy prego test at the grocery store.

Julie wrote: Are you kidding?!?!

I wrote: It's an answer.

On Saturday, Julie and I trekked to Regina's Grocery on a pregnancy test quest. Julie needed to know her future, and the first step was to know if a child was in it. We entered the store midday: fewer people, fewer witnesses. Moving in stealth mode, we canvassed the aisles. I had only worked in the produce section, so I knew the pregnancy tests were not shelved between the zucchinis and the broccoli florets.

It was difficult to walk with purpose and remain incognito. Julie grabbed a stranded cart and pushed all the while eyeing the products. When a customer wheeled towards us, we turned and pretended to read labels.

"Raine, did you know some green beans are all natural?"

I eyed her. "When wouldn't they be all natural?"

Julie jabbed me with her elbow knocking some 'go with it' understanding into my head. At one point, Old Sue Ellen Dawson

102

chugged her way down the aisle nearly hitting Julie.

"Excuse me darling. Would you help me?"

As she asked, she leaned near Julie's face, leaving about five inches of space.

Old Sue Ellen Dawson studied a bit and said, "Oh Julie, it's you. Would you help me? My eyes aren't what they used to be."

"Um, sure," answered Julie, rolling her eyes.

"I know this might embarrass you, but I need some hemorrhoid cream. Could you help me find it?"

"Uh, well, I don't know."

"What's the matter with you? Don't you want to help a senior citizen?"

Old Sue Ellen Dawson paused a moment. Adjusting a hair comb, she added, "Honey, you don't know what hemorrhoid cream is do you?"

Julie remained silent unable to determine what to say. I could tell Julie had no clue. I, on the other hand, was well versed in the cream. Granny had, on many occasions, called me to her restroom and announced, through the closed door, to get her hemorrhoid cream out of her cosmetic bag. She would tell me that her watermelon grew some Russet potatoes with eyes. The cream decreased the bumps in size. That was when I asked her why she kept the cream in her cosmetic bag. She laughed and explained the product also reduced black circles beneath her eyes. Granny added that if hemorrhoid cream doesn't shrink it…it can't be shrunk.

I interrupted the silence by saying, "Ms. Dawson, I know what it is. Do you know which section of the store we would find it?"

She gave me a sweet smile and said, "Sure. It's in the feminine product aisle. Isn't that where we are now?"

"No, we are in the green beans aisle."

"Ahh," answered Ms. Dawson. "I guess I didn't count my aisles carefully. I must have messed up when I talked with Sarge. The correct aisle is three to the right of the canned food aisle."

Ms. Dawson pushed her cart forward, and we followed. Half

way to the feminine product aisle, Ms. Dawson literally ran into her old friend, Charlotte Kranz. After apologizing for the accidental cart crashing, the gray hairs began gabbing.

"Sue Ellen, how are you feeling?"

"Fine, except for the roids."

"Don't I know it. I have had a bout of them myself."

Mrs. Kranz turned to Julie and I and explained, "When you get to our age, we don't care who hears about our old age woes. You will understand after you have kids. That's when you will get the varicose veins, and your legs will look like a road map to Canada."

She turned back to Ms. Dawson and asked, "Did you hear about Abner's new girlfriend?"

"Girlfriend?" answered Sue Ellen Dawson.

"That's what I said. Girlfriend. She's a much younger woman and is dating him only for his money."

"Gold-digger. Do I know her?"

Charlotte Kranz whispered loud enough to be heard over a jet engine's roar, "Jeanie Pips."

Sue Ellen Dawson appeared appalled. She shot back, "That hussy. That's why she had her hip replaced six months ago. She wanted to walk without creaking."

"The way I hear it…there's a lot of creaking going on, but it's not due to walking."

The woman emitted a dirty guttural laugh laced with intermittent cackles.

Julie looked at me, and I looked at her. The whole idea was to get in and out without witnesses. Julie's eyes started to look misty. If we didn't get Julie's test done soon, she was going to sprout Niagara Falls.

Finally, the older friends finished gossiping, and we continued our hemorrhoid cream quest. After turning down the maxi pad aisle, Julie pointed to the pregnancy tests. She stopped to look while I grabbed a tube of "roid cream."

Ms. Dawson thanked me for the help and rolled off –

probably to hit someone with her cart.

I returned to Julie and looked at the boxes without touching.

"Girls," said a gruff voice.

Crap, I thought, it was Marge Hanks, aka Sarge, resident store manager.

Sarge's raspy voice questioned, "How may I help you? I've seen you browsing the aisles. What are you looking for? Perhaps I could help?"

"No, no help needed," I responded.

"Julie? Do you need help?"

"Nnn ooo," Julie uttered.

Her no turned into a landslide of tears.

A maternal emotion traipsed through Sarge's gruff exterior. She wrapped her arms around Julie and asked, "Baby, what's wrong?"

Julie's cry developed into an agonizing sound that was often reserved for only unfathomable pain. The resonance made my soul shiver, and I cried with Julie. Sarge looked from Julie to me. At that point she earned a lifetime of respect from me.

Sarge swept Julie into her arms and carried her to her personal office. I followed not sure what I should do.

Sarge closed the office door and sat in her extra-large computer chair. For about five minutes, Sarge rocked a crying Julie. I watched and continued to leak companion tears.

"Enough," ordered Sarge. "Now tell me what's wrong."

Julie blinked tears and began. She spilled the beans about everything…and I mean everything. She started with detention, went to the dance, and concluded with the hallway nasty.

"Well, that explains what you were doing in the feminine hygiene aisle," mused Sarge.

With the power of an ox, Sarge twirled Julie from her arms and stood her upright. Gazing into Julie's eyes Sarge said, "I've never told anyone this, but I had a baby when I was in high school. I had a body that wouldn't stop which is what got me into trouble.

Boys wanted to date me. And, if they didn't want to date me at the moment, they dreamed of dating me in the future. A person with my looks had to be careful that a romp in the hay wouldn't clog their facial pores or lose their virginity. Parents don't say this, but losing your virginity jump starts the aging process."

Sarge's memories roundhoused me. I think Julie was clocked with Sarge's verbal fist too. Sarge never noticed because without losing a beat she continued, "At first I declined because I wanted to focus on my studies, but then there was Skip. He was so handsome. He stood about 6' 5" and had rippling blond hair that moved gracefully in the wind. Sporting his pilot's glasses, he reminded me of a splash of the sun's rays reflecting ocean water."

Sarge looked up and to the right. Her mental world traveled to a memory filled with hopelessness and pooped on dreams. With a burst of energy, her voice converted to a sultry, husky tone. She began a hypnotic monologue, "Lust overpowered my studies...I became more focused on my womanly sexual powers than the manipulation of numbers to solve algebraic equations. Not to be graphic, but my body pulsated with pheromones which rode the sexual winds of lust. I can almost feel Skip's hands traveling over every dip, curve, and protrusion of my body."

Sarge droned on about moonlight, sheets, and burning loins. I was ready to upchuck my chocolate covered cereal. But Julie...well, she was mesmerized by the monologue. She nodded at appropriate times and even uttered a few "no ways," "ohs," and "I understands."

The sisterhood of heartbreaking love affairs was taking place before me, and my mental translator was on stupid mode – none of this made sense to me. Sarge continued, and finally she relayed a part I understood.

Sarge said, "My hormones locked up, and I knew I was pregnant."

I interrupted and asked, "How did you know you were pregnant?"

Sarge answered, "My boobs hurt."

Julie looked at me and nodded like "I told you so."

Interrupting again, "But that doesn't mean you are pregnant."

Sarge and Julie's eyes swiveled to me. Translation: shut up.

Sarge said, "Now I was in high school and pregnant. After finally telling my parents, they sent me to a special school for sexually deviant girls."

Julie butted in, "That's what they called it?"

"What?" Sarge asked.

Julie restated her question, "The school – it was called A School for Sexually Deviant Girls? Sheeesh, I am so toast."

Sarge smiled and answered, "No, that was not the name. That's what my dad called it. The school was for pregnant girls. It was actually called New Horizons. The school was designed so pregnant girls didn't have to be around their friends during gestation. The whole matter could be kept a secret."

Julie nodded, "Oh. What happened to him?"

"Skip?" she asked. "Not sure."

"The baby?"

Sarge breathed in and out...very slowly, all the while unconsciously rubbing her stomach. She answered, "She is fine."

Julie asked, "May I ask her name?"

"Little Bird," answered Sarge. "She has a real name, but that is what I call her. My little girl had to fly away to have a better life."

"Oh," said Julie. "You placed her for adoption."

"Yes," breathed Sarge.

Julie asked, "Do you know where she is?"

Once again, Sarge took in air with intense purpose and answered, "Yes." She mentally calculated her next words and continued, "She's here in Runge. I live close to her without her knowing the truth."

Julie questioned again, "Don't you want to tell her?"

"Yes."

"Why don't you?"

"I don't think she knows she is adopted. By not telling her, I am giving her another gift."

I interjected, "Jeeze, what is worth not knowing your parents?"

Sarge looked at me with sorrowful eyes. "Raine, I know this won't make sense especially with what's going on with Dander."

I interjected again. "Dang, how do you know about Dander?"

Sarge smirked and said, "Shopping aisles are steeped in Runge's latest and greatest news. That's how I knew about Principal Dander. It's also how I keep up with Little Bird. When she comes in with her mom, I listen and watch. I want Little Bird to be happy – and she is. I'm so proud of her accomplishments."

"Ok." I said. "Maybe I don't know about mommyhood, but I do know how it feels to wonder about family."

"That's my point," Sarge said. "She doesn't wonder. Her world is a circle of all that is good and right. If I crack her circle with this news, what she knows and has experienced will pour out and seem like a lie. That's my gift...her life is contained within the circle."

I asked, "Who is she?"

Julie silenced my question by resting her hand on my shoulder. "Raine, she can't tell you. That's her gift to herself. Little Bird is her circle."

I said, "You must be pregnant. You sound all grown up."

Sarge said, "Being pregnant doesn't make you grown up. Being pregnant forces you to think in a grown up way. So, let's find out if you are pregnant. I'll get a kit from the shelf."

Sarge left the office and returned after several minutes. She sat back in her seat. Taking control of the situation she said, "From the directions, it looks like we mix a little of this stuff and your urine. After several hours, we will know. It's the most popular kit, so it must be good."

Julie asked, "So what do I do?"

"Pee in this cup. Now don't be an overachiever and fill the

cup – we only need a little."

Sarge handed Julie the kit's urine container. Without looking back, Julie walked into the office restroom and shut the door. She returned with a cup of glistening yellow liquid. Sarge mixed the pregnancy test powder with the pee and stirred.

"Okay, girls, come back tomorrow, and I'll let you know."

Julie asked, "But you said it took only a few hours."

"Julie, the kit takes a few hours, but the store closes in an hour."

We walked out of the office and left the store. We didn't speak until we were just in front of my house.

Julie said, "I thought…"

BBRRRRRRRR convulsed a lawn mower.

I leaned close to Julie's ear and said, "I can't hear you."

Julie cupped her hands and placed them near my head. "I thought I would know today."

I mouthed "me too."

Chapter Thirteen

Letters

We sat on Granny's lawn watching Scooter mow. He moved from the Snyder lawn to the Carmichael lawn. During the gas filling intermission, I opened the mailbox and removed several letters. One letter…a familiar aroma…equaled Mom. I opened it and read:

Dear Raine,

It's true. Rob is your father. There was no way to tell you, but I'm glad you know. We fell in love when he taught me math. Who would have thought then he would become Runge High School's principal. Wow, I am so proud of him. I still love him. I guess I've always loved him. I'm hoping to come back to Runge to be with him. If he will have me…

I'm sure you are wondering about Gordon. We were never really married legally. One of the bingo patrons had us say our vows between bingo games. To keep things cosmically aligned, we will go back to the bingo parlor and have a patron declare us as a bad bingo.

Cheers,
Mom

I handed the letter to Julie. She read it and shook her head. Julie said, "Your mom is whacked."

I rolled my eyes and responded, "That's one way to say it. Jeeze, things just keep getting better. I'm about to lose it. Why can't I have a normal family relationship?"

Julie said, "If I were some kind of doctor, I'd call this Broken

Circle Syndrome."

"What?" I asked.

"You have a broken circle. It's just like what Sarge talked about in the office."

"Crap," I answered. "You are right. My circle's cracked."

Julie said, "I'm going home. I just want to go to sleep so that tomorrow will come faster."

"Right," I answered as Julie walked away.

I went into the house. Granny sat in her customary position: shower curtain, avocado smear, and Gunsmoke on the television. I looked for Dander, but he was not in the room.

"Where's Dander?"

"Visiting his other kids," answered Granny. "Hey baby girl, how was your day?"

"Interesting."

"Anything you want to talk about?"

"Got a letter."

"Your mom?"

"Yup."

I opened the letter and placed it on the shower curtain. Granny grimaced as she read. A portion of the avocado smear plopped on her lap hitting the letter. She belched and said, "Well if that don't chap my dimpled saddlebags. That girl is so mixed up. I don't know what she's thinking."

Julie and I met outside Regina's Grocery at 7:55 am. Sarge unlocked the door and let us in early.

Julie asked, "Did you look?"

"Yes," answered Sarge. "Before I tell you, let's go back to the office."

"This can't be good," Julie said.

Sarge said nothing. We reached the office, and Sarge closed the door.

"We need to make a plan," Sarge said. "Yes, you are

pregnant."

"I knew it. Crap, crappity crap," said Julie.

I looked from Julie to Sarge. A bond grew between them before my eyes. I was surprised Julie didn't cry. She actually seemed relieved.

Julie asked, "What's the plan."

Sarge continued, "We need to start on prenatal care. It's important for the baby to have the best start possible. When was your last period?"

Julie thought a second and said, "I guess about 8 -9 weeks ago."

Sarge looked at Julie dead on and said, "Now the hard part. We need to tell your parents."

"No can do."

Sarge's right eyebrow rose a quarter inch.

I jumped into the conversation and said, "Julie's dad has anger management issues."

"And," answered Sarge.

"He sort of takes his temper out on people – namely Julie and her mom."

"Can we tell your mom?"

"Maybe."

"Can't we keep this a secret a little longer?" I urged.

Sarge paused and then said, "Yes, but not much longer. What about the dad? I'm assuming it's Jess."

I said, "Dang the grocery aisles do have the pulse on Runge's gossip!"

Julie answered Sarge's question with another question, "Does he have to know? I have too many things I'm thinking about and then to have to include him…well, it's too much."

Sarge used her sergeant-like voice and answered, "Yes, you must tell him. It's not like he won't figure it out when your belly pooches."

"Fart, I hadn't thought about that. Ms. Hanks, do you think

you could tell Jess?"

"No, but I will be with you. Where is he right now?"

"NOW?" bellowed Julie. "Let's tell him about the same time I tell my parents. I could use a few weeks or months to work up my courage."

Sarge said, "Okay. Let's wait a bit, but you will need to tell your family and Jess before you start showing. My concern is prenatal care. You will need to eat fruits, vegetables, and whole grains."

I mused, "You sure seem like an expert."

Sarge said, "It's not being an expert. It's common sense."

Julie said, "Do you think I could work here? That way I could buy the extra food that we don't normally have at home. Dad is more of a meat and potato sort of person. If there's anything extra around the house, he gets upset about using his money, but if I work and bring it home, he'll be okay with it."

Sarge clapped her hand on her knee. "That's a great idea. You can work, get paid, and I can watch over you. You will start today. It just so happens I need someone in the produce aisle." She paused and looked at me.

I asked, "What about me?"

Sarge looked at me remembering the last official day I worked at the Regina's Grocery. She announced, "No openings."

I left the store and walked home, alone. I grabbed the front door, but it seemed jammed. Wedged between in the door frame was an oddly angled piece of wood. I pulled it from the door frame and a note fell. Unfolding it, it read:

Unkept Promises MUST be punished!

I shivered. What was going on? I looked around but only spotted Scooter mowing a lawn. No unfamiliar people hugged the shadows. I moved inside and found Dander reading the newspaper.

"Look what I found." I said to him.

He laid down the paper and shifted his gazed to the note.

He said, "Must be a joke. I get stuff like this all the time. When you are a principal, kids do stupid stuff like this."

"But Dander, you are not the principal anymore."

"True, but I still have lots of students who like to harass me."

"Well we need to tell Granny to be careful."

"Raine, relax. Don't tell her anything. It will just worry her."

"But the last time we saw something about promises was in your office following the fire."

"True, but I still do not think this has anything to do with that. You know," he continued with a smile spread across his face, "With Granny at the food bank, it would be a great day for the two of us to do something."

"Ugh. I don't know."

"Come on. It will be fun."

"You think a little time together will make it a Father/Daughter trip?"

"Maybe you should think of it like two people becoming friends. From there we will decide how to proceed."

"What do you want to do?"

"Well, Raine, we could go to Crampton Park and go for a hike."

"Question?"

"What?"

"You have a little ticker problem. I don't think a hike would be good."

"It wouldn't be that long of a hike. Exercise would be good for me."

"Right, but I don't want to give you CPR again."

"Well, why don't we do something I used to enjoy: photography. We could go to Crampton Park and take pictures of the wildlife. That way we can do a little hiking and snap some pictures."

I thought about it a bit and said, "I guess so."

Dander pawed his head stating, "I have one problem. My camera is at my house."

"We can find something else to do."

"Nope, we can't. The camera is mine, and I want it. I'll just go over there and get it."

"What if the Mrs. is home?"

"She can't deny me the camera. I'll just walk in and take it."

I almost laughed remembering the way he shuffled into Granny's house several weeks before.

We pulled up to his bland ranch style house: brown exterior and shutters painted a slightly darker shade of brown. Squared off hedges accented the freshly mowed lawn. I looked for Mrs. Dander's car, but it seemed to be missing from the boring landscape.

"Let's go, Raine."

"No way. I don't want to go inside your house."

"Come on. No one is home. Besides, I want to show you some of my framed pictures."

What the heck, I thought and climbed out of the Buick.

Several steps into the house we heard, "Mommy's not going to like you being here."

"Yeah, Mommy's not going to like you being here."

Dander responded, "Hi kids. I didn't think you were here. Where's your mom?"

Marian took an uppity body stance and popped her nose in the air. She threw back her shoulders and said, "She's out."

Dander asked, "Where?"

Marian said, "Mommy said she would rather you not know."

Kimmi chimed back, "Yeah, not know."

Dander smiled and knelt before Kimmi. "You are so beautiful."

"Thank you, Daddy."

"I miss you, Kimmi."

"I miss you too."

"Where's Mom?

Kimmi's plate shaped face smiled innocently, "Mommy says we are not supposed to tell you about Scooter coming over to mow the lawn."

Dander froze for about 15 seconds, which can seem like an eternity when you're waiting to see what will happen next.

He mused, "Mow the grass? Just how often does he mow the grass?"

Marian interrupted, "It's none of your business."

Kimmi added, "Yeah, it's none of your business."

Dander asked again, "Don't tell me. I don't want to know. But I do know something that I can't tell you."

"What?" asked Kimmi.

"I can't tell you," said Dander.

Kimmi's lower lip stuck out, "Why Daddy?"

"Well, Kimmi, it's not fair for me to tell you something when you won't tell me something."

Marian snipped, "Kimmi, Daddy is trying to trick you."

Kimmi's lower lip quivered and she said, "But I don't like it when Daddy knows something that I don't know."

"Don't tell him, Kimmi!" said Marian.

"I have to know what he knows!" whined Kimmi.

Dander looked at her and slightly tilted his head.

Kimmi uttered, "Ohhh, she's with..."

"Don't do it," said Marian.

"With...ohhh..."

"Don't, Kimmi," said Marian.

I decided to play along, "Ahh, Kimmi doesn't know. Let's go, Dander"

"But I know, I know."

Marian ordered, "Don't, Kimmi."

"She's with Scoo."

Marian clapped her hand over Kimmi's mouth.

"Scooter?" Dander and I said together.

Kimmi smiled, "Right!"

116

Kimmi turned to Marian and placed her hands on her hips. She said, "See, Marian, I didn't have to say it. They guessed."

Dander's hand shot to his head and pawed his scalp.

I said, "Woof, I didn't see that one coming."

Dander said, "So that must mean…"

Kimmi answered, "Scooter mows Mommy's grass a lot."

Marian and Kimmi watched from the front windows as Dander went to and from the house stuffing his belongings into the Buick. Periodically, Kimmi tapped on the window and waved. He returned her wave and continued packing. Dander shoved, stuffed, and sandwiched household items into the Buick with the efficiency of an elephant inserting a tampon.

After he added a can of roasted coffee grounds, I asked, "Did you get the coffee pot?"

"Funny, Raine. You know Granny has a coffee pot," answered Dander.

"I'm not trying to be funny. Don't you think you are overdoing this?"

"No. Maybe. I don't know. I just know I don't want Scooter touching my favorite things."

"Dander. Think about it. You really think he hasn't used the coffee pot?"

"Right, Raine."

With that, Dander went inside, grabbed the coffee pot, and launched it into the air, landing mid lawn. It shattered into approximately a bazillion pieces. Kimmi frantically tapped again. She clapped for Dander and left the window. Seconds later she returned with a vase and tossed it into the front yard. Shards of glass littered the lawn.

"Yay, Daddy! That was fun. Do it again!"

With the final item stowed, I said, "Let's go back to Granny's."

"Well, Raine, I need to do something. It's either take pictures, or I break Scooter's favorite mower."

I snickered and uttered under my breath, "Mechanical or biological."

"Huh? What did you say?"

"Nothing."

He started the car and drove to Crampton Park. I stared out of the window enjoying the quiet of the ride. We were just about there, and Dander said, "You know, I always wondered why he mowed our lawn so often."

I laughed. It's not that it was that funny, but mowing the grass and an affair don't sound romantic.

I asked, "So, where do you want to start taking pictures?"

"Let's sit on the picnic table by the pond and watch. Sometimes turtles will climb on tree limbs lying in the shallow water. I've seen egrets and herons along the water's edge."

We trudged from the Buick to a picnic table, lugging the camera equipment and sweating all the way under the Texas sun. I personally didn't give a rat's butt whether we saw anything. Sweat trickled down my shirt, and I noticed Dander had "pretty juicy" armpit rings. The lake water rippled a bit, and I heard a sound near several submerged limbs. I watched as a turtle climbed on a limb, stretching his head towards the sun.

Dander brought out his camera. Aiming, he manually focused the lens until the turtle sharpened into view. SNAP! SNAP! The camera sounded as each picture was taken.

"Wow, that should be a great picture," said Dander. "Why don't you try to take a picture?"

"I don't want to take a picture of a turtle."

"Well, why not a bird."

"Bird, smurd. This is stupid. There are thousands of turtle and bird pictures."

"Raine, that's true. But you are forgetting the most important thing."

"What's that?"

"You would be the one capturing the memory."

"So."

"So, the second you take the picture, you have captured a memory from the world and stored it on film. Every time you see the picture, you will remember that you were the one to not only see, but also capture the moment. It's a period of time that you will *never* be able to get back."

"That's some lecture Dander. Jeeze, give me the camera."

I took it and peered through a small square. It seemed to magnify the view a bit.

Dander helped by saying, "Turn the lens back and forth and it should sharpen your view. Whatever you see, that is what will be printed on film."

"Don't treat me like a child. I know how to take pictures."

"Sure, anyone can take a picture, but not everyone can capture art on film."

"Okay, let me just take a picture."

Dander reached over and grabbed the camera. He said, "You're not ready to take pictures."

"Sure I am."

"Not hardly. Let's just sit and watch the lake."

I rolled my eyes and said, "Pleeze."

I looked at Dander, and, except for his eyes dancing around the lake, he remained motionless, so I sat still too. It felt like it was a standstill challenge– I could definitely beat him.

My eyes traveled the shoreline. The longer I sat, the more I saw…things like grasshoppers leaping into the shallows, and a fish breaking the water's tension. Dander tapped my shoulder and pointed to a bird standing on pencil-like legs.

Dander whispered, "It's a white-faced ibis."

The bird used its long down-curved bill to probe the water for food. Periodically, the ibis lifted its head and allowed gravity to aid it in swallowing. Dander handed the camera to me. In stealth mode I moved the camera to my eye and twisted the lens to focus. Another white-face ibis walked near the first ibis. As it flapped its brown shimmering wings, I snapped as the wings reached their full extension.

"Did you see that?" I asked.

"Beautiful," answered Dander.

"I took the picture. Do you think it will look as good as the real thing?" I asked.

"Never. But it is gratifying to show others."

We stayed all afternoon, snapping picture after picture. At the end of the day, we had three rolls of film to be developed, so we drove to Regina's Grocery. Dander walked to the film drop display while I moseyed to see Julie working in the produce section.

"Hi, Julie," I said.

"Hey, Raine," she answered.

"You doing okay?"

"As good as can be expected."

"You want to come over after work?"

"I have to go home, but if I can get out of the house, I'll come over. By the way, my dad came by and wanted to know why I took a job."

"Ouff. What did you say?"

"What do you think I said?"

"You like fruit?"

Julie smirked and said, "No, doo doo head, I told him I wanted to earn money for college. It just popped out of my mouth. I was impressed with myself."

"That was good."

Dander waved for me to follow him as he walked out of the Regina's Grocery.

Julie said, "Whoa, what's going on here?"

Dander turned and called out to Julie, "Father – daughter outing."

She looked at me and said, "You have got to be kidding.

120

Ending or starting?"

"Ending."

"How was it?"

I said, "Actually, it was fine. We took pictures at Crampton Park by the lake. I better go. I can't wait to show you the picture. I took a picture of an ibis. Never saw one before."

Julie eyed me, "So, you had an outing, and you had a good time. Me thinks 'The Big D' has started to earn your trust."

"No way. Well, not in the way you think. Did I tell you about the note I found wedged in our door?"

"No."

"It said: Unkept Promises must be punished."

Julie slid a strand of hair behind her ear and folded her arms.

"Raine, whoever is doing this does not like Dander. Since he is at your house, that places you in danger."

"Maybe, but don't you think it could be someone who read the newspaper and copied what they read?"

"Raine, it's time to go," interrupted Dander.

I cut my eyes to Dander and back to Julie and said, "Julie, I'll talk to you later."

"Yeah, okay," answered Julie.

Chapter Fourteen

The Arrival

Dander and I arrived home. As I made my way towards the house, a yummy smell wafted its way to my nose. I thought: chicken and rice. Something happened. Granny only made the meal of doom when she felt guilty for something. I helped her set the table waiting and wondering what she did, or who was on the receiving end of her wrath - Dander or me?

Sitting at the table, Dander rubbed his hands in glee. He didn't realize he might be sitting at his last supper. Granny and I watched him shovel the rice and chicken on his plate.

"What a grand meal, Granny!" announced Dander. "Did Raine tell you about the pictures we took today?"

"Pictures, eh," said Granny, looking at me.

I looked up from my rice and slid Granny a glance. Her fork stabbed a chunk of chicken breast several times with little reverence for the meal's presentation.

Granny's shoulders rolled back prior to asserting, "Okay, Dander. Let's get something straight. I've raised Raine since she was born. No one, and I mean no one, will ever replace me."

"I know Granny," answered Dander as he smiled and continued chewing his food. He was absorbed in food happiness, and he truly had no idea Granny was jealous.

"Just so we have that straight. Now, Rob, there's something I've been meaning to tell you," stated Granny.

"Mmm yeah. What's that?"

Here it comes. I snapped to attention. Dander did not even

know his head was placed on a chopping block, and Granny was going to slice his dumpling.

Granny said, "Well, I spoke to Phyllis."

Dander's eyes sparkled like a teenage boy's eyes after touching his first set of boobies.

"What did she say? And when is she coming home?" asked Dander.

"Rob, it was a difficult conversation."

"How so?"

"I told her not to come back until she's ready to grow up."

"Why is that a problem?"

Granny grunted with dismay, "Because she's never going to grow up."

Dander looked up from his peas. His whole demeanor changed from foodie to principal with an attitude. "Well, who gave you a badge declaring you police chief of the grownups?"

Things were getting good now.

Dander added, "Granny, let's face it. I've made quite a few mistakes, but Phyllis is not one of them."

I guess he was waiting for Granny to reply, but she pressed her lips together and stared at him.

He continued, "I love her. I want to marry her."

Granny responded, "Horse cucumbers. You wouldn't know love from your weenis."

"Excuse me. I most certainly would know my penis from love."

"You old poot, I said weenis – meaning your elbow skin. You being a high school principal never knew the name of elbow skin? You know, that baggy skin hanging from your elbow. You can pull it, see?" She pulled her skin about an inch from her elbow. "I think I made my point."

With that, Granny left the dining room. She grunted as she returned to the kitchen, her weenis trailing behind her. And left Dander finding his weenis, like a child's new discovery.

Dander and I finished the meal in silence. He huffed and puffed through his chicken and rice. Several times he bit down on the fork which created an irritating metal sound, making my stomach hurt. I shoved the last bit of food into my mouth and carried the dishes to the sink.

The doorbell rang and Julie cranked the door open yelling, "Hello!"

"I'm in here," I called to her.

Julie entered the house and said hello as she passed Dander and Granny in the living room.

The silence in the house made me whisper, "What's Dander doing?"

"Sitting and staring."

"What's Granny doing?"

"Sitting and staring."

"What are they staring at?"

"Each other."

"That's it?"

"That's it."

By 10:00, the sitting and staring duo went to bed, slamming the door to punctuate their anger. Julie and I made our way to my bedroom where we began a sacred beautification ritual – zit popping. Every woman needed to remove zits playing havoc with their skin. If the epidermis was not monitored, creamy centered areas festered and screamed to be visually center stage. A friend, only a really good friend, helped search and destroy these facial violations.

Since Julie was pregnant, she decided to be first. Using maximum light, I visually scrutinized every pore. I positioned my face to her face as close as possible before it blurred. Scanning from right to left, I was determined to leave no pore intruder unpopped.

"Hold your breath Raine! It's making me nauseous."

"Just because you're pregnant doesn't mean you should be rude."

"Hurling on your floor would be rude."

My fingers squeezed a nice juicy blackhead just between her eyebrows. Black hardened gook squirted upward.

"Julie, you won't believe what I got out."

I presented *the yuck* on the tip of my fingernail like a royal gift.

She responded, "That is so gross." She paused and asked, "Do you see anymore?"

Just as I worked in another area of her face, we heard the floorboards creaking in the hall. Typically this would not be strange, but we knew the twins were in bed.

I stared in Julie's eyes, and she stared into mine, our eyeballs bulging.

In unison we whispered, "Unkept Promises must be punished."

Julie added, "Lights – off – now."

She rolled towards the lamp and turned the switch to drench the room in darkness. We maintained in a statue like pose and listened. Typical household sounds flooded the house – some normal and some abnormal. The floorboards creaked again and stopped. Listening for a bit more, we heard nothing but Granny's rhythmic snoring.

Julie had more courage than me. She descended to the floor and crawled toward the door.

"What are you doing?" I asked.

In an authoritative whisper Julie said, "Don't be an idiot. We got to find out what's going on. Get down - let's go."

"No way."

"Raine, get down here."

With that she grabbed my shirt and jerked downward.

"Jeeze, Julie. What are you doing?"

"We are saving Granny."

"What about Dander?"

"Well, I can only save one person at a time. Shut up. Let's go."

125

We crawled to the door and slowly twisted the door knob. The goal was to make the least amount of noise possible, but in an old house, doorknobs squeal. A creak from the hallway floor boards sounded. I tried to scream for help, but nothing would come. Fear officially paralyzed me. The punisher was coming for us!

Julie pressed the door closed, and we braced against it.

A rapid fire of hallway movement reverberated down the stairs and out the front door. I screamed and gripped Julie.

"Get a freakin' grip!" Julie responded. "We need to make sure Granny's okay."

Julie opened the door and headed to Granny's room.

"Wait."

"What?" answered Julie in exasperation of my childlike needs.

"What if there's more than one person here."

Julie stared at me for several heartbeats and grabbed the lamp, yanking it from the socket. After handing it to me, she grabbed my blow drier.

Armed, we trekked through the hall to Granny's room. The moon's light gave just enough illumination to see an empty hallway. I sighed thankfully.

Julie twisted Granny's doorknob and opened the door slightly. We eyeballed the room and spotted Granny sleeping. Her avocado mask laying in chunks on her pillow.

Julie pointed to the closest. Step by step I inched my way across the room to the closet. I opened the door with my left hand and readied the lamp with my right hand. Nothing.

CREAK! The floorboards sounded near Granny's bed. At this point I had two choices: Scream for help or hide. Since I was officially paralyzed, I decided to come up with a modified second choice: hug the closet door and become invisible.

Movement was in front of me. Even though I was paralyzed, my sense of smell worked just fine. The aroma of guacamole dip grew stronger as the movement grew closer.

"Granny?" I meekly asked.

"Whaaaat!" screamed the voice.

I heard the person take several steps forward, crash into the wall, and fall. Dander's door opened with his night stand light illuminating the hallway. Granny was flat on her back with me hugging the closet door. Between seeing Granny's green tinted face and realizing Dander slept in his underwear that should have been worn by a man 50 pounds smaller, I felt numb.

"Are you okay?" asked Dander.

He leaned down and extended his hand to help Granny. She eyed it and said, "I'll get up myself. I heard a noise and thought someone was breaking in."

"Ah Granny, that was just me. I was doing some yoga."

Granny's eyes widened, and she responded nearly gagging, "…in your underwear? Weren't you afraid those small drawers would cut you in half doing the downward facing dog?"

Dander shook his head while the rest of us just stared at fruit bunched into a small container. I did not want to look but I could not tear my eyes away.

After several moments of silence, Julie asked, "Well, if you were doing yoga then who went out the front door?"

"I didn't hear the front door," Dander answered.

The four of us spent the next 10 minutes checking behind every curtain, chair, and closet. The house was absent of strangers but not of uncertainty.

Julie and I returned to my bedroom and crawled into my double bed. We chatted about plausible reasons for the hallway noise, but we found none. With our conversation muted, my mind shifted to Julie's baby.

"Julie?" I asked.

"Huh?"

"Can I feel your stomach?"

"Why?"

"I don't know."

"I guess, but you won't feel the baby yet."

I reached forward and touched her ribs. She grabbed my hand and moved it to her tummy. The rise and fall of her belly let me know Julie was there, but like she said, I felt no baby – not even a bump.

"You think it's really in there?" I asked.

"IT is a baby. And yes, *it's* in there," Julie added.

We chatted until we drifted to sleep.

When I awoke, Julie had already left for work. I looked around the house for intruder clues, but found none. I tossed back some cornflakes and spotted Dander's wallet. With a quick glance for witnesses, my fingers slid over the leather and opened the tri-fold wallet. In the first third of the wallet, I discovered picture after picture of his kids, all three of them. The second section contained his credit cards and driver's license. Held in the final section was nothing. It seemed odd to have so much in two sections and squat in the third area, so I slid my finger into the third slit of a pocket. Sure enough, there was a hidden treasure. With a quick shimmy, I retrieved a ragged photo. Two people were locked in a romantic embrace. Bile tap danced into my throat when I realized it was Dander and my mom. The whole situation did not seem real. How could my mom and Dander really do it. EUWWW!

I figured Dander owed me for inserting himself into my life's history. He also owed me for the mental image of him doing yoga in his underwear, so I grabbed a wad of cash and tucked it into my pocket. I left the house and headed toward Regina's Grocery to pick up the pictures.

At the grocery store, I looked for Julie. Not finding her, I paid for the developed film and sat outside the store flipping through the pictures. Snapshot after snapshot made me remember the ibis' delicate movements and the sunbathing turtles. Amazing. Flipping to the next picture, I squeezed my eyes shut. I opened them again but the picture remained unchanged. It was of me stretched across my bed, sleeping. Another picture framed my eyes and nose. The camera would have had to be fairly close to capture that angle. Other pictures showcased Dander's office – post fire. In the final picture, the words Unkept Promises took in the balance. A creepy feeling chilled me. Someone had been in my room taking pictures and with the same camera that had taken pictures from the fire.

The disturbing feeling continued to race through my veins but was replaced with anger. I jumped up and returned to the produce section to find Julie. I guess I had tunnel vision because I bumped into Mrs. Dander.

"Excuse me!" she huffed.

Wasn't worth it, I thought. I zeroed in on Julie and continued my trek.

Julie asked, "Whoa there cowgirl, what's going on?"

"You won't believe what I found in my pictures."

"What?"

"Me. Check this out."

We huddled, flipping through the pictures.

"Julie, look at this one."

I handed the picture to Julie and she pulled it closer to her eyes. She looked at me and asked, "Is this from the fire?"

I nodded.

Julie mused, "Oh my gosh. Who would have taken these pictures?"

"I don't know. When I retrace the camera's movements, it was only at D's house before we got it. Even then, after we took pictures at the park, we dropped the film off here to be developed."

Julie answered, "But that means, someone from Dander's house took the camera, took the pictures of you sleeping, and most likely started the fire."

A moment of silence passed between us. The hair on the back of my neck lifted, so I turned to see who was near. Mrs. Dander went eyeball to eyeball with me.

Her eyes pinched together and she said, "You are not going to imply that I took those pictures."

I continued staring at her and wondered…what kind of soap

opera was this?

Mrs. Dander continued, "You probably took those pictures to frame me. I can't believe you took pictures of yourself in your bedroom. The fire pictures are over the top. You definitely take after your slutty mother."

I continued staring at her. Her nostrils flaring, she added, "You little conniving twit. All you want is to add drama to my life. I've had it with Rob taking your side. You were the one who made him leave his real family."

Interrupting her I said, "Just hold on. Me, want him? Lady, you are sooo screwed up. I am surprised Scooter would even want a thin green bean bodied woman like you."

"Just what do you mean? Scooter wanting me. I don't know what you are talking about."

That's when Julie laughed. It was the kind of laugher filled with a robust amount of witchiness, sarcasm, and an added edge of fanatical lunacy. Regina's Grocery shoppers stopped mid cart roll and looked. People in the produce section dropped their veggies and stepped back, and mothers hid their children behind them.

An older gentleman asked his wife, "What's going on?"

"You'll like this Henry. It's a woman versus woman fight. You didn't even have to pay for that HBO."

Henry's eyes sparkled with anticipation.

Sarge broke through the circled up crowd and asked, "Just what is going on in here?"

Julie and I looked at each other and shrugged our shoulders.

Mrs. Dander said, "These young ladies have decided to sexually harass me."

Sarge questioned, "Well, Grace, just what did they do to make you think that?"

"They told me I had a thin body and even Scooter wanted me."

I interrupted, "No, no, no. We said your body…"

Mrs. Dander cut me off and pointed to me. "See, Sarge, she's starting again with my body. You, Raine, are one twisted little girl. No wonder you took pictures of your own sleeping body."

Sarge's eyebrows lifted, but other than that she presented little emotion.

The older gentleman looked at his wife, and she gently elbowed him and offered him a sly smile.

I gasped and answered, "That's not..."

Mrs. Dander continued, "Raine is just jealous that she's not a real Dander."

Sarge continued, "Grace - follow me."

"I will not!"

"Grace, don't make me tell everyone about your produce fetish."

"You think just because you're the manager of Regina's Grocery you can threaten me?"

"No, I think that you are making a scene and..."

"And what?"

"You have two choices," stated Sarge.

"So now I have choices. Two of them to be exact. Well, let me give YOU two choices. Choice one: Get the hell out of my way."

Despite the interruptions, Sarge plugged away. "First choice is to come to my office to discuss this or..."

"Or what?"

Grace's hands perched on her narrow hips. Her body language looked like a hyperventilating slimy eel. Sarge must have recognized Grace's inability to hear logic. A melancholy emotion steeled with resolve stiffened Sarge's body.

Grace said again, "Or what?"

Sarge turned and walked towards her office.

Grace continued saying, "Or what?"

With each addition of "or what," Grace grew louder.

Finally, the older gentlemen asked his wife, "Is that it?"

His wife shrugged her shoulders.

He said, "If that's what a catfight looks like, I haven't missed anything on that HBO."

"Enough!" boomed Sarge. "Girls, go to my office."

Julie and I did not need to be asked twice. The produce crowd parted, allowing us just enough space to ease out, and the path closed quickly.

Grace turned a full circle, looking at the crowd around her. A dark cloud of damnation clapped thunderously. She walked towards Sarge's office yelling, "There will be hell to pay if you don't come back here. I will not tolerate being treated like this by a Regina's Grocery worker. I've got rights. I'm going to call my senator to tell him about your poor management skills and the inequality between workers and shoppers. There must something in the Bill of Rights that cries out for financial satisfaction for this injustice."

Sarge guided us into her office and as a response to Grace's tirade, she slammed her metal office door shut. Moments later, Grace pounded on the door and said, "I want those pictures from my camera."

Julie, Sarge, and I stared at the door.

Sarge said, "Now, girls, explain to me what is going on with these pictures."

No words were needed to explain the photographic evidence, so I extended the picture package. Sarge flipped open the photo packet and visually perused picture after picture. Some pictures she paused a little longer than others and finally she placed them in her lap and looked at Julie and me.

"Interesting combination of pictures...Where did you get them?"

Julie and I looked at each other. I hesitated and wondered if Sarge would think Dander started the fire. It just didn't make sense with the love letters. Was he showing off? Did he think he was a stud who wanted the town to appreciate his manhood?

Mrs. Dander beat on the door again. "Give me my property!"

Sarge rolled her eyes. She thumbed towards the door and

132

asked, "Did she take the pictures?"

I cleared my throat, paused, and mustered the following explanation, "I took the pictures of the wildlife, but I don't know who took the rest."

Sarge scratched the top of her right thigh and thoughtfully posed the assumption, "If you took the wildlife pictures, I'm guessing Princess Beating Door or Principal Dander took the rest."

Julie added, "It looks that way, but it also makes Raine look guilty."

Sarge shifted in her chair causing her muffin top to cascade downward adding several muffinette layers to spill over her pant line.

She said, "See what you mean. Those pictures appear to incriminate the whole Dander clan."

"Not me!" I retorted.

Julie shook her head, "Yeah, even you. Do you really think the police will believe you and Dander just picked up the camera the same day you took the pictures and had them developed. Heck, even Marian could be a person of interest."

"Julie, really, a person of interest. Where did you get those words?" I asked.

Julie adjusted her Regina's Grocery name tag and answered, "We don't move a lot because my dad is an angel."

"Your dad has been a person of interest?" I asked.

Julie answered, "Yup, several times. He's got quite a temper."

"Noticed," I added, absent mindedly rubbing my cheek. "Think Kimmi would be considered a person of interest?"

Sarge fielded that question, "Nah, too young and stupid. She's a pretty simple girl. It's almost like she has different parents than Marian."

Fists hitting the office door covered Sarge's words.

Sarge grimaced, "This is getting annoying."

Gripping the door handle, Sarge opened the door bellowing, "What do you want?"

Surprised, Grace squeaked, "The pictures."

"Fine," answered Sarge, closing the door. She seized the pictures and sorted them into categories: wildlife, sleep, fire. Then Sarge removed the negatives and replaced them with a set from her own pictures. At that point a mischievous smile took over her face.

"What?" I asked.

Sarge rummaged through her own pictures and held up a picture of a person holding a large red fish. My eyes initially zeroed in on the trophy fish, but slowly the person holding the fish came into sharper focus. It was Sarge wearing a string bikini. Words cannot describe the fluff billowing over the bikini's elastic.

"Nice fish," I uttered.

Julie's face remained stoic.

Sarge added her picture negatives to Raine's picture packet, along with a few of her vacation shots.

Julie whispered, "Won't she know those are your pictures?"

"No, my pictures are of wildlife. She will never know the difference, except she won't see pictures of the fire and Raine sleeping. But, Grace won't know that until she gets home."

Sarge opened the door and handed Grace the pictures.

Gripping the pictures like a trophy, Grace asked, "Now was that so bad?"

Sarge widened the door's width and walked forward two steps, her body filling the space.

"Listen Grace. You rant and rave childishly and then asked if that was so bad. Go crawl under your rock."

"Now Sarge, there's no need to get testy. I was just making a comment."

A red lace pattern crawled up Sarge's neck. Her lips thinned as she said,   "Why I've got a comment I'd like to show you."

Julie jumped from her chair and pulled Sarge backwards, closing the door in the process. Sarge sat in her chair with a humpff, the wheel mechanism groaning in protest. Except for an occasional squeaky grocery cart rolling past her office, we sat in silence. Finally, Sarge cleared her anger and said, "That woman is a menace to pond scum. Now, girls, is there anything else I need to know about?"

"Yes," I answered.

"What then?"

"Unkept Promises."

"You mean like what was written on Principal Dander's office wall?"

Julie piped, "Raine's getting notes with that same message."

"Tell me about it."

I gave her a quick recap of the drama. Sarge nodded several times as if to show she was listening. Sarge stated, "Girls, something is definitely going on in Runge. I think we need to lock up the negatives and photos in the store's safe. It stands to reason that Principal Dander does not have anything to do with the fire, pictures, and the threatening notes. But, if I ponder about it, his actions with Raine's mom started the drama."

I asked, "So what do I do about it?"

Sarge massaged her neck and moved up to her temples. "Where are the notes?"

"Well," I paused. "They are hidden in my room."

"Hmmm," Sarge stroked her chin. "Where?"

I answered, "Under my dirty clothes."

"Ok, not my first choice as a hiding spot." Sarge said as she stroked her chin again. "You need to get the notes and give them to Granny. I'm not sure about the sleeping pictures. It's rather odd. You could go to the police or you can do nothing but wait. Something will surface to provide guidance. I would, however, talk to Granny. Let her know your fears and concerns."

I asked, "What if we talk to the police?"

"Well, if you tell them, they will probably say someone is playing a trick on you. Girls, you must admit the fire and letters could be considered a historical event in Runge. Someone is going to add to the drama with the pictures. It's human nature."

Sarge added, "Think about the time Gilbert's wife, Sue Ann, had her twins in his fishing boat. Gilbert was trying to reel in a 50 pound yellow catfish. The whole time he reeled, she was yelling 'My water broke!' Gilbert thought she meant the fish broke the water's surface. Now when fishermen reel in a big one they're yelling 'My water broke!' Yup, this town sure loves drama. There will be one piece of every dramatic event that keeps on keeping on."

Sarge nodded her head up and down, applauding her monologue.

Julie asked Sarge in a serious adult voice, "So you're saying 'Unkept Promises will be punished' will become a normal thing to say?"

"Now girls, I'm not saying people are going to go around punishing non promise keepers, but in a small town like Runge, people like a little spice. Leaving messages around the town, well, it adds…"

"Spice," I finished her rambling.

Sarge parroted back, "Yeah spice, like cinnamon."

"More like cayenne pepper," Julie added under her breath.

Chapter Fifteen

Unveiled Secrets

I left Julie in the produce section, and I went home to talk with Granny. The walk provided time to mentally distance myself from the emotions of the Regina's Grocery drama. Granny needed to hear only the facts; she'd add the drama on her own. But when I rounded the street corner, a police car sat in our driveway, adding a bit of zip to my walk. I chugged to the house, noticing Mrs. Lapp rocking on her porch. She must have been there a while because her jar of Texas tea was half gone.

Fear flooded my body. What was going on? Did someone die? It was at that point I heard laughter. Police and laughter did not match. It was like pickles and cooked spinach.

In the kitchen, four sat at the table: Granny, Dander, and the two officers. Ironically, the officers were the same policemen who had succumbed to my mom's dance of the hypnotic dancing melons. Strewn across the table were pictures of me at all stages of childhood.

Granny looked up and said, "I'm showing the officers pictures of you growing up."

"Why?" I asked, unable to imagine anyone wanting to specifically see pictures of me.

"Well, these gentlemen think you might be involved in a bit of trouble."

"Umm. Like what kind of trouble?"

One officer piped up, "We received a tip that you're going around threatening folks with letters and pictures."

"And would this tip be from Mrs. Dander?"

137

"Can't say ma'am."

"And when was this 'threatening' supposed to have happened?"

"Can't say ma'am."

"Well, what can you say?" I looked at his badge and added, "Officer L. Mahoney?"

"We received a tip that you're going around threatening folks with letters and pictures," Mahoney paused, shuffled through a few baby pictures and continued, "And you were one cute baby."

I asked, "Okay so it's a tip. Doesn't mean it's true. It could be that someone is making up something. People in Runge like drama, so why are you really here?"

Officer Mahoney pulled out a small pad of paper and pen. He flipped it open and read, "Just where were you about an hour ago?"

I could see where this line of questioning was going – right in the rotten fruit crapper.

I answered, "I was with Julie and Sarge."

"Where?"

"Regina's Grocery," I answered.

The officers looked at each other. The second officer, Ken Matey, scribbled a few notes and asked, "Could we take a look around your room?"

Granny jumped into the conversation, "Sure, she has nothing to hide."

The officers pushed back from the table and stood, waiting, looking like presidential body guards.

Granny cocked her head to the right, "Boys, why are you standing there?"

Officer Mahoney cleared his throat and replied, "Where is Raine's room?"

Dander responded, "I'll show you."

I interjected, "Uh Granny, I have several unmentionables on the floor. I better pick them up."

I jumped up and tried to sidestep the officers and Dander, but

Granny grabbed my arm and said, "Now, Raine, I'm sure the officers have seen their share of unmentionables."

Officer Matey shot Mahoney a glance and stifled a snicker. Both men seemed to puff out their chest at Granny's remark.

I knew it would only take me a few seconds to tuck the notes out of sight, so I pleaded, "Granny, really, I need to pick them up."

Granny pulled me down, "Sit, Raine. It will be fine."

The three men trumped up the stairs. Out of view Granny asked, "Just what the asparagus is going on."

"That's why I came home. I wanted to tell you."

"So, tell me already."

"Granny, do you remember when Dander and I took pictures at the park?"

She nodded – as if she thought she remembered but the details were missing from the memory.

"Well, along with the pictures that should be there…well, there were pictures that shouldn't be there."

"Like?"

"Like, pictures of me sleeping and a picture of the wall in Dander's old office. You know, the wall with the words: Unkept Promises must be punished."

Granny paused to let the information percolate through her brain. She questions, "Where did you get the camera?"

"Dander and I picked it up from his house the same day we turned in the film to be developed."

Once again, Granny thought and asked, "Anything else you want to mention?"

"Notes."

"What notes?"

"I've found notes, here, at the house with the words Unkept Promises."

"Show me the notes."

"Can't – they're in my room."

Granny sprang from her chair and started up the stairs while shouting, "Officers, don't go in the room! Unmentionables!"

"What Granny?" questioned Dander.

I could hear the floorboards creak as the men searched my room. Granny made it only three stairs steps before the upstairs creaking ceased. She froze, sighed, and headed back to the kitchen, tail tucked between her legs.

So we waited – Granny and me, for the apple to be juiced. My stomach twisted, and Granny did not look much better. Her fingers tapped her face wrinkles while her feet shuffled to the beat of the mental horror film music playing through her mind.

I heard the men heading downstairs. Officer Mahoney's eyes zeroed in on my eyes which added to my stomach pain.

He asked, "You want to explain the meaning of these notes?"

Dander insisted, "I told you. Raine found them around the house. She's innocent of this craziness."

The officers pivoted their eyes at Dander commanding him to shut his talking fruit hole. The three men sat at the kitchen table with Granny and me. With the number of people at the table it was like a Thanksgiving meal only I was the main course.

Officer Mahoney asked again, "You want to explain the meaning of these notes?"

At that point I had nothing to lose, so I explained everything to the officers starting with the fire and the strange way my mother's husband showed up and ending with the pictures of me sleeping. When I finished, I felt drained and yet relieved. I guess I did not realize how much the information weighed me down.

Officer Matey took copious notes. Periodically he flipped through them, seemingly trying to elevate his importance. Finally, he asked, "Raine, anything you want to add?"

I shook my head.

Dander announced, "Well, I want to add something."

Officer Matey turned, raising an eyebrow like Spock in the Star Trek series. It would have been funny had the situation not been so tense.

"Well," started Dander. "Raine told me about the notes, but I told her that principals often get strange unexpected gifts typically after a student's office trip. I've received them for years, so when Raine told me about these notes, I didn't get too worked up. But now that the facts are laid out...well, I suppose..." He pawed his head several times and continued, "I should have noticed there was a problem."

Officer Mahoney commented under his breath, "You think the fire would have tipped you off."

Dander grimaced.

Granny shifted in her chair making the chair scrape against the linoleum floor. One quick look and I knew Granny was going to mentally blow. Even the officers noticed. Mahoney fingered his gun while the second officer nudged his nightstick. Dander was the only person more focused on pawing his thinning hair than Granny's mental shift.

Her wrinkles hung lower, shoulders rounded, and her hands flew in the air.

She stood and shouted, "You!"

Moving around the table she positioned her face about four inches from Dander's face. "YOU!" she bellowed even louder.

The policemen and I scattered but remained close enough to watch the showdown. Once again, Granny sputtered, "YOU!"

Dander's expression was like a basset hound carrying around football sized hemorrhoids. "What?" he asked.

Her body twitched and she yelled a fourth time, "YOU!"

"What Granny?" he answered. His sad droopy eyes sank lower and lower until they almost rested on his double chin.

"YOU! You brought evil to this house. You have placed my Raine in the line of fruit crazed bats ready to do battle with some Unkept Promise. What's the matter with you?"

"I don't know how you can blame me."

"NOT BLAME?"

She plucked a fly swatter from a nail on the wall and whacked

141

him. Dander's mournful eyes accepted his punishment, but the corner of his mouth trembled. I was not sure whether he was going to cry or lose his temper.

I personally didn't want to see either so I surged forward to pull Granny away. The officers grabbed my shoulders and tugged backwards.

Officer Mahoney leaned his back against the kitchen cabinet and smiled, trying to hold back a snicker. He said, "This is better than the day Cherry Martindale fell from the parade float."

His partner shook his head. "No way, Cherry was wearing crotchless underwear."

They shared a quick look at each other and giggled like a boy farting in a locker room.

Granny flipped the fly swatter downward making Whack, Whackity Whack sounds as the webbed plastic ricocheted off Dander's head. Finally, Dander grabbed the flyswatter, bent it in half, and tossed it.

Granny, using her best southern twang, said, "As John Wayne said, 'Life is tough, but it's tougher when you're stupid.'"

"I know life is tough. I live with you."

Granny swaggered towards the discarded fly swatter, grabbed it, and whacked him again, using the strength God gave her to sting his skin.

Dander twirled a finger around three strands of hair. He blustered, "Well I got a John Wayne saying for you, 'A man ought to do what he thinks is right.'"

"And just what is that supposed to mean?"

"It means I'm doing the best I can with what I know."

During the verbal duel, Officer Mahoney sidestepped the action and began rummaging through the pantry. Finding chips, he tossed the bag to his partner and tagged cookies for himself.

I looked at Officer Mahoney and he shrugged. Whispering he said, "Snacks - Nothing better than eating while watching drama."

"This is not some movie. This is real life."

The officer laughed. "Raine, from the outside looking in, this is life at its funniest."

The three of us paused to watch. I guess it was funny.

Granny blustered, spittle streaming from her lips creating a tiny rainbow of color. "Horse flies! My daughter spent time with you and look where it has gotten us now. This reminds me of another John Wayne saying. 'If you've got them by the balls, their hearts and minds will follow.' I'm tellin' ya - Phyllis grabbed you by the balls long ago, and we still can't be rid of you."

"Woman, I told you once, and I'm going to tell you again: I love Phyllis, and we will be getting married! Let me add one more John Wayne quote to this battle: 'In this kind of war, you've gotta believe in what you're fighting for.'"

Granny shook her head, wrinkles shifting into an unnatural position. "Rob, don't mean to remind you, but you are still married, and Phyllis is not here."

"My marriage was on the fritz long ago. It took the fire to shake me into action. I will marry Phyllis."

"You," Granny said slowly in a tired voice. She whacked him softly on the head and sat at the kitchen table. "Woof, I'm tired."

Dander sat with her at the table and then turned to look at his audience. The three of us looked at each other and sat with them.

Officer Matey continued as if nothing happened, "Raine, you need to call me or Officer Mahoney if you discover any more notes, and please stay away from Mrs. Dander." He cleared his throat and added, "She has a habit of creating drama."

"You think?" commented Dander.

The officer paused and leafed through his notes. He continued, "The sleeping pictures of you and fire scene make me wonder. You are sure the camera never left the Dander's home until that day."

Dander answered, "She's sure because I'm sure. I don't know how anyone could have gotten in this house and taken pictures of Raine sleeping."

Officer Mahoney sighed, "Okay folks, with the fire, pictures, and notes either one of you is lying, or there is a situation brewing in Runge."

"Really?" sighed Granny sarcastically.

Officer Matey sarcastically commented, "I know. It's hard to believe there could be problems in a small town."

Granny answered, "I know. I always thought Runge was such a safe place. It must be teenagers causing problems. They are not watching good wholesome shows like Gunsmoke and Dallas."

The officer's eyes caught and disbelief registered between them.

Officer Mahoney slowed and paused a downbeat, "All-righty then." He continued, "Raine, could you meet me at Regina's Grocery tomorrow morning around 10 to show me the pictures."

"I guess."

"Yes, she will," answered Granny with much more conviction.

The officers left, and I felt drained, so I went to bed for a quick nap. The moment I shut my eyes a dream began. Ms. Prine stood at the front of the classroom and yelled SLACKERS. Notes fell from the ceiling, each containing the words UNKEPT PROMISES. Julie's sad face stared in a full length mirror reflecting her growing belly. Rudy McGarza stood inches from my face waiting for another kiss. His spit poured out of his mouth soaking my body.

At that point of the dream, a portion of my mind kicked in with a thought. I think I am wet. Did I pee in my pants?

My eyes opened and I realized I was wet.

Julie laughed and laughed. In her hand she held a spray bottle and was still spritzing me with water.

"Get up, you sleepy head."

"Why did you do that? I was taking a nap."

"I'm off work. Let's do something," answered Julie.

"Like?"

"I don't know."

144

"Come on Julie. You woke me by spraying me, so you must have something in mind."

"Okay, okay. I do. Let's go see Jess."

"Haven't you seen enough of him?"

Julie flipped a dirty look and answered, "Jeez Raine. It is what it is – move on. I love him, and I'm having his baby."

"Does he know?"

"No. But I am getting up the courage to tell him."

"Did you tell your parents?"

"Heck no."

"Julie."

"Raine. Come on. For today, let's just have fun. ACK! Don't comment on fun."

"Let's go to the school and check out what's going on."

"Great. Let's go."

Chapter Sixteen

Information

By the time we walked to the school, sweat had trickled down our backs and pooled just above our butts. Surveying the school work area, I saw workmen scattered about the school. We edged around the building until we found an unlocked door minus workers. Julie slid into the main hallway, and I followed.

Julie said, "Let's check things out. For fun, let's see how long it takes for us to get caught."

"Okay," I answered and for good measure I shot her one of my best *you have got to be kidding looks*.

"Don't look at me like that. We might be in high school, but that doesn't mean we can't have fun."

I shrugged my shoulders, thinking about her comment.

I asked, "Circus kind of fun?"

"Nah, more like Carol Burnett meets a karate expert at a Powder Puff football game."

"Got ya."

I lead the charge, tip toeing to avoid footstep echoes. Julie mimicked my moves down to my left to right ninja cadence. Every few steps I plastered myself against the lockers, hiding in the hallway shadows.

By the time we neared the main office, not one worker had spotted us, even though the area teemed with workers: some sleeping, others eating, and one working.

Right over left, right over left we moved, trying to maintain complete silence. I turned to check on Julie and hit something.

"Ahh Ms. Raine and Ms. Julie. Nice to run into you, literally. What are you doing here?" asked Coach Whipley, aka Coach Kernel Corn.

I don't know about Julie's mind, but my brain shuffled through possible excuses: lost, see if we could help, school meeting…"

Julie interrupted my thoughts and created an excuse, "Coach, we were taking a walk when I had to use the restroom, so we came inside to pee."

Coach Whipley smiled. "So, you want to stick with that story?"

"Yup," Julie and I said in unison.

Once again, he smiled and crooked his finger indicating we were to follow him. Four televisions sat on a large desk rolling feeds of the school. He stopped one feed, rewound and played the VHS tape. There we were sneaking through the halls like the stooges mimicking ninjas - stoonjas.

Coach Whipley's eyes sparkled and he chuckled, "Now this is some funny stuff." Whipley threw back his head and laughed, deep and meaty all the while displaying his corn kernel tooth.

"It's not funny," Julie raged, a rose color shimmied from her neck to her face.

Hormones I thought. He was in for it now.

Julie continued, "If you were a girl, you would understand."

His laughter caught a wave of confusion and he stared at us. I could not imagine where Julie was going with this line of thinking, so I decided to ride her hormonal thought wave.

He cleared his throat and asked, "Understand what?"

"You know."

"No, I'm afraid I only know what I saw on the monitor." He skipped a beat and continued, "That is – two girls trespassing."

"No, what you saw is two girls needing to find a restroom."

The Kernel shifted in his seat sorting through Julie's ramblings. He leaned forward, pushing rewind followed by the

VCR's play button. For the second time, I watched Julie and I stoonja our way down the hall. Never thought the word stoonja could be used as a verb.

"That's it!" Julie emphatically stated. "Now I've got to tell you the truth."

"About time," he answered.

"I am on my period, and I need to change my pad!"

He stared at Julie. What could he say? Would he want proof?

"Right now?" he managed to stammer.

"Yes. Right now. Since you want to laugh at us, do you want to discuss my heavy flow?"

Poof! Coach Kernel Corn's head shot up and you could see anger beginning to take hold. He answered, "Now see here. I have no idea what you are up to, but I fully believe your period has nothing to do with you being in Runge High School. You do not now or in the future, ever need to talk to me like that again. Get on out of here."

I'm not sure we could have moved any faster. With the school in her rear view mirror, Julie added, "Should have asked him for a maxi pad."

"Julie, you are so bad," I responded and pushed her.

She laughed and added, "Stop it. You are going to hurt the baby."

"What baby?"

Before either of us turned to see who asked the question, we knew who it was…Jess.

He asked again, "What baby?"

Julie ran into his arms and sobbed. "Ah crap," he responded.

He wove his fingers through her hair, kissing her forehead. "You sure?"

As Julie nodded her head up and down, Jess gazed toward the heavens and said again, "Oh no."

He swallowed hard, not once but twice. Then he asked the stupidest question ever asked by a man with a used cucumber, "Why me?"

Julie's shoulders tightened and Jess stepped back. Personally I moved away, too. I had seen this look when Julie discussed her alleged period with Coach Kernel Corn.

"What?" asked Julie. "Why would you say - why me? You mean why us."

Jess shook his head, "I didn't mean it like that. I just meant..."

"What?" asked Julie, again. "This didn't just happen to you. It's happening to me - Son-of-a....."

"No," said Jess grabbing Julie's face between his hands, cupping her cheeks in love and fear. "Listen to me. I love you. We will get through this together. I just need to think. You have known longer than me so give me a sec to think about it. To allow it to sink in. To ...I don't know...just stop and let me think."

He released her face and looked down at his shoes. "Ah Julie. What are we going to do? You're sure, right?"

"Yes," she answered.

"Did you go to the doctor?"

"No."

"Then how did you know."

"Sarge Hanks got me a pregnancy test."

"What? Sarge Hanks knows? Who else?"

I answered, "Me."

Jess continued, "Who else?"

In a soft voice, Julie answered, "God."

"Come here sweetie," said Jess, extending his arms. "This is what we are going to do for now. Nothing. I mean, you might miscarry or might even decide not to have this baby. What will our parents say? My dad is going to lose it on me."

Julie retorted, "Your dad? Pleazze."

"What do you mean?" asked Jess.

I interjected, "You haven't told him?"

"Told me what?" asked Jess.

Julie looked at me and I looked at Julie.

"Told me what?" asked Jess, again.

"Well…" answered Julie.

"Spit it out," I prodded.

Julie continued, "Hmm, well."

"Ahh jeeze Julie. Tell him," I prodded once again.

"Someone better tell me before I get really upset,"

Not mincing words, I announced, "Julie's dad beats her and her mom."

"What?" Jess gasped. "Are you kidding me?"

"No, it's not like that," pleaded Julie. She began spewing sentences in rapid succession to defend her dad. "We sometimes make him mad, and he loses his temper. He can't help it. He's really getting better. Once you get to know him, you'll understand."

With each excuse, Jess grew madder and madder, clenching and unclenching his fists.

"He hits you?" questioned Jess. He shook his head back and forth not believing the added information about Julie. "I'm going to kill him."

Julie panicked, "No, Jess. It's not like that. He promised he wouldn't do it again."

"Has that stopped him?" asked Jess.

Julie remained silent.

"Answer me. He promises not to do it again, but he always does, right?" continued Jess.

Julie whispered, "Yes."

Jess shook his head and a tear slid from his eyes. "Julie, my first step dad did the same thing to my mom. As a little kid, I hid under the desk and watched him hit her over and over again." He paused recalling the memory and then shook his head to remove it. With conviction he added, "I will NOT allow him to do that to you."

"How do you plan on doing that?" I asked. "It's not like you live in their house."

Jess turned his gaze at me, "Don't you worry. I'll think of something."

I flipped back, "Just like your avoidance of the baby?

Remember you said you two were not going to do anything because Julie might miscarry or decide not to have this baby."

Julie spit out, "Stop it Raine. Jess loves me and we'll figure out something."

"This is rich. You are protecting Jess just like you protect your dad."

"Raine, I said to stop it," added Julie.

Shaking my head in disbelief, I said, "When you decide you need me, I'll be at Granny's house."

I mustered my best 'go suck fruit flies' stare and shot it at Julie and Jess. Then I walked away. I listened for a ...'wait Raine' or 'hold on a minute,' but silence walked beside me. My mind told me to look back. Maybe the two were watching me, hoping I would return. The urge gripped me like trying to resist scratching my nose. A nose must be itched, so I turned and looked back. Jess and Julie were hugging, and I was not part of their world.

Chapter Seventeen

The News

I arrived home and noticed the open garage door. Boxes and garbage bags framed three sides. Since anything was better than going inside to Granny and Dander, I decided to reorganize part of the garage. I had no idea where to begin, so I reverted to an age old technique for task selection: eeny, meeny, miny, and moe. My moe was the part of the garage I hated the most - the area with piles of clothes sandwiched between the garbage bags and boxes. Gripping the clothes, I pulled and flipped them over my head to the other side of the garage. After a couple of pulls, a treasure surfaced - my childhood toy box. The painted teddy bear on the lid had faded, but he still welcomed me to play. I opened the box and a musty mildew smell rose and so did additional memories of laughter and love. The depth of the box made it difficult to see the contents, so I flipped the switch to turn on the garage light, but nothing happened. Hmm. I thought. Grabbing a fresh bulb, I removed the old one to replace it. I gripped the bulb and turned. A piece of paper fell from the outlet. I grabbed it and stepped in the outside light to read it. It said: Unkept Promises must be punished.

I screamed. Fear bulldozed my warm fuzzy feels of moments ago. Granny and Dander ran out of the house.

"Are you okay?" asked Granny.

I extended the note in my hand to Granny.

Fear with an added bit of holy crap flooded her body. Granny handed the note to Dander. He read it and said, "Call the police. Enough is enough."

152

By the time the officers left, exhaustion consumed me. I gripped Feeffers with the vengeance a wolf would use to maintain ownership of a deer leg. The comfort allowed a quick sleep launching into a delicious dream of eating warm funnel cakes on a carnival midway. Just as my teeth plunged into the gooey cake, a noisy - CA-WHAP, CA-WHAP jolted me from my dream.

I laid there and listened. My first thought was Unkept Promises was in the house. I lifted my head to pull the cover folds from my ears. I listened again. CA-WHAP, CA-WHAP - it sounded from inside Dander's room. Fear snaked through me. I continued listening. Surely I was dreaming. Movement and the strange sounds were definitely in Dander's room. A supernatural pressure began to build within me similar to gas after a heavy meal. The pressure grew until I needed to release my raw unbridled anger. I grabbed my lamp, holding the stand like a weapon.

Gripping his door knob, I twisted it slowly. Another CA-WHAP...I squeezed my head through the narrowest of openings. Moonlight streamed through the windows, illuminating a naked Dander doing yoga... with my mother? A squash belly twisted over hypnotic melons - the whole mess jiggling. My mind tried to make sense of this vision. Slowly, puzzle pieces began to slide together.

It was not yoga but my principal doing the nasty with my mom - next to my room. This was all kinds of wrong. They never knew I was there. I could not tear my eyes away from the squashing-melons.

"Raine," called Granny out in a whisper. "Where are you?"

I pulled my head out of the room and grabbed and hugged Granny.

"Granny," I whispered. "I have bad news and bad news."

"Give it to me straight. I can take it," answered Granny.

"Phyllis and Dander are making fruit salad."

"No way!"

153

Granny bolted from my embrace and opened Dander's door.

"What the hell is going on here?" demanded Granny as she flipped on the bedroom light.

"AHHHHHHHHHH!" screamed Dander like a little boy who caught his green bean in his zipper.

Granny walked out of the room, slamming the door. She yelled, "Get your clothes on and meet me in the living room. We are going to talk!"

Once again, Granny's mind flipped a switch and a new train of thinking barreled down her one-tracked mind. She began yelling her monologue as she walked to the living room, "Just what do you think you are doing in my house, under my roof. I invited you over because your skinny boned - green beaned wife got rid of you when she discovered you cucumbered Phyllis. What the heck do you think I'm made of? I can't handle this kind of pressure. This Unkept Promises nonsense scares the raisins out of me, and now I have to have an intruder in my home. And to find out it's my own daughter! Holy pap smears. I can't handle this. Do you have your clothes on yet? Hurry up. I'm getting tired of talking to myself. Raine you get in here too. We are going to hammer this out and I need your input."

I sat on the floor near Granny, listening to her. I was feeling kind of happy because now I knew the noises in the house have probably been my mom the whole time. It was enjoyable for Dander and mom to feel Granny's wrath. They deserved it. Maybe Granny would kick Dander out of the house.

WHACK! Granny smacked my head. She told me, "Don't think I don't see you smiling, Raine. I know you are thinking Dander is leaving. But no, I want him right here where I can watch him."

Granny and I turned to see Dander and Mom walk down the stairs, holding hands.

"Sit!" commanded Granny.

They sat, side by side, with a stupid look on their face. I recognized the same look when I discovered Jess and Julie in the school hallway after the dance. Mom's face looked slightly embarrassed and Dander's face goofy.

"This is how it's going to be. ONE - Dander, you need to think about your future.   Divorce, no divorce, get back with Grace - whatever the future is - you need to decide. TWO - there will be no veggie tossing under my roof until Rob has made his decisions about his future. THREE - Phyllis - I'm tired of your flighty ways. You never seem to find what you want so you hop from man to man. So, I'm telling you. You will find a job. You will not leave again. You will be more of a mother to Raine. FOUR - Rob, you need to spend time with your kids. I am talking about Marian and Kimmi. They need the confident man you used to be, not this saggy, wishy washy fruit fly of a man. FIVE - I will not be awakened in the middle of the night again. SIX - you three talk."

With that, she marched up the stairs and returned to her room. I scratched my head wondering what had just happened.

My mother got on the floor. She pulled me into her arms and started kissing me as she said, "Ahh baby, I'm home. I'm so glad you are finally with your parents. We love you soooo much."

"Stop it!" I grimaced from the affection. "Mom, pull your head out of your crack. Granny is my only parent."

"You will not talk to your mom like that," stated Dander in an authoritative manner.

My mom turned to him and fluttered her dewy eyes. She turned back to me, "Raine, did I ever tell you why we named you Raine?"

"This is not a freaking game of 'Let's Remember.' This is life and it sucks."

She continued, ignoring my interruption. "Rob and I named you because you were born during a wonderful earth soothing rain. You have always remained a soothing part of my life. Other than Rob, you are the best thing that ever happened to me."

"Excuse me?" I interrupted again.

Dander added, "What your mom means is that you *are* the cornerstone of our love."

"Ahhh Rob. How do you always know how I feel? I love you so much," said mom in a sultry voice which made my stomach churn like smelling a rotten egg fart.

"Granny said NO MORE VEGGIE TOSSING!" I said in my personal authoritative voice.

Dander retorted, "Now Raine, we are in love. We can't help that our words reflect that. You need to get one thing through your cute pumpkin head. We are a family. Let me say it again. We are a family. You have a mom, dad, granny, and two sisters. Granny is right. Marian and Kimmi need to be part of our lives. I'll talk to Grace tomorrow about spending time with all three of my girls here - at my new home."

My mom clapped her hands in delight, "Ahhh Rob. I can't wait. Finally, I will have all my children and my sweetie with me."

I said, "You two are weird. I'm going to bed."

Leaving, I could not help but think they were having some major reality issues. I crawled into bed and gripped Feeffers like my last salvation. Poor Feeffers, his button eyes bulged as I clutched his midsection. Pulling the covers over my head, I curled in fetal position and started crying.

My door opened and I heard movement. I prayed it was Granny, but I suspected it was the parental unit ready to cause me pain in the form of tenderness.

Someone sat on each side of my bed. My mom pulled back the covers and said, "Honey, I know you are upset, but change is like that. It can be uncomfortable. However, for our family, it's the best thing possible. We are finally together."

"Raine," said Dander clearing his throat. He continued, "Take some time and let the possibilities wrap around your heart."

I sat up and looked from one to the other. How could I respond? I needed space - and lots of it. I got out of bed and slipped my sweats over my night clothes, crawled out of my window, and walked.

I heard mom say, "Don't go!"

156

Dander answered, "Don't worry. She will be back. She always comes back."

My feet naturally took me to Julie's house. I stood outside her house, and every hair on my body stood. Something felt wrong, very wrong. It was too quiet - no blaring television - no blazing lights. I crept up the front porch steps and peeked into the house. A small light illuminated Mr. Twain, slumped on the couch, with his front shirt covered in sweat and blood droplets. I saw the rise and fall of his chest. Okay. He is alive, but Julie? Mrs. Twain? Unkept Promises slid into my mind.

Adrenaline jump started my legs and powered me home, faster than my mom changing husbands. Knowing the front door would be locked, I crawled up the tree and into my room. My mom and Dander were cuddling on the floor waiting for my return.

"You have to help!" I screamed. "Something has happened at Julie's house."

Dander took control. Whether it was the terror in my voice or the fact he trusted me, he did not ask further information. He announced, "Phyllis, call the police. Raine, let's go."

He sped down the street leaving a trail of curling rubber. We arrived with Officers Matey and Mahoney trailing us.

"Stay," Officer Matey signaled.

Dander and I sat in the car. He grabbed my hand and held it, saying, "Raine, it will be okay."

I thought about his words and remembered the blood. I thought - maybe...maybe not. One thing for sure, this day was a changing point.

Officer Matey and Mahoney moved toward the house, guns drawn. The officers peeked in the open front door and spotted Mr. Twain on the couch.

I heard one of the officers loudly announce, "Runge Police Department. We are coming in. Runge Police Officers coming in. Mr. Twain, Mr. Twain. Are you okay?"

Whether it was the silence of the night or the fact that fear increased my sensitivity to sound, I heard Mr. Twain respond in a gravelly voice chock full of a southern accent, "Geeet off my property!"

"Mr. Twain, this is the Runge Police Department. We need to know if everything is okay."

"I sayid, geeet off my propertee!" Mr. Twain responded again, followed by a loud crash. Officer Matey and Officer Mahoney moved inside the house.

"JULIE!!!" I screamed. I gripped the car door, flung it open, and ran to help.

I'm not sure how, but Dander bolted too and grabbed me, pinning me to the ground.

"You will not go in there," huffed and puffed Dander. "It's too dangerous."

I screamed, "You don't understand. Mr. Twain is dangerous. He's hit me, and he'll kill her if he finds out she's pregnant."

The secret slipped. I closed my eyes and shook my head.

"He hit you? I'll kill him."

He gave the top of his head a quick paw and then barreled his way to the house. His forward motion overtook his surplus belly weight. He hit the ground in a belly flop and laid there teeter tottering, up and down on his squash abdomen. This allowed me enough time to jump up and sit on him.

I had just enough weight to hold down an out of shape man. Dander remained stationary, huffing, puffing, and trying to regain his breath.

I said, "Dander, he is a dangerous man."

Dander tried to respond, but he could not regain enough oxygen.

We remained sitting on the front lawn center stage to the action. Mr. Twain was tucked in the back of the patrol car. Mrs. Twain was found in the kitchen, badly beaten. And Julie – was not found.

The paramedics arrived and took a stretcher in the house.

Dander and I could see enough through the front door to watch the paramedics strap Mrs. Twain on the gurney. They hauled her down the front porch stairs and positioned her just outside the ambulance tailgate.

The sheet did not cover her injuries worth a squat. Droplets of blood appeared like confetti. Her nose was inches out of place and her mouth three times its regular size. I watched as Officer Matey hovered over Mrs. Twain's ear, questioning her about the attack. She only had enough energy to lift her swelling eyelids. I wanted to go to her, to let her know everything would be okay now that Mr. Twain was cuffed and stuffed in the back of the police car. But mainly I wanted to find Julie.

I looked around, trying to find my friend. Runge's finest emergency workers scrabbled all over the area. Somehow between the moving forms, I spotted my mom, Granny, and Julie racing to us. All three dog piled Dander and me.

I stated, "Julie, I thought you were hurt like your mom!"

She answered, "My mom? Where is she?"

In unison, we pointed to the ambulance. Julie released an anguished cry which made every person in the area stop mid motion and watch Julie run to her mom.

Mrs. Twain shimmied her hand out of the straps and cupped Julie's face. I moved closer to see if somehow I could add comfort. Dander shadowed my every move. The two of us nearly morphed into one person. Mrs. Twain looked at us and then reached out her hand. At first I thought she wanted me to come closer, but when she crocked her finger beaconing to the top section of my shadow and I realized it was Dander she wanted. He leaned over and hovered his ear inches above her mouth. Seconds later he stepped away and the paramedics loaded Mrs. Twain. I watched as Julie surveyed the area.

Spotting her dad in the squad car, she roared towards him screaming, "I hate you! How could you do that to me? I thought you loved me. I thought you would get better when we moved, but you didn't. You are always going to remain evil. You bastard! You tried to kill my baby. If it weren't for mom, you would have done it too. Mom protected me and what did she get for it?"

Julie slapped the squad car window with her hand and continued her tirade. "I'm talking to you! Do you hear me? I asked you what did mom get for protecting me?"

Mr. Twain never look up. His eyes remained glued to his lap. Julie slapped the window again. Officer Matey grabbed her hand and said, "Stop." He paused long enough for Julie to refocus. Then he continued once again. "You need to tell me what happened."

He flipped open his pad of paper and readied his pen. Julie looked at the officer and back at her father. She announced, "This time I'm going to tell the truth...all of it."

Mr. Twain looked at her, the corner of his mouth twitched.

Julie smiled, "Oh, did I finally get your attention? I'm not even going to leave out the part where you hit Mom trying to get to me, or the part where you tried to kick my stomach to kill the baby!"

Officer Matey scribbled every tidbit of information. The rest of us remained glued on Julie's words. She continued yelling, "I hate you! I hate you!"

Officer Matey interrupted Julie and asked, "So what happened just after Mr. Twain tried to kick you in the stomach?"

Julie just stopped and stared at Officer Matey. Then she looked around and noticed her audience. She puffed up her shoulders and tears streamed down her face.

Officer Matey asked again, "So what happened after Mr. Twain tried to kick you in the stomach?"

Granny poked the officer in the upper arm and spouted, "I know your momma taught you better manners than to pester a woman when she is distressed. You scallywag."

Folding Julie into her arms, Granny continued, "You are a bad, bad officer. You should console her before barking questions at her."

"Sorry," Officer Matey apologized.

Granny released Julie and turned to the officer and popped

him on the backside adding, "Now run on and give me a few minutes to calm down Julie. I'll let you know when you can talk to her."

Officer Matey deepened his voice, "Granny, don't ever hit an officer."

Granny puffed up retorting, "If you need a spanking…"

At that moment, Dander nudged Julie to the side and grabbed Granny, pulling her into his belly, smothering her comment.

Dander said, "I'll see to it that she doesn't…"

Granny struggled until Dander released her.

"You oversized piece of squash crap. I could have died. You nearly cut off my air supply."

Dander shook his head responding, "The officer would have cut more than that off if you didn't respect him!"

Granny's response was an exaggerated eye roll. Under her breath she added, "Give me some scissors and I'll cut something of his off and yours too for that matter."

She paused a moment for effect and continued speaking to Julie, "Darling, what happened?"

Officer Matey stepped back from Julie but stayed within earshot.

Julie looked at her audience and began. "Mom was in the kitchen cooking dinner when Dad came home from work. I'm not sure what set him off, but he began yelling about the house being dirty. That's when I walked in and tried to help. Sometimes I'm able to calm him down- but not this time. He fumed and sputtered something about Jess and meeting his father. Dad wanted to know why he was the last one to know I had a boyfriend. I didn't know what to say, so I just stared at him – waiting for some sliver of an idea to make its way into the front of my brain. Dad stared back and then said in more of a statement than question – 'I bet you two have already had sex. You girls are all the same - you can't keep your legs together. So, are you?' I had no clue what he meant so I just stared at him. He answered his own question by saying, 'You are pregnant.'

Julie took a deep breath and looked at the house. I'm sure she replayed her father's abusive temper tantrum in her mind. Tears glazed her face, and Julie took in air and continued, "That's when Dad's anger multiplied by ten. His face reddened and his brow line sank over his eyes. He pulled back his fist and plowed me to the floor, kicking my stomach. He yelled, 'You little betraying whore, I will remove the baby one way or the other!'"

Julie took a deep breath trying to push down her anger and fear. She lifted her shirt and exposed the darkening areas on her stomach. She paused, and she seemed to look within her herself to complete the story. "Mom pushed me to the side and yelled 'Julie get out of here. Run!'"

Julie teared up again and added, "I left watching him throw her down and kick her. She took my punishment for getting pregnant. Did you hear me? She took my punishment. I deserved it, not mom or the baby."

My mom looked at me and mouthed, pregnant?

Granny interrupted, "Just stop. That's the biggest load of bull slop I've ever heard. What do you mean punishment? Things happen. No one deserves to be beaten. Talked to. Given extra chores, but beaten...NO!"

Once again Dander took charge, "Julie, your mom asked me to take care of you until things are settled. We need to get you to the doctor to make sure you and the baby are okay. Then we will check on your mom."

Dander turned to Officer Matey and asked, "Do you have any more questions for Julie? I need to take her to the emergency room."

Officer Matey glanced at Granny. She lifted her eyebrows and squeezed off a pinched smile. The officer's body language shrank. He answered, "Um, no. I'm good. Call me at the office to update me on Julie's medical status."

Chapter Eighteen

Friendship into Sisterhood

My heart ached waiting to hear news about Julie and her mom. It was like my pain would slice me in half. Julie might not be a blood relative, but she was bound to my heart like another artery. I'm not sure when I actually fell asleep because I must have looked out of my bedroom window a zillion times, checking to see if Dander returned. About two in the morning, Dander pulled into the driveway. The car's headlight beam penetrated my bedroom window waking me.

It would only take one look at Dander's body language to know if Julie and her mom would be okay. My heart beat harder. I saw his dark silhouette sway in the car window. It looked like he was talking to himself. What was taking him so long to get out of the Buick? Was he trying various versions of the truth to see which one would stun me the least?

Without warning, another silhouette popped up from the back seat. Julie! It was Julie. I raced down the stairs, out of the house, and flung open the back door of the car.

"Julie! You are here. Are you okay?"

I crawled into the backseat and wrapped my arms around her. She looked tired but otherwise there were no bandages.

"I'm fine. Mom will be okay too, but she is going to stay in the hospital to be monitored."

"Praise God," I responded.

I wanted to ask about the baby. I looked down at her belly.

Julie caught my glance and answered, "Baby is fine."

"Thank goodness."

Julie did not answer. She got out of the Buick and headed up the sidewalk to the house. I followed with Dander trailing us. Julie climbed the stairs and went to my room, climbing into the bed without uttering a word. She fluffed her pillow several times and laid down, back facing me. I followed suit.

The next morning, I left Julie sleeping and wandered into the kitchen where I walked into an intense discussion between Granny, my mom, and Dander. Huddled like a football team discussing the next play, I leaned near the pack and listened. I heard intermittent words like: *Unkept Promises, Julie, and the girls*.

I interrupted, "What's going on?"

The three swiveled to face me. Mom walked forward, rubbed my arm and announced, "It's happened again."

"What?"

She cleared her throat, "Well, a packaged wrapped in yellow wrapping paper was placed on the front porch. This time it was addressed to Julie."

"That's nice," I responded.

My mom shook her head, "You don't understand."

"What's not to understand? Someone wanted to give a get well gift to Julie."

Again my mom shook her head. "No, the wrapping paper had little yellow ducks and a baby rattle on it. Raine, it was a baby gift."

"Who would do that?"

Granny answered, "We don't know. But the strangest part is the note."

"Granny, please don't tell me it had something to do with Unkept Promises."

Granny, Mom, and Dander stared at me. Dander answered, "The note said: Unkept Promises will be punished."

"Don't you think this is weird?" I said. "Julie has never received one of these notes but now that she is in our house...Well.

She's got one. What is the connection?"

Dander pawed the front of his head and then slid his hand over his face. Melodramatically he whined, "It's me. All me. I've brought this danger to you. It's because I fell in love with Phyllis. That *is* the only connection."

"Yup. I agree," interjected Granny. "You went all pulpy with my daughter when she was an impressionable teen, so now, your pulp continues to spew forth as the fruit flies dive bomb my house."

"Mother!" shouted my mom. "You are talking about my future husband."

"Mother, nothing. Anything Dander touches goes to crap in a handbag including his so called marriage."

I have never heard Granny talk like this. Was this how she felt about me? Was I crap?

I blustered, "Granny, if you really believe that, you are calling me crap too."

Granny's face went ashen. "I never thought about it like that. You are the best thing I've ever had in my life. Well, Rob, you did manage to create something good."

My mom's face pinched and contorted trying to determine how to handle the personal attack. "So, Mother, are you calling me crap?"

"Well, let me think about it. Flighty, insecure, jobless, slut..." Granny paused a second and continued, "...daughter, mother of Raine...well, you are only 1/2 crap."

"Mother, that is not very nice."

Granny added, "Phyllis, why don't we focus on what we are going to do about this situation instead of coming up with a human comparison to crap."

"Now see here, Granny," began Dander.

The doorbell rang and the crap discussion silenced. We looked at each other. Granny mouthed: Unkept Promises is at the door.

Each of us grabbed a weapon of mass destruction: Granny a

meat mallet; Mom a butcher knife; Dander an ice pick; and me, I stood behind the crappers. Dander peered through the window and announced, "False alarm. It's Sarge."

He opened the door and invited her inside the house.

Sarge began, "Wow, do you always welcome your guests with dangerous kitchen utensils?"

Granny gathered the weapons and returned them to the kitchen.

Sarge continued, "The grocery aisles are steep in the events of last night. I wanted to check on Julie and see if I could help."

"Julie is still sleeping," I explained.

Julie peeked her head around the wall and answered, "Not anymore. The crap conversation poked my eyes open."

Her face now sported a small bruise, but otherwise, there were no visual reminders of her father using her as a kicking bag. Sarge grabbed Julie's shoulders and pulled her in for a hug.

"You okay?" Sarge asked.

"I will be."

"Do you want to talk?"

"Sure."

"Let's walk around the block and chat."

Granny cleared her throat and responded to the suggestion, "Ya know that crap you referred to earlier?"

Julie and Sarge gawked at Granny trying to make sense of such a random question.

"Umm, yeess," answered Julie.

Granny hesitated and then announced, "You just got crapped on."

"Granny, what are you talking about?" asked Sarge.

Granny answered, "Unkept Promises left a gift for Julie. That basically means he or she is watching the house so I don't think it's a good idea to go outside. In fact, I think we should all stay together until this whole promise crap is solved."

Sarge walked to the window and pulled the curtain to the side.

She analyzed the area like an operative preparing for a military resurgence. "I don't see anyone now except Scooter mowing and your neighbor, Mrs. Lapp, having a morning cocktail. Have you called the local authorities?"

"Just about to," said Dander. "I wanted to open the present first."

Sarge grabbed the gift and listened. She turned it right and left, giving every side a quick visual. Then she set it on the table and watched it.

Granny watched the antics and asked, "You done this before?"

"If you have to know, Granny, in one of my previous occupations, I worked with military weapons."

"Well that does explain a lot." Granny nodded her head agreeing with herself.

Continuing her analysis, Sarge announced, "I must take this outside just in case there is something harmful."

Her muscles flexed beneath her Regina's Grocery work shirt, and her demeanor changed from grocery manager to Agent 007. Walking with purpose, she moved the gift outside and saddled herself between several of Granny's backyard rusty treasures. Sarge stuck her hand in the front of her shirt, reached between her breasts, and pulled out a pocket knife. With a quick flick of her wrist, the blade removed the wrapping paper. Sarge spent a few minutes inspecting the gift wrap and finally set it down. Then she opened the box and looked. A smirkish smile passed over her face but was quickly covered over with a steely tough girl appearance. She picked up the box, turning and twisting it for various views of the mystery gift. Finally she reached inside the box and removed a very flat, yellowish object. Sarge sniffed it, pulled off a corner, and ate the piece.

She turned to the house and proclaimed, "It's a slice of cheese...processed cheese."

Granny muttered to herself, "I guess she would know."

Sarge walked to the house and presented the cheese like a

trophy. "Someone wrote a message on the cheese with black pen. I would speculate that the pen had a fine point. There are no extra bits of cheese next to the letters."

"Well," stammered Granny. "What does it say?"

"Ahh, yes. It says: Promises are like fake cheese."

Julie asked, "What does that mean?"

Granny chuckled, "Means Dander's full of rotten fruit. Someone just does not like anyone near you Rob. Other than what you did to my Phyllis, what did you do to piss someone off?"

He pawed his hair, arranging several strands over his ever widening bald spot. "Nothing that I know of."

My mom cleared her throat. "Rob, that's not exactly true. You had an affair. Is it possible Grace is seeking revenge?"

"I guess. But, umm, I never thought of that. Do you think she would harm my kids?"

Smiling, my mom placed her hand on his shoulder and tenderly massaged it. "No, babe. She would never hurt your kids. She would just hurt you."

"Phyllis, that's not a nice thing to say, but I guess I understand. However, I don't think she is that warped to send cheese with a message."

Granny snickered, "She married you didn't she?"

"Mother!" exclaimed my mom. "Do not talk about my future husband that way ever again! I'm warning you. I will take Raine away, and you will never see her again."

Sarge puffed out her chest and made herself seem two feet taller and three and a half feet wider. "Now, let's calm down. We need to stay focused on the situation at hand."

Granny answer, "You're right, Sarge. Besides, Phyllis will move in a week or two, so I know Raine will go nowhere."

"That might have been," my mom responded. "But that was the old Phyllis. The new Phyllis stays and cares for her daughter. I finally have the love of my life in my arms."

"There she blows!" Granny shrieked. "The old Phyllis is back."

Mom glared, "What do you mean by that?"

Granny chuckled. "Phyllis, the love of your life should have been Raine. That's being a mother. Rob is just an itch in your inner fruit. Once you pick it - you'll move on."

"I said enough!" ordered Sarge. "Inform the police of the cheese note. Julie, you come with me. We are going to walk and talk. I can promise each and every person here that I WILL keep Julie safe. She will be back here soon. Oh and Rob. I would suggest talking to Mrs. Dander about the notes. Perhaps she is getting them too."

Sarge beaconed Julie to her. They left through the back door, screen door slamming.

Dander waved his hand in front of him and said, "This whole thing is no good. So if we are theorizing the conclusion would be: all of these notes, fire, and gift are all because of my love for Phyllis. I got to sit down. I need to think."

He walked into the living room and sat in his armchair. He laid his head back and closed his eyes. Periodically he would grunt or mumble to himself. The rest of us stood around him and waited. Truthfully I'm not sure why we watched. For me, I'm sure it was morbid curiosity. What was he going to do now?

Finally, he opened his eyes and announced, "I need to make some phone calls."

He grunted his way out of the arm chair. He made his way to the phone and dialed 0.

"This is Robert Dander. I'm need to speak with Officer Matey."

He paused to listen.

"Yes, I'll hold."

He paused again.

"Yes. Officer Matey, this is Robert Dander. First, Julie is now at Granny's house and recovering fine."

Paused again.

"Yes, the baby is fine. But I need to tell you about the note and gift left for Julie. Sarge opened the gift and found cheese."

Dander paused. Paused some more.

Dander rolled his eyes, "Quit laughing...Yes, I said cheese...A slice...No, this is not a joke...You don't understand. The note *was written* on the cheese. Really, stop laughing. You are irritating me. Sir. Do you have to announce this to all of your cop buddies? Sir, REALLY. If you can hear me over your snorting, I will call you back in an hour. I'll just put the cheese in the refrigerator so the evidence will not be melted by the time you choose to take this seriously."

Dander returned the phone to its cradle. Then he looked at Phyllis and mouthed: love you. He took a deep breath and another. His third deep breath was so deep I thought his double chin would slide through his mouth and dangle down his throat. And with that, he dialed a number, one that he knew from memory.

"Hello, Grace, this is Rob, your husband. We need to talk. Grace. Grace. Grace." He looked at us and said, "She hung up."

Dander dialed in the number again. "Grace, before you hang up. You need to listen."

Grace must have said something quite poetic because Dander responded, "Yes, Grace. I've been there and back. Hear me out. We need to talk about a divorce."

He pulled the phone away from his ear. Grace's deep, throaty ramblings jetted through the phone like she was standing in the room. She answered, "Divorce! What do you mean divorce? I want to do more than divorce you."

The rant continued with some unexplainable words and sounds. Clarity returned and we heard, "You have never been a good husband. After all I've done for you. I have never once strayed...not like you."

Dander answered her accusations with one word, "Scooter."

Grace hung up.

Chapter Nineteen

Changes

About ten minutes later, the front door opened, and Julie and Sarge entered the living room smiling. It was as if nothing bad had ever happened. Perhaps my family could shake off the Unkept Promises crap.

At that moment the front door creaked and a shoe poked its way through to widen the door. Tension swept over the room.

Everyone froze, expect Sarge. She must have felt her personal perimeter in danger of being breached. Her military sixth sense zoomed into overdrive and she flung open the door, grabbed the intruder and pinned them to the wall.

"Shitake mushrooms! What now?" shouted Granny.

Dander responded, "What the hell are you doing here Grace?"

Mrs. Dander squeaked. She tried to speak but only a squeak penetrated the airwaves.

Sarge asked, "Does anyone know why Mrs. Dander is sneaking into this house? Someone? Anyone?"

The prisoner twisted, only moving centimeters. Granny narrowed her eyes and walked to Grace, standing inches from her face. Granny asked, "Have you lost your mind? This is my house. You don't belong here. And by the way, are you the slug that has been showering us with Unkept Promises crap? Answer me, you flying fig of a fart knocker!"

"Granny!" I interrupted. "I hate to interrupt you but it's hard to talk when she is plastered against the wall." I let my words sink into her brain and added, "Sarge, let Mrs. Dander breathe."

Sarge took her hold down a notch or two, more like three or four notches, allowing Mrs. Dander the opportunity to slurp in several deep breaths. Her bulging eyeballs receded, and a normal color filled her face.

"Th th th ank you," stuttered and puffed Mrs. Dander, seeming genuinely thankful.

Dander moved toward his wife and ran his hand over her shoulder. He began in a soothing tone, "What are you doing here?"

"You asked for a divorce. It should have been me telling you I want a divorce. You are the one who fathered a child while we were married. You shouldn't be happy. You shouldn't feel entitled to go on as if nothing ever happened between us."

It was weird to see Mrs. Dander passive and meek. Sarge must have sensed the change in her too. Within seconds, Sarge completely released her hold, and Mrs. Dander turned and slid into Dander's arms. He held her, stroking her back. Nuzzling into his chest, Mrs. Dander wrapped her arms around him. The two of them were completely lost in their world leaving the rest of us to contemplate what the heck was happening. Mrs. Dander tilted her head up which caused Dander to look down.

Mrs. Dander whispered something unintelligible.

"What?" asked Dander, moving his face closer to hers.

Then, Mrs. Dander reached up and grabbed the back of Dander's head, forcing it down. Their lips now touching, Mrs. Dander wasted no time slipping him the tongue. It was a full throttle lip lock with spittle slinging from left to right.

There was an audible gasp, some dry heaving, and one shrill laugh in the room. I think I was the dry heaver, but it was my mom's laughter.

I think Dander went numb from fear because he went with the motion of the kiss but his eyes were open, wide open. Mrs. Dander continued kissing, making her tongue swim like a fish in and out of the water.

"Grace, just stop," laughed my mom. "I know what you are

doing. You will not make me jealous. Rob loves me, not you."

Grace pulled away from Dander and asked, "What do you mean you're not jealous?"

While she questioned my mom, Mrs. Dander used her hand to break the spit strings left hanging in the air. Dander used his hand to dry his face.

Laughing, my mom answered, "When Rob is truly enjoying his kiss, his eyes are shut."

"How the hell would you know?"

"I, on the other hand," continued my mom, "like to watch the person I'm kissing to see if he is enjoying our kiss."

Disgust launched across Mrs. Dander's face. Her pencil thin lips grew thinner, her nose wrinkled, and her shoulders bunched. "You are such a slut."

"Now, now, Grace," interrupted Dander. "You and I both know talking like that is not going to help solve our situation. Let's sit at the kitchen table and talk about things." He paused for a bit and added, "Come on Grace."

Dander stood and motioned his hand like an arrow pointing out the kitchen. Grace held solid to the floor. Her green bean body swayed slightly as if she was weighing the pros and cons of actually discussing the concerns at hand.

Thirty seconds went by, and all of us remained captive to the brewing issues. Sarge cleared her throat and announced, "Hmm, folks. I don't mean to leave this happy festival, but I need to restock some shelves." Sarge edged out of the door and stuck her head back inside for one final goodbye, "Julie, I'll check on you tomorrow."

The hostile situation continued. The second hand of the kitchen clock clicked away the time. Sixty seconds went to one-hundred-twenty seconds. Two minutes was not a long time except when anticipation was involved.

Granny snapped and announced, "Grace, put on your granny panties and drag your green bean butt to the table."

Granny cupped Grace's elbow and tried to direct her to the

kitchen.

Mrs. Dander pulled her arm away and bellowed, "Don't touch me! I have a good mind to drop you to the floor like I did in the hospital."

"Now, ladies." inserted Dander. "No one will be dropping anyone to the floor. Granny, Phyllis, and girls, why don't you let Grace and I have some privacy in the kitchen."

Several hours later, the back door slammed, and we peered out of the window and watched Mrs. Dander walk to her car. Dander smiled as he walked into the living room. He scooped up my mom and flung her in a circle around him.

"Phyllis, it's finally happening! We are going to be a family."

"Oh, Rob. I am so, so very happy. What happened?"

Dander set her down and grabbed her hands, kissing them. "Honey…my love…Grace and I worked out some of the divorce plans. Of course we will have to see a lawyer, but at least we have a direction."

"Rob, give me details."

"Well, we first talked about you. I told her everything."

My mom's eyes went wide. "Rob, you told her everything?"

He chuckled a masculine macho rumble and answered, "Well, maybe not everything."

"Whew. Thank goodness!" answered my mom. "Go on."

I rolled my eyes.

"Basically, we are going to divide everything down the middle, including custody of the girls."

I decided it was time for me to add some of my own comments to their conversation. "So, she sounds like she was pretty fair about the divorce. Don't you think that's a bit odd for Mrs. Dander? She has quite a temper so this personality reversal seems odd."

Dander smiled, "Well, I neglected to mention that I did bring up her affair with Scooter."

"No way!" added my mom. "So what happened?"

174

"She laughed and tried to brush it under the table. But when I told her that Kimmi said that Scooter mowed our lawn a lot...well...she knew she was screwed."

Granny asked, "How's that?"

"Granny, my daughter can't keep a secret. Grace knows that Kimmi will unleash more information than I will ever need to prove adultery on both sides of the marriage."

"So," added Granny. "You knocked up a student and had a child out of wedlock. That should cook your ass-paragus and good!"

Once again, I saw Dander's face transform from happiness to gut wrenching sadness. "Well, I suspect, that, well. Um."

"Aw, spill it already," bellied Granny.

I knew what he was getting at. I've seen that look all my life, so I finished his sentence, "That Kimmi is not his child but Scooter's."

Dander added, "Who is to say she's even Scooters? Who is to say she hasn't had more 'Scooters' in her life that I don't know about."

"Well at least she didn't rape a young impressionable girl," verbally slapped Granny.

My mom's eyes narrowed and she hollered, "Enough! You wicked woman! You think you were a perfect mom? I spent my life fearful that you would do something stupid. Remember my first grade Valentine party? All you had to do was bring cupcakes. But NO! You did bring cupcakes alright, but instead of cake batter you layered Oreo's and Cheese Wiz. Kids called me Wizzy for years! Or what about the time you brought your collection of dentures to show and tell. I simply called you to bring my bag of seashells. You had to go and improvise. Now, what did you tell me? Oh yah. The dentures could tell their own story. What the heck does that mean? And now you are claiming I was raped? I was eighteen. Yes, he was my teacher, but he was also twenty-two. No, it wasn't right, but love is love."

Granny slowly eyeballed the group. It was evident she was

working through a range of emotions. It was not often that Granny worked herself into the tear stage, but droplets of salty tears formed in her eyes until they bubbled over her eyelids. Snot pooled at the base of her nostril and she said, "Phyllis, all I ever wanted to do was give you the best in life. But when you became pregnant, I felt like a failure. Every time you ran off with another man, and goodness knows there were enough of them, I felt like life's crap bird laid a big one on Raine and me again and again."

My mom took in Granny's monologue and said, "I screwed up many times. Yes, you and Raine got hurt in the process, but meeting Rob was never ever, EVER a mistake. Our beautiful daughter is a gift. My biggest mistake was not spending more time with Raine."

Using the back of her hand, Granny wiped the snot and tears from her face. She drew in a plug of snot and asked, "I just don't know what's happening to you. Who the hell ARE you?"

"Mom, I'm telling you that I'm a changed woman."

Dander cleared his throat and announced, "So, since everyone is making announcements, I have to make one of my own."

At that, he stood before my mom and knelt on one knee. "Phyllis, will you marry me?"

Mom wrapped her arms around Dander, and yelled and I mean yelled, "YES!!!"

Granny slapped her head and said, "Aww, dang crap bird got me again."

The doorbell rang. Granny said, "Who would be here?"

Dander smirked, "I have another announcement. I probably should have said something earlier, but now that you are going to be my mother-in-law...well."

The doorbell rang again. Dander continued, "This is going to be my week to have the girls, so Granny, you will be able to get to know your granddaughters."

The front door opened, and Mrs. Dander pushed Marian and Kimmi into the house. Each girl held a suitcase, pillow, and a lost look.

"Dang crap bird," Granny said at the same time Mrs. Dander slammed the door behind her.

By the end of the week, Granny had 8 people living in her home. Mom, Dander, Kimmi, Marian, Julie, Mrs. Twain, Granny, and me. Julie's mom left the hospital but needed additional care, so Granny brought her home. We wedged everyone in the home creatively. Granny slept in her room. Julie, Mrs. Twain, and I slept in my room. Dander and my mom stayed in another bedroom. And Kimmi and Marian... ended up in the living room. Granny had the bright idea to section off the room with a sheet. The girls slept on a pallet of blankets and old towels. It actually was quite comfortable. At least that was what I explained to Kimmi. Everything was going well until personal bubbles were punctured by the close proximity of the living quarters.

Chapter Twenty

Hormonally Challenged

I made a point of avoiding Marian and Kimmi. Actually, Kimmi was not too bad, but Marian, ARG! I guess I took my avoidance too far because Mom decided I needed an intervention while I was sitting on the toilet. We have an unspoken rule in my house: If the bathroom door is closed, someone is inside making a number one or number two, or a three which is a combination of a one and two. Sometimes there is a number four, but that's only when we are sick.

"Get out Mom. I'm concentrating here."

"No, we need to talk."

"Can we talk after I finish going to the bathroom?"

"No, there is nowhere else I can talk to you in private."

"Well, hurry up," I demanded, grabbing a towel and covering my lower body.

"Raine, I need you and Julie to be nicer to Marian. She's having a hard time adjusting to all the change."

"And I'm not?"

"I understand what you are saying, but I need you to be the bigger person and help bridge our families together."

"Mom, what do you mean by bridge?"

Mom patted my leg and answered, "Rob and I are going to be married. We want you girls to act like sisters."

"First, Mom. Don't ever pat my leg while on the toilet. It's gross. Second, I'm not now or ever going to be a sister to those girls."

"But you already are sisters. You have the same dad."

"Maybe. But even Dander said he had doubts about who's the

178

daddy."

"Wow, Raine. Just a minute, we need some fresh air in here." She went to the window and cracked it about six inches. She continued, "You must be battling a firm poo."

My mom paused, took in fresh air, and continued, "Raine, we are not going on doubts. The girls have been raised by him, so he is their father. Now, I want you to start being nicer to the girls."

"Are you kidding me? I've not said a word to the girls. I have been completely kind because I have a lot of things I want to say."

"Ignoring the girls is in itself not being caring and loving to your sisters."

"Okay, Mom, I'll try. Now will you please get out of here?"

As she left, my mom smiled and said, "You might consider some fiber in your diet. It would help to avoid straining a number two delivery."

Twenty minutes later, I left the bathroom and found Julie and her mom in my room, crying.

"What's wrong?" I asked.

Mrs. Twain answered, "Mr. Twain is getting out of jail and wants to renew our marriage vows. Julie wants me to get a divorce."

"But what about the baby?"

Mrs. Twain pulled Julie into her arms and rocked. Julie cried softly.

"What the heck is going on?" I asked.

"Well, Mr. Twain wants Julie to remain at Granny's house."

This did not make sense to me. "What do you mean he wants Julie to remain at the house? What about jail? What about his temper? What is going on?"

"When you grow up you will understand. A husband and wife should never be separated. All the charges have been dropped and Mr. Twain will be picking me up. Granny will take care of Julie. I just have to go back to my husband. We are married so he will always come first."

I closed my eyes, wondering about her thought process. "Mrs. Twain, you say your first duty is to your husband. He beats you and your daughter as well your grandchild. Are you willing to give up a relationship with your future generations?"

"Raine, like I said, you will understand when you get older."

"No, Mrs. Twain, **you** will understand when you get older."

Julie cried out, "Mom, please don't go!"

A car horn blared and Mrs. Twain grabbed her suitcase, kissed Julie, and left. Julie sobbed, and all I could do was hold her. Granny came in and wrapped her arms around us. My mom came in too and added her arms to the giant hug sandwich. Julie was triple wrapped in love, yet, I knew, it would never be enough to heal her heart. I had to find some way to at least make her look around and see the future she had with her child. Jess, I thought. That's it.

I left the house to use the pay phone at the corner of Paco's Tacos and Regina's Grocery. I dialed Jess's number, allowing it to ring only three times before nerves just about caused me to place the phone back on the receiver.

"Hello," answered Jess.

"Um, Julie needs you. Her parents do not want her. Since you know, she's pregnant with your baby; I thought you might like to check on her."

"Who is this?"

"Raine."

"Oh."

"She's at my house. You really need to be there for her."

"I have to clean my room first. Then I'll come by."

"Okay," I answered. Clean his room...Odd answer. A bit of shock paralyzed my mind. Would he actually come by? Would Jess care that Julie was pregnant and unwanted by her parents?

On the walk home I decided I would try to be nice to Marian. Mrs. Dander was not exactly up for the mom of the year award. Maybe Marian was feeling many of the same emotions Julie was feeling. I truly thought that was bull, but at least I could tell Mom I tried.

I went upstairs and told Julie we were going to ask Marian and Kimmi if they wanted to play cards. Julie laughed. She asked, "Why?"

"My mom wants me to be sisterly with them."

"Them?"

"Yup, them."

"Well, okay. Might as well, all I'm doing right now is feeling sorry for myself. Ya know, Raine, I always thought my dad would leave me, but I never imagined my mom would go too."

What was I to say? She was right. Her dad was an idiot, but he was still her dad. Her mom, however, deserved a better life than to be a punching bag.

"Julie, I want you to know that we will always be together. When we get grey hair, I will pluck them for you."

"I know, Raine."

"Do you know that I sister love you?"

"Yes, and I sister love you."

I had nothing more of value to say, so I just asked, "You want to play them in Go Fish?"

So, thirty minutes later, the four of us were sitting crossed legged on the floor. Kimmi was the only person playing the game who seemed to be enjoying herself.

"Raine, do you have any threes?"

"Go Fish, Kimmi."

"Again?"

She pulled a card from the discard pile.

Marian asked, "Julie, do you have any threes?"

"Yes," answered Julie.

"No! Those are my threes!"

Marian lovingly stated, "No, Kimmi, that's not the way the game works."

"Well, I want the threes."

Kimmi threw the cards and folded her arms. "Then I'm not

playing because this is not fair."

I answered, "Fair enough."

Grabbing the cards I straightened them, slid them in the box, and tucked in the lid.

"Wait, wait," stated Kimmi. "I was kidding. Forget about the threes. I will fish for some other numbers. Let's keep playing."

"Nope, you said you didn't want to play, so we are done," I answered.

"That's not right," said Marian. "She's just a little kid. We can keep playing."

"Nope," I answered again. "Kimmi is spoiled and needs to learn a lesson."

Marian's face steamed red, "No, you need to learn to be nicer to people. You are a horrible person."

"Yeah horrible!" repeated Kimmi. "All I wanted to do was play cards."

Julie interjected, "Now, now. Let's not do this again."

"Aww shut up, Julie," snidely stated Marian. "You are no better. Ya know. The only thing I smell when I'm around you is fish."

Julie appeared confused, "What do you mean by fish?"

"With your legs always up, the air takes on a fishy smell."

Kimmi added, "Yeah, you smell like fish. Hey, Marian, if she smells like fish can we play Go Fish again?"

I responded to Marian's comment, "That doesn't make sense. You are crazy like your mom."

Marian worked up a smug expression and replied, "Since Julie's legs are always up, that's why she's pregnant."

"What?" asked Kimmi. "You can have a baby by spreading your legs. Oh no. My legs were not together when I played cards. I am going to have a baby."

Kimmi ran out of the room looking for Dander.

He stormed back and asked, "What is this about Kimmi being pregnant?"

Marian said, "Ah Dad, you know how she is just repeating

what she hears. Julie said something about the baby and..."

"No, Daddy," interrupted Kimmi. "Marian said that when legs are up you smell like a pregnant fish."

Dander blinked. "Huh."

Marian interpreted, "What Kimmi means is we were playing Go Fish when Julie said something about being pregnant. Kimmi is confusing all the different parts of the story. You know how she twists and repeats things."

As he left the room, he pawed his head and replied, "True. So very true."

Kimmi asked, "I didn't know that's what I meant. I thought that spreading your legs made a fishy smell and babies."

Marian smiled and told Kimmi, "Don't you worry about it honey. Why don't you go outside and play in Granny's recycled stuff. You might find a treasure."

"Ohhh, that would be nice."

Kimmi left, leaving Julie, Marian, and me alone.

Julie was the first to speak to the enemy. "You said Raine was horrible. You treat your sister like a dog and then you say disgusting things about fish and legs. And, by the way, you leave my baby out of it. He or she has done nothing to deserve your insults."

Marian's voice went up an octave responding, "Getting testy are we...I must have hit a nerve. Maybe now you two know how it feels to live where we are not wanted."

"What the heck does that mean?" I asked. "You think we have anything to do with this? If you want to be mad at someone, be mad at your dad and my mom. They dragged three innocent kids into this mess. And since you are wanting to get ugly...Your dad may not be the real dad of Kimmi."

Marian tensed, "Shut up You don't know what you are talking about."

From the other room we heard Dander call out, "Girls, go outside and play. I can't read the newspaper with such racket."

"This is not over," Marian whispered as she stormed outside.

"You got that right," I volleyed back.

That night, Julie and I went to bed. I thought about the day and remembered Jess. He never did come to see Julie. I was glad I never told her about the possibility. I shut my eyes, and sleep consumed me.

I started dreaming right away. I was in the Runge School Library with Grandpa Perth and Runge's first librarian, Claire Fitzson. He hugged me and said, "Babe, you will have a decision to make in the next few days."

Ms. Fitzson opened a book and handed it to my gramps.

"Ahh yes," he said in response to her gesture.

He presented the book like a trophy saying, "It says here that gestation lasts forty weeks."

Gramps leaned in and pointed to an illustration showing the development of a baby. Then he flipped several pages and thumbed the area referring to nutrition.

"Raine, you will need to make sure Julie goes to the doctor and eats right."

"Gramps?" I started. "What does this have to do with a decision?"

"Oh yeah," he laughed at himself. "Claire and I were just going through the baby book. I thought you would find it interesting. That whole fish bit Marian talked about really cracked us up here on the other side. That's when several of us got to discussing babies and Julie."

"Gramps, what about it."

Ms. Fitzson pushed Gramps out of the way and said, "He'll go on and on if you don't keep him focused. The decision is about Unkept Promises. How are you going to handle it?"

"Handle what?"

Ms. Fitzson answered, "Girl, you are more like your gramps than I would like to admit. I just told you. Unkept Promises. What will you do?"

My bedroom window opened causing my dream to end and

Gramps and Ms. Fitzson to vanish. I looked and spotted Jess entering my room. Julie was already out of the bed and hugging him.

She whispered, "I've been waiting for you."

He touched her hair and wove it around his finger. "Honey, I've missed you, too."

I could not believe it. I was watching the reunion of the Mr. and Mrs. Horney, so I closed my eyes but my ears pulled in every word.

"Raine called me today."

Julie responded, "She did?"

"She told me about your parents leaving."

I heard Julie start crying, kissing, and Jess say, "Don't cry my love. I'm right here. There, there. It will be okay. I'm here. Remember, we are going to always be together. "

"Really?"

"Yes, really. I love you."

That was when I heard the smacking of lips and a few umms and ahhs. I thought surely they are not going to do the nasty right here in my bedroom.

Julie said, "Jess, let's get in the closet. That way we can have some privacy."

No way, I thought. Taking a quick gander at the floor, I saw all the stuff from the floor of my closet piled against the wall. I took another look and saw two center cracked moons. Smothering my face in my pillow, I tried to remove the image of the vegetable butts. A scream resonated in my mind, bouncing between my right and left ear.

The closet door closed and I thought to myself. Should I tell them to stop? Should I pretend to sleep? After volleying my choices, I decided to try to pretend to be sleeping. I gripped Feefer's ears and stuffed them in my ear canals like earplugs. Unfortunately, I could still hear the slapping of sweaty skin. Finally the two fell asleep just as did I.

The next morning I awoke with Julie in bed with me and the

window closed. I left her sleeping and crept down to the kitchen. On the table was an open newspaper. The headline read: Coach Whipley Named Principal. I sat at the table and read:

Coach Whipley Named Principal

On July 26, 1983, Mr. David Whipley, who has been the long time athletic director of Runge Independent School District, assumed the principal job after Robert Dander left. A swirling controversy over the alleged sexual affair he had with a student has given Runge citizens grave concerns about the educational welfare of the town's children.

Previously, a fire broke out in the office area. The major clue was the message: "Unkept Promises will be punished." There is an open investigation to determine who caused the fire, and if there is any correlation between Dander's alleged affair and the fire.

The repairs following the fire should be completed by August 15, allowing school to reopen for the 1983 - 1984 school year on September 1. Principal Whipley says he is excited about this new opportunity afforded him by the Runge School Board.

Well, it was official. Dander was out and Whipley in as principal. School was going to begin in September, and life was going to continue despite the punishment by Unkept Promises.

I grabbed the newspaper, went upstairs, and laid it on the bed next to Julie.

She rolled over and asked, "What's this?"

"Coach Kernel Corn is the new principal of the high school."

She gave the paper a look and laughed. "I guess the new principal will tell the teachers about the school stoonjas."

Julie paused and added, "I've got to ask a strange question."

"What?"

"Raine, should I be this big already?"

She lifted her shirt and exposed a baby bump.

"Wow, are you sure that you are not further along than what you think?"

"Raine, my first time ever was at the dance in May. I've counted days and I should be due around the end of October."

"I'm not an expert, but you do seem big."

Granny has a knack for walking in at an awkward moment. She opened my bedroom door and gawked at the protruding belly.

"Holy Watermelons!" she announced. "Julie, are you sure you are not further along than you think?"

"No Granny," Julie replied. "It was my first time with Jess at the dance."

"My, my, my," answered Granny. "Have you been to the doctor yet?"

Shaking her head Julie said, "No."

"I'm calling Dr. Pooley right now. I'll get you in there today."

Granny left, and we could hear the rotary phone dial spinning.

Julie asked me, "Can Granny get an appointment that quickly?"

Chuckling, I stated, "They are afraid of her. They will do whatever they can just to keep her out of the office."

Sure enough, we were at the doctor's office two hours later. Granny, Julie, and I sat in the waiting room leafing through pregnant woman magazines.

Julie hovered over Granny's ear and asked, "What is Dr. Pooley going to do to me?"

Granny whispered back, "He's going to look at your inner fruit."

"My inner fruit?"

Granny pointed to her feminine parts and responded, "You know...your inner fruit."

Horrified Julie said loudly, "NO WAY, NOT MY INNER FRUIT."

Julie got up and sprinted to the restroom.

I started to go after Julie, but Granny grabbed my hand and pulled me toward the chair.

"Ahh, no worries, Raine, she'll come out. I'm sure Julie is wrapping her mind around what is going to happen."

Julie returned ten minutes later.

"What did you do?" I asked her.

"Raine, if Dr. Pooley looks at my inner fruit, I had to make sure there were no pieces of toilet paper clinging to my vine."

Granny leaned over and added, "A woman's got to do what a woman's got to do."

Stunned, part of me wanted to laugh, but the other part of me knew one day I would be checking for t.t.p.b. - tiny toilet paper balls.

A nurse called Julie's name, and the three of us entered the sanctuary of the fruit vine checker. Julie disrobed and covered herself in a white sheet. The nurse looked at Granny and me. She asked, "Julie, do you want them in here?"

Confused, Julie asked, "Where do you want them to go?"

"I mean," the nurse explained. "Would you rather be examined without an audience?"

Granny looked at the nurse's name badge and answered for Julie, "Of course she doesn't want an audience – so, Nurse Simple, get out."

"My name is Nurse Stimple, and I am required to be here during the examination."

Sensing she might be over her head in the examination room battle, Granny said, "Julie, would you like us to stay?"

"Granny, I would like you and Raine to stay."

Nurse Stimple answered, "Well then. We shall begin."

The nurse asked her loads of questions about her seed, vine, and picking. Julie seemed embarrassed but answered diligently. She did well until Nurse Stimple asked her to lay back and place her feet in the stirrups.

"Excuse me."

Nurse Stimple explained, "Julie, you need to lay back and place your heels in the lopsided circles called stirrups."

Julie looked at them and the nurse. Looking horrified, Julie said, "Ummm. No."

The nurse forced a smile and said, "Julie, if you don't do this, the doctor can't examine you to see if the baby is okay."

Julie closed her eyes and leaned back and slowly slid her feet to the stirrups.

The nurse continued, "Now, slide your butt closer to the edge of the table. Julie, your knees can't be touching."

"Nurse Stimple, I can't pull them apart."

Granny sidled to the table and said, "Well hell Julie, if your knees had been together in the first place, you wouldn't be pregnant."

"That is highly inappropriate," barked Nurse Stimple. "Although I agree, it's too late for that discussion now. So, Julie, spread it."

Julie's knees parted and the doctor walked in the room.

"Good afternoon ladies," announced Dr. Pooley. He immediately pulled his stool between Julie's legs and asked, "So, Julie, how have you been feeling?"

"Fine."

"Any morning sickness?"

"No. Well, sometimes, but it's not too bad."

"Are you exercising?"

"Sort of."

"Have you been taking vitamins?"

"No."

"Do you...?"

Julie interrupted him and asked, "Do you always ask questions when you look at a patient's inner fruit?"

Dr. Pooley pushed the sheet down and looked at Julie, his eyebrow lifting. He asked, "Are you related to Granny?"

Julie popped back, "Maybe not by blood, but I consider Granny my grandmother and Raine my sister."

"Oh," he answered.

He snapped off the gloves and rolled his stool near Julie's

face. He began, "Let me apologize. My name is Dr. Pooley. I am going to be your doctor who will help you on this incredible journey towards motherhood."

"Nice to meet you," she answered, shaking his hand.

"Now, Julie. As I review my notes, I see that the baby was conceived the beginning of May. That places the due date at the end of January."

He pulled out a measuring tape and said, "Nurse Stimple, help Julie out of the stirrups. I need to get a measurement of Julie's stomach."

Dr. Pooley measured and measured again. He did a little head scratching and measured again. He compared his measurements to a chart and asked, "Are you sure you conceived in the early part of May?"

"Yes. That was my first time, so yes."

"Okay. So let's listen to the baby's heartbeat. First I'm going to put some gel on your stomach which will allow the fetal Doppler to move easily."

The doctor swirled the Doppler around until a washing machine sound filled the room.

"That, my dear, is your baby. Sounds strong and proud."

He moved the Doppler around some more and the washing machine sound filled the room, once again.

"Oh my," said the doctor. "Well, that explains the large measurement. You are carrying twins."

Julie cried and I stared at Julie's belly in shock. Two? Two babies?

Granny, however, danced a bit of an Irish jig and announced, "This is a good day. You have been blessed."

A bit insulted by Granny's rejoicing, Julie cried out, "We should not be celebrating this. What am I going to do? I can't be a mom, much less a mom of twins."

The doctor said, "You have three choices when you have an unwanted pregnancy. You could allow someone to adopt, terminate

190

the pregnancy, or raise the baby - I mean babies."

Julie flinched. "You know, Dr. Pooley, if every unwanted pregnancy resulted in termination, than I would not have my sister friend Raine."

"That's right," added Granny.

Dr. Pooley appeared stunned, "Ladies, I didn't mean to appear uncaring, but my job is to provide choices for Julie. This is a life changing event."

Julie fumed, "My babies, my life…I will have them."

"Love, love, love it," danced Granny around the room.

"What are you doing, Granny?" I asked.

"I love when a pregnant woman's emotions course through her veins faster than Superman flying to face his enemy. Julie has entered the hormonally challenged arena. Heck, I myself have been known to become hormonally challenged."

"You ain't kidding," responded the doctor.

"Watch it, Dr. Pooley. That's my grandmother you are talking about," chastised Julie, twisting her body to punctuate the comment.

"Careful!" said Granny. "Your gyrations will make your sheet go airborne and PRESTO your garden will be displayed. Listen, Julie, Dr. Pooley can't help it that he's inconsiderate to pregnant women as well as women going through hormonal changes. Ya know. I have a great idea. Let's try to get a law passed that would shelter women from verbal emotional trauma. Hmm. I guess we would need a woman who is hormonally challenged to wear a sign that says: Caution: This woman is hormonally challenged. Carefully monitor every word, facial expression and gesture when confronting her. If provoked, she may verbally unload a hostile response or turn on a downpour of salty tears. If a hormonally challenged woman wore the sign, then it would be legal to assault idiots who verbally challenge our hormones."

Nurse Stimple cleared her throat and suggested, "We could even educate the public through a bombardment of hormonally challenged commercials. The first advertisement might sound something like this:

This is a hormonally challenged woman.

This is a hormonally challenged woman's emotions.

This is a hormonally challenged woman's rage after an insensitive remark.

Got it? YOU BETTER!"

Granny smiled, "Well, Nurse Stimple, you are really growing on me. I like you."

Julie added, "Me too."

"Ya'll just crack me up," I tossed into the verbal arena.

Dr. Pooley said, "Okay, I'm not sure how to handle creating laws supporting hormonally challenged woman. I'm concerned I won't survive the wave of emotions. But ..." He paused and smiled, "I could use your idea as advertising. I'll give out t-shirts to my menopausal and pregnant woman with the words: Help, I'm Hormonally Challenged, and Dr. Pooley is my Superman! It would showcase my ability to handle the hormonally challenged women with a sense of humor."

The examination room became a battlefield of which idea could out shine the another. The group became louder and louder causing laughter to echo down the doctor office's halls. The door to Julie's examination room opened and Old Miss Sue Ellen Dawson, the oldest town spinster *and* the blindest, blasted her way into the room. She was naked except for a sheet draped over her melons and vineyard.

She yelled, "I'm not sure what is going on here, but I have been on a table bare assed for thirty minutes, and all I hear is laughter and hormonally challenged women comments. I'll give you a comment: Get your white coat in my room, and give me my exam. My nipples are so cold they're cutting slits in my cover-up sheet."

She turned around and walked out giving us an eyeful of her sagging buttocks.

Dr. Pooley grinned and rolled his stool away from Julie. "Ladies, I must leave. It has been a pleasure." He turned to Julie adding, "My dear, I look forward to delivering your twin blessings. I'll see you in a month. Oh, and, my staff will get you information on your pregnancy and birth preparations."

He left muttering, "Hormonally challenged women. That's just flat out funny."

The door closed and Julie started crying. "What am I going to do? Twins? I don't have a home, parents, or a good paying job. I can't believe this is happening to me. My parents left me and now twins."

Granny wiped away a few tears. "Honey," Granny said. "Listen, when Phyllis found out she was pregnant, she said the same thing, except about the twins. Ya know, I told her that everything will be alright. I wasn't sure how, but it would be alright. And that's what I am telling you – everything will be alright. You at least have some brains in your head.

Now, Phyllis, on the other hand, isn't exactly known for her clarity of thinking. And being pregnant, hormonally challenged, and - well let me just come right out and say it - she's flat out an idiot.

I was not so much worried about the baby coming into the world as finding the baby's father. I personally had fantasies of grabbing his balls, dipping them in honey, and drop kicking them into a fire ant nest. Had I known it was Principal Dander's sperm…well, the school would have had a soprano speaking principal."

Granny paused and then added, "Raine has turned out pretty well - despite her mother and father. Somehow, someway, we will get through this. As long as I'm living, you can stay with me."

"Thanks Granny," said Julie, still crying. "But I need to figure out a way to raise my kids. Hmm. That sounds funny. Kids...I need to finish high school and go to college. I must figure out a way. Set a goal. I need to talk with Jess. He's going to lay a brick when he finds out about the twins."

Granny murmured, "Lay a brick or two."

"Maybe he will feel happy," I added.

Julie rolled her eyes. "He nearly passed out knowing he was

going to be a daddy and now...twins? I wonder if he has told his parents they will be grandparents."

Granny pursed her lips and snidely commented, "Remember this is Runge. The news will surface, if it hasn't already."

"I know. You are right. If Jess doesn't have the guts to tell his parents, I guess I should do it with him. Let me get dressed and let's go back to Granny's house." She closed her eyes for a brief second, sighed, and added, "I need a nap."

We left with a bag of informational pamphlets and went to the car. Granny inserted her key in the door and froze. She whispered, "Girls, get back in the building and call the police."

"What's going on?" I asked.

"I said go inside!"

Chapter Twenty-One

More Danger

Julie's voice got about an octave higher, "Granny, you are scaring me and the twins."

"You should be scared. Look," said Granny, pointing.

We saw a note sticking out of the front tire, pierced by a six-inch knife.

I said, "I'm guessing the note will say something about Unkept Promises."

Granny grabbed my arm and Julie's arm and started dragging us back to the office building, "We aren't going to find out. Whoever this is...well, they are getting more aggressive. When we get inside, we are calling the police and then Sarge."

"Why Sarge?" I asked.

"Cause she's like a German shepherd juiced up on steroids. She'll keep us safe."

Within an hour, the police had investigated and driven us home. Sarge met us at the house. She stood in the doorway, arms folded, and eyes darting left and right. Standing next to her, Kimmi stood, arms folded with her plate shaped eyes wider and more round than normal.

Everyone gathered in the front room and sat on sleeping pallets and pillows.

"Daddy?" said Kimmi. "Why would the Unkept Promises person want to hurt us?"

"Well baby, sometimes people don't think clearly, so they do and say things that are wrong," answered Dander.

"Like Granny?"

"Well... um...not exactly."

Granny tapped her fingernail against the coffee table. "Well, I can certainly understand how Kimmi might believe I don't think clearly. However, Kimmi, just because someone looks at the world differently doesn't mean they are dangerous. I am what they call right brained. I think outside of the box."

Kimmi looked around the room and under the couch. She asked, "Where's this box?"

"Exactly," responded Granny. "Now that we got that straight, we need to make a plan...a safety plan. Sarge, you want to guide us on this one?"

"First, no one should go out of the house alone. Second, I am staying here at night."

I hated to interrupt but I couldn't help but ask, "And just where are you going to sleep?"

"I'm not," she said.

Her expansive body seemed larger, grander, and more intimidating than ever. I nodded up and down, allowing her to continue.

"We need to figure out who is leaving the messages."

Kimmi added, "And the knife in the tire."

"Right, Kimmi," added Sarge.

"Can I help?" asked Kimmi.

"Sure. You can let me watch you. That way I can exercise my eyes."

"Okay, Sarge," answered Kimmi, smiling happily.

The rest of the day and evening Sarge asked questions and took notes. She read her notes multiple times and made an announcement. "Well folks. I have some thoughts, but before I begin, I need everyone to be brave, especially Kimmi."

Squatting at eye level with Kimmi, Sarge's bottom hovered inches above the floor creating a floating sideways smile. In a soothing voice, she asked Kimmi, "Can you listen and be brave?"

Kimmi beamed ear to ear and said, "Trust me. I will be the queen of help."

Phyllis announced, "Aww look. Double smiles."

Fear gripped me. Sarge's physical position primed her to offload internal combustion. Marian sensed the possible explosion so she grabbed a couch pillow, burying her face.

Granny yelled, "Incoming!" and tucked her face into the crook of her arm.

Looking around her expansive hind quarters, Sarge asked, "Why does everyone think I'm going to fluff?"

Granny chuckled, "Fluff? Is that what you call it? That fluffing could be lethal."

Granny started giggling and followed it up with a loud peal of energetic laughter. Everyone in the house started laughing too. With the tense Unkept Promises situation, laughter seemed the least likely emotion to feel, but it was the emotion resounding in the house. Suddenly Granny shouted, "Aw JEEZE! I just wet myself."

She ran from the room which kicked up our laughter two notches. A few minutes later, Granny returned in a silky orange floral blouse and cool striped mint pants.

"That's enough," Granny ordered. "We have work to do. Sarge, lay out your concocted plan."

Sarge squinted her eyes and drank in Granny's mismatched outfit. The corner of Sarge's mouth twitched as she tried to suppress laughter. She took a deep breath and regained control.

"Sarge, did you hear me?" asked Granny. "I said to lay out your plan."

After another deep pull of air, Sarge answered, "Have you ever noticed the last two notes arrived after an event of some kind? For example, when you returned from the hospital, a gift and note were at the door."

I added, "Don't forget the slice of cheese."

"Right," Sarge responded. "And the slice of cheese. Then

when you went to the doctor, the note was found by the car."

Kimmi insert, "Stabbed with a knife."

"Yes, Kimmi," answered Sarge. "Let's not forget the knife. And, as I was saying, it seems there is a developing pattern. I think whoever is doing this is also watching you. I want Mr. Dander to take the family and Granny to the park. Let's call it the Dander's first family outing. I'll stay here and watch for someone to deliver a note.

"And then what?" I asked sarcastically. "What's your plan if the person actually delivers a note? You going try to capture them or take pictures for proof?"

Sarge stared at me and asked, "Your tone makes me feel like you are doubting the plan. Do you have any other ideas?"

I didn't. But I didn't want Sarge to know that nothing except chirping crickets filled my head. I acted like I was thinking and started out saying, "Well, we could..."

"Horse pucky! You don't have any other ideas," interrupted Granny. "If you did, you would have said them long ago."

"Yeah, horse pucky!" repeated Kimmi.

Marian asked, "Kimmi, do you even know what horse pucky is?"

"Sure, it's the puck in horse poop. You know, the stuff that looks like corn kernels," responded Kimmi, smiling and nodding her head like she answered a million dollar question.

"Okay, so I don't have any other ideas, but I just feel like we are setting ourselves up for trouble," I answered, gnawing on my index fingernail.

Julie pulled my finger away from my mouth. She smiled shyly and said, "Raine, if anyone can do this, it's Sarge. Let's go to the park. What's the worst that could happen?" She paused a downbeat and continued, "We swing and then eat a snack?"

"I can swing real good, Raine. Do you want me to show you?" asked Kimmi.

"Sure Kimmi, show me how to swing," I sighed. "Okay, let's go."

"Yippee! We are going to the park! Can we have a picnic too! Will they have high swings at the park too?" questioned Kimmi.

"Sure," answered Dander. "Sarge, we will be at the back playground...the one lined with pine trees."

Sarge nodded her head in understanding. Her shoulders rounded and her eyes darted left and right, taking in every movement and sound. As I watched, her demeanor changed from reasonably soft and fluffy to the mode of a German shepherd.

Granny asked, "What do we want for snacks?"

"Cookies," chimed Kimmi and Julie.

Marian said, "Nothing."

"Chips," I added to the list.

Granny nodded her head and opened the pantry, pulling out a barrage of sugary and salty snacks. Kimmi jumped up and down asking Granny, "Can I help pack the picnic basket? I've never been on a picnic. I've seen picnics on TV, but I ain't ever been on one. Do you think the ants are as bad as they talk about on the TV? I think this will be fun. Well, it will be fun unless that Unkemmp Promass man tries to stick a knife in the tire again."

Granny looked at Dander. She asked, "Kimmi has never been on a picnic?"

Dander's eyes bounced from Granny to Kimmi to Granny again. He said, "Ummm, I was the principal of a high school. The job kept me pretty busy."

Silence filled the kitchen. Granny pushed a bag of chips into a basket and muttered, "But you had time to..."

"Granny!" I interrupted.

She swiveled her head in my direction, almost menacingly. Clasping her hands together she gripped them measuring the strength she had to refrain from uttering what she really thought about Dander's lack of time.

Granny finally replied, "Well, you know what I mean."

We piled into the Buick and drove to Campton Park, leaving Sarge at the house with the boogey monster.

With the park entrance ahead of us, Dander slowed to almost a crawl. He said, "Girls and Granny, you will need to stay where I can see you."

"Why Daddy?" asked Kimmi.

Marian answered, "Cause Sarge is watching for Unkept Promises. If she finds him or her, we need to go and see who has been so mean to us."

As Dander slid the car into park, Kimmi shot out of the car and began running while my mom stayed hot on Kimmi's trail.

Mom called to Kimmi, "I'm going to beat you to the swings."

"Not way," answered Kimmi.

Kimmi slipped into the swing and began pumping her legs jetting her to climb higher and higher. Mom mirrored her and pumped her long legs in time with Kimmi. Each time Mom neared the ground, she parted her legs to keep them from dragging the dirt.

Dander eyed the swing duo and grabbed his camera bag. Without peering down, he walked toward them the whole time digging in his bag to locate his camera. Then he sat on a park bench and began to snap pictures.

Granny nudged me, "Looky over there. Robert likes the view."

"Huh?" I responded. I looked at Dander and watched as he absorbed the movement of my mom's legs and the parting of her knees.

Julie snickered; Granny sneered; I suppressed vomit; and Marian rolled her eyes and walked away.

"Don't you go too far," said Granny using a parental tone. "Remember what your dad said."

"Yeah, yeah," answered Marian. "But Dad's clearly too occupied in a fish casserole to even notice I am gone."

While Julie and I seesawed, Marian stood in the tree line visually transmitting weapons of mass destruction. She clearly did not like us. Of course, I clearly did not like her either. I can't believe my mother really wanted me to be sisterly to her. I could sooner talk warts off a frog than effectively communicate sisterly love to Marian. I felt like I needed to get revenge. I constantly asked myself why I was so angry at Marian. Was it because she was such a witch? Was it because of sibling rivalry? I felt like I needed to do something to Marian…to get her back.

I pushed the seesaw off the ground and asked, "Julie, do you notice Marian's evil looks at us?"

"Yup."

"What do you think we could do to Marian without actually touching or harming her?"

"Why do you want to get revenge?

"I don't know. I just want her to know I hate her without actually hurting her."

Julie pushed up on her side. "Well," Julie started. "What about if you were extra nice to her so that she wondered what was going on."

I pushed upward. "Good one. What else?"

"Hmmm. What about you dip her toothbrush in the toilet?"

Julie pushed up. I thought a second, returned the seesaw push, and answered, "Nice one, but I'm not sure about that one. That's a little bit too gross even for my taste."

Julie pushed and suggested, "Okay, if you don't like that one, why don't you fart on her pillow?"

I laughed and pushed up. "You have got to be kidding."

"No," she answered, pushing up. "I do, I mean did, it all the time to my dad. He made me so mad. I knew I couldn't hit him back, so I waged war using my 'fluffs' as a weapon."

When Julie said fluffs she made air quotation marks.

I sat on the ground holding Julie in the air. "Ya know, Julie. Granny would call that being passive aggressive, and I, on the other hand, call it efficient. No preplanning required except tanking up on some gassy foods. I would allow a buildup and then crack open a fluffy fluff on Marian's pillow."

I pushed up and asked, "Since you are an expert, any fluffing suggestions?"

Julie returned the push and answered, "A well planned fluff can make for an unpleasant face plant, so you'll want to dig your butt deep into the pillow and release. If you maintain that position for at least thirty seconds, maximum smell is absorbed into the pillow. Then I fold the pillow and cover it with the bedspread. Think of the bedspread like a piece of a fluff preservative."

I heard my name called and noticed Dander motioning us to come to him. Julie, Marian, and I walked to Dander. The three of us not talking but still walking side by side like a group of military troops ready for battle.

He waved his camera, seemed to dance a mini jig, and announced, "I'm going to take pictures of my daughters and Phyllis. Julie, you can help me make sure everyone is looking and their eyes are open. "

He ordered, "Let's take the picture on the jungle gym. Phyllis, stand next to it. Kimmi, climb to the top and find a comfortable sitting position. Marian and Raine, position yourself somewhere in the middle."

Julie smiled at me. I knew she was probably envisioning my desire to fluff on Marian's pillow. I commented to Julie, "I know what you are thinking!"

She answered, "What? Me?"

I guess Marian felt excluded from the conversation so she asked, "What is she thinking?"

"Oh you know."

"No, I don't know, and that's why I'm asking."

"Well, Julie's thinking that this is pretty stupid and that she's glad she's not in the pictures."

Julie cocked her head and took in my answer. She replied, "Maybe, but I have a feeling there's more stink to it than that."

Before I could respond, Dander announced, "Ready? Set. Say Cheese."

He snapped several rolls of film, smiling the entire time.

Finally, he finished his photo session and announced,

"Kimmi, are you ready to play your favorite game?"

"Yes, yes, yes!!!" answered Kimmi. "Really! It's been so long since we played. Yeee haw!! I am excited! Me first. Okay everyone, close your eyes."

I asked, "Um. I don't mean to be rude, but what are we doing?"

"Aww, Raine, you know. We are playing my favorite game."

"Pretend I don't know, and tell me."

Kimmi sighed frustrated, "I'll hide something and then you got to find it. If you are close, I say getting warm, warmer, warmer, hot, hotter, fire hot or maybe I say cold, colder, or blue balls."

Dander barked, "Kimmi, you shouldn't talk about balls."

"Why not?" asked Kimmi. "That's what you say when you get out of the shower. I thought that meant really cold."

Granny laughed, "This one's a card. I just love her."

"Granny," responded Kimmi. "I'm not a card. I'm a little girl."

"Sheesh," interjected Marian. "Let's play the game. This is such a load."

Kimmi perched her hands on her hips and announced, "I'm going to hide the pine cone real good. Keep your eyes shut until I give you the magic of wood. Weally, shut youw eyes! When I come back, I tell you hot or cold."

I heard her trudge through the leaf litter until the sound became more and more distant. I strained to place an ear lock on her location. I heard a car door slam followed by another car door slam. I waited and waited, but I did not hear Kimmi return. I opened my eyes and tried to find her.

Dander must have opened his eyes about the same time because he asked, "Where is she?"

Marian added, "Kimmi, Kimmi don't hide."

"She's not here," announced my mom.

A car rounded the road's bend and screeched to a halt. The sudden assault of sound caused us to perform a synchronized turn which showcased Sarge bulldozing her way out of the car.

"It's Scooter. It's Scooter!" screamed Sarge.

"What? What? What do you mean?" asked Dander.

"Unkept Promises. I saw him and he saw me!" cried Sarge.

"Slow down. What do you mean?" asked Dander.

"I was in Raine's room visually monitoring the perimeter. The only thing I saw was Scooter mowing. He kept looking around which is what drew my eyes to him. Suddenly he left the mower in his yard, went to his truck, and grabbed something. Then he walked across your yard and left something on the porch. He made a quick jog back to his lawnmower and continued mowing."

I asked, "So did you look in the bag?"

"Of course. That's when Scooter noticed me. As he was mowing a strip away from the house, I pulled the bag into the house. He turned towards the house and our eyes locked. We remained locked for what seemed like minutes, but I'm sure it was only a few seconds. Then he left the mower, got in his truck, and took off."

Granny asked, "So what was in the bag?"

"A cheap ring with a note attached which said Unkept Promises must be punished."

Marian commented, "After the knife, I guess it could have been worse."

"Well," continued Sarge. "It was pretty bad. The ring was stuck in dog poop. Well at least I think it was dog poop."

"Oh my gosh," responded Granny.

I added, "Where's the ring now?"

"Right here," answered Sarge, pulling the ring out of her pocket.

"Whoa!" I yelled. "Wasn't that in the poop?"

Sarge grimaced, "Unfortunately."

A synchronized chorus of "EWWWW" resounded from every person within earshot.

"Wait!" shouted my mom. "Kimmi's missing. Do you think Scooter got her?"

Marian frantically yelled, "Kimmi!!!! Kimmi!!! Where are

you? This is not funny! Come out!"

"Spread out!" Granny hollered. "We got to find her. I just hope Scooter didn't grab her."

Julie replied, "How would he even know we are at the park?"

"Oh my!" uttered Marian. "It's my fault. I thought Scooter was my friend. After all, he and my mom have been dating, so I ..."

Dander grabbed Marian's arms. He filled in her statement with a question, "What did you do Marian? Tell me. NOW!"

Emotion consumed Marian. She pulled away from Dander. Her hands clenched and she fell to the ground, falling into a fetal position. Sobs mixed with words drenched the airwaves.

Dander grabbed her arms again and lifted her up. "Marian, I don't have time for this! Your sister is missing. What did you do?"

Between intermittent sobs, she choked out, "I tol-tol-old Scooter wh-what was hap- hap-pening. I thou-though-ght hee hee hee was my fr-fr-i-end."

"How could you, Marian?" yelled Dander. He released her arms with more force than he intended, causing her to hit the ground.

Marian wailed even louder and curled up into a tight ball, rocking. My mother ran to Marian. At first, it looked like my mom was going to cradle her, but then my mom's face creased and she snapped into trauma momma.

"Get over it!" shouted my mom. "You sister is in danger and all you can do is rock like a baby. SUCK IT UP!"

Marian's tears stopped and she uncurled. A moment passed and Marian stood and yelled, "WHAT THE HELL DID YOU SAY TO ME, SLUT?"

"I said to get over it. Your sister is in danger."

"That's what I thought you said!" Marian curled her first and bashed my mom in her face. My mom went flying backwards. Not so much from the force but from surprise.

Dander pushed Marian out of the way and scooped up my mom. He glared at Marian and retaliated, "I never thought it was possible. I never did. How could you become your mother in such a short time?"

"My mother is a saint compared to you!"

Granny stood between the battling trio and said, "Must I remind you that Kimmi is missing. If that little girl is hurt because you three had a piss poor fight, I personally will add a button to your butt hole."

"Mother!" reacted my mom. "How dare you!"

Granny's mind flipped and she used her orthopedic shoe to pop my mom in the split of her butt cheek. The force of Granny's shoe did two things. It stopped the fight's momentum and forced the three to remember Kimmi's plight.

Sarge seized the moment to say, "We need a plan. Julie, here's a quarter. Go to the pay phone and call the police and apprise them of the situation. Then come back to this exact spot. Kimmi might just come back and I don't want to miss her. I also want you to be here to brief the police on the situation. Marian and Raine, you need to search the north side of the park."

Sarge pointed to the north side and continued, "Granny, you search the south side."

Once again she pointed - this time to the south. Facing Dander and my mom, she pointed to the east and said, "You two - that way."

Marian and I took off at a brisk pace, yelling Kimmi's name. From each direction we heard Kimmi's name echoed. With the addition of sirens ricocheting off the pine trees, the whole situation seemed like a living horror movie. It was at this moment I was confident Scooter had Kimmi.

I said, "Marian, I know Scooter has her."

"I know," answered Marian, sniffing back tears. "Let's go back. We need to tell the police what we know."

We ran as fast as we could back and noticed Julie, Granny, Dander and Mom had already returned from the search. They were surrounded by policemen, each scribbling notes as questions were answered.

Officer Matey asked, "Who other than Scooter could have taken Kimmi?"

Dander slowly said, "Grace."

"Your wife?" asked Officer Matey slowly, giving my mom a quick onceover - I'm sure reflecting on her hypnotic melons. "Why would your wife take her own daughter?"

"Soon to be ex-wife," interjected my mom.

Dander hesitated before answering, "Well, we have not exactly been on good terms. She has been having an affair with Scooter, so I don't know if she planned this with him."

"So why do you think Mrs. Dand, - the future former Mrs. Dander, would take her own daughter?"

Pawing his head, he answered gravely, "It was a promise I didn't keep when we got married. That's what the Unkept Promises is all about. It's the only thing that makes sense."

The officer scribbled a few notes. He walked a few steps to his squad car and radioed dispatch to be on the lookout for Grace Dander and Scooter Wheeler.

By early afternoon, we were told to go home. Mom, Dander, and Granny went back to the house in the Buick. Julie, Marian, and I climbed into the back seat of Sarge's car. Sarge climbed into the front. She blew out a long breath and started driving back to Granny's house.

She said, "That didn't go the way I planned. I never thought someone would take Kimmi. What did I miss?"

The drive continued in silence, but halfway home, Julie announced, "I don't know about you, but I can't go back. I have to keep looking for Kimmi. I mean, if Scooter has her - well...he might do things. What if a 'few seconds earlier' is the difference in keeping her safe?"

Sarge screeched the car to a halt and turned to look at us. She asked, "This could be dangerous. Are you sure you are ready for this?"

Marian steeled a strong expression and answered, "I'm in."

I answered, "I'm in."

Julie answered, "I'm in. Let's get Jess. He'll help too."

"You sure?" asked Sarge.

"Just drive. He'll help."

As we drove, I thought about Julie. I had never heard Julie speak to an adult with attitude. I guess becoming a mother and wanting to protect another child changed a person. But then again...why didn't it help Mrs. Twain want to protect Julie? For that matter, why didn't my mom want to protect me? She just kept leaving me. Maybe motherhood is not in birth but in attitude.

Sarge hit the brakes in front of Jess's house. Julie hopped out and ran to the front door. Within minutes, the two sat in the front seat holding hands.

"Before we set out again, let's make a plan," stated Sarge. "We need to -"

"Find Kimmi," interrupted Marian. "We should stop talking and start driving around for Scooter's van or go to Scooter's trailer."

Jess turned around, "How do you know he has a van or a trailer?"

Marian's face creased and she said, "Shut up."

"What did I do?" asked Jess.

Julie explained, "It's a long story, but Marian knows a lot about Scooter because her mom and Scooter spend a lot of time together."

"That did it!" yelled Marian. She jumped over the front seat and started whacking Julie's face.

"What the hell?" yelled Jess in the form of a question.

He grabbed the crevice of Marian's forearm and she crumpled back to the backseat.

Sarge stared at Jess's pressure point manipulation and asked, "How long have you been a black belt?"

"Two years," answered Jess.

"I told you we needed Jess," said Julie smugly.

Marian looked out of the car window and massaged her arm.

I, on the other hand, would have laughed, but my fear for Kimmi overpowered my tickle bone.

"Once again, I will say," stated Sarge. "Where should we begin?"

In a soft voice, Marian said, "The policemen will be at my house, but they will have no idea where Scooter lives. He keeps it private, so let's start there."

The four of us gave her a look. She replied to our glance, "So I know where he lives. What's the big difference? He took me there a couple of times. No one will find it. It's hidden in the back woods off Shirley Slick Road and Crab's Loco Ranch Road."

"Okay," answered Sarge. "I know those roads. There are lots of little caliche roads veering off the main road. Why don't we let Marian sit in the front seat so that she can guide me to his house?"

Once we arrived at Shirley Slick Road and Crab's Loco Ranch Road, Marian said, "After the third bend in the road, you will need to take the next caliche road to the left. Travel slowly until I tell you to stop."

We went about a hundred yards forward, branches brushing the top and sides of the car.

Finally, Marian called out, "Stop right here and put your lights on bright so I can see."

Sarge stopped and Marian hopped out. She went to a mesquite tree and removed a false bark front. She tapped in several numbers into a keypad. Suddenly a series of tree branches opened - one to the left, then next to the right, and the last branch to the left.

Chapter Twenty-Two

Boobie Trap and Chicken Pecks

Marian climbed back into the car and said, "Go until you see a red brick in the middle of the road. Go around it to the right. Do not go over it."

"Why?" asked Sarge.

"Boobie trap," answered Marian.

Sarge voiced her concern, "What are we getting ourselves into? I would have never thought Scooter was this twisted."

Marian shook her head. "You don't get it. He's really nice. We played lots of games and had family time. Dad was gone so much that it was nice. Scooter is paranoid. But mostly, he thinks people want to steal his mowing equipment."

"Really, why would anyone want his stuff?" I asked.

Sarge shook her head and said, "This is getting too dangerous. Let's go back."

"Can't," answered Marian. "There's one way in and one way out. Go until I tell you to stop. Scooter may have added more security, so keep your eyes open."

The five of us peeled our eyes for hidden security.

A hundred yards later, Marian ordered, "Stop. Now go to the right...easy....easy... At this point we need to go to the left of the oak tree. This will be the road that takes us by Scooter's trailer. We will know that he's home if Dinner walks out of the front door."

"Dinner?" I asked.

Marian nodded, "Yeah, that's his pet chicken. He calls her Dinner because that's what she is going to be in a few weeks."

As Sarge edged forward, she asked, "How will we see Dinner? It's too dark."

Marian answered, "Scooter has little lights, kinda like Christmas lights, that turn on when there is movement. If Dinner walks around the yard, she leaves a trail of lights."

"So, you are telling me that Scooter will know we are there because of security lights," summarized Sarge, as she stopped the car.

Marian growled, "Why did you stop? We have got to get Kimmi."

Growling back, Sarge turned toward Marian. At the same moment, her foot slipped off the brake, and the car began to slowly roll forward. Sarge, unaware of the car's movement, answered, "Marian, we are going to lose the element of surprise if the little lights pop on."

The car rolled and suddenly we were bathed in light.

Marian announced, "We are here."

"Crud," answered Sarge.

We surveyed the area and saw a boneyard of lawn mowing parts. Blades, lawn mower shells, handles, and motors littered the property. Wedged between two mighty oak trees was the rusted trailer. Several windows were broken and the front screen door was missing its screen. A chicken trotted out of the door like the trailer was her home.

"Dinner," we whispered in unison.

"Here's the plan," started Sarge. "I don't think he has seen or heard us so I'll see if I can look in a window to spot Kimmi."

"Don't bother," said Marian, pointing. "Scooter has already seen us."

Scooter stepped out from a brush. He wore a full camouflage outfit and had black grease paint on his face. He slung his shotgun from its sling into shooting position. With a quick flick, he cocked his gun.

"You are trespassing," uttered Scooter in an "I'm not takin' crap off anybody" voice.

Sarge was the first to recover from the shock of seeing G.I. Mental Case come out from the trees and underbrush.

She said, "Sorry. We were driving around and got lost. We will..."

"Where's Kimmi," interrupted Marian. She got out of the car and ran toward the trailer.

"Little girl, you stop right there," ordered Scooter. He swung his gun in her direction.

She stopped but then continued edging her way toward the trailer. "You won't hurt me. You love my momma too much to do that."

"Maybe so. But I can shoot your traveling companions."

He spun around and aimed the shotgun at Sarge's car.

"Okay, okay. I'll stop," intervened Marian.

Scooter lowered his gun and said, "I want everyone out where I can see you."

We climbed out of the car and huddled in a clump. Jess pulled Julie behind him protectively, and Sarge tried to shield all of us with her body. This was the first time I thought Sarge's backside needed more width.

Scooter ordered, "See that shed?"

I noticed the shed which consisted of chicken wire, rusted tin, and about ten wide-eyed chickens.

He continued, "Get on in there and don't turn around until I close the door."

As we shuffled into the structure, it was evident it was not going to hold us. Jess entered first. Chickens began clucking. Julie followed. The clucking increased. The hens shuffled in their nest area, stirring up dust, feathers, and chicken manure odor. The birds tried to fly, but with five people and ten chickens, there was not enough room for wing extension.

Marian said, "Scooter, we won't fit."

"Don't care."

"We'll squish the chickens. You don't want to accidently kill your food," reasoned Marian.

"No worries. Dinner is right there," Scooter said, thumbing to the chicken trotting into the trailer.

Scooter tried to shut the chicken coop door, but Sarge's oversized watermelon butt restricted its closure.

"Move in further," ordered Scooter, as he used his body weight to latch the door.

With each push, our bodies became wedged like a church fart. With a final heft, the door latched.

"Now don't think of even gettin' out of here," ordered Scooter. He added, "I don't want to use this gun and mess up your pretty faces."

He burst into a round of horror movie laughter. "I wish you could see this. Sarge's butt fat is sticking out of the chicken wire. It looks like eggs trying to squeeze out of the coop."

He continued laughing, and as he walked into the trailer he added, "Enjoy the chickens."

Paralyzed, we said nothing. We were handling our capture well until the security lights clicked off. Fear mounted - in us and in the chickens. After a few minutes, the security lights clicked back on, so we were not sure who or what activated them.

"YEOUCH!" yelled Jess. "What stung me?"

"Well, whatever it was, it just stung me," stated Julie.

I swiveled my eyes into a nesting box and came eyeball to eyeball with a disgruntled hen. She cocked her head, left and then right, trying to figure out what kind of bird entered her domain. The hen clucked and pecked the tip of my nose.

"Gosh dang-it!" I uttered. "We are being pecked not stung."

Julie was the first to speak, "I don't want to be pecked. Get me out of here! And the smell. Oh my gosh!"

"Chicken poo," Sarge responded. "There's no other smell that rivals it. Well, except pig excrement. Scooter must never let the chickens out because there's about six inches of the stuff under my feet."

Sarge lifted a foot and her shoe made a sucking sound as it pulled out of the manure.

"This smell is making me sick," announced Julie.

I suggested, "Breathe out of your mouth."

Julie tried to cover her mouth but was unable to wiggle her hand upward. She said, "I think I'm going to throw up.

"Don't you dare," ordered Marian.

Julie retched twice before a volcano of vomit spewed from Julie's mouth and hit Marian in the face.

"I'm sorry," slobbered Julie. Droplets of vomit clung to the side of her mouth. Giving a quick shake of her head to remove it, she vomited again.

"EEEEWWWW!!! Help me!!!" yelled Marian. "I'm not feeling so good!"

"Breathe through your mouth," I yelled in anticipation of receiving a vomit face plant.

I begged, "Come on, you gotta breathe through your mouth!"

In the small confines of the chicken coop, the five of us pushed away to find shelter from the raining chunky gut soup. Marian retched twice and her stomach's contents launched forward and hit my face. Losing my footing, I rocked backwards, and pushed into Sarge's body. The added pressure on Sarge's side of the coop popped the latch, and she tumbled out of our prison.

"We need to hide," I ordered, wiping the vomit from my face and flicking it on the ground. "Do you see Scooter?"

"He's gone," announced Kimmi happily.

I looked up and Kimmi stood before us like an apparition. She held Dinner's leash in one hand and a lollipop in the other.

"Is this a game?" asked Kimmi. "Looks like fun, well, not the chicken poop and frow up."

Marian scrambled out of the people pile. She squatted before Kimmi, grabbing her shoulders. "Kimmi, where is Scooter? Are you okay?"

Kimmi shook Marian's hands from her shoulders and took

214

several steps back. "Why would you play in poop and frow-up? You stink. That's just not right. Scooter told me never to play in the chicken coop - there's too much poop."

"Stay focused," ordered Marian. "Where is Scooter?"

Kimmi answered, "Aw, Marian. Why are you so upset? Scooter's not here. He went to town to get me tape," answered Kimmi. The hen cocked her head left and right. Growing bored, she circled Kimmi, spiral wrapping the leash around her legs.

Seeing Kimmi and Dinner in the middle of Scooter's lawn mower graveyard seemed surreal.

"Aw, Dinner, you are going to trip me if you do that. Scooter would not be happy if I squished you. Let's go back inside to watch TV," said Kimmi, more to herself than to us.

Sarge said, "Wait. Why don't you stay with us? You can tell us about your adventures with Scooter. Why don't you start with how Scooter brought you here?"

Kimmi grabbed a mower shell and sat on it like a chair. She answered, "Well." She picked up Dinner and began petting her. "Um, well. I was hiding the pine cone when I noticed Scooter's van. Scooter always has candy and my tummy told me it was time for candy. So, I walked to Scooter's van and asked him for some. But he didn't have any so he said he was going to take me to get some. Wasn't that nice? He really is a nice guy."

Marian asked, "What happened then?"

"Ya know, Marian," started Kimmi, turning her head to the right. "You *never* wanted to know about what I done before." Kimmi hesitated before she asked, "Are you okay?"

"Ah you know. I just missed you," Marian answered.

"Me, too," I piped.

Julie and Jess answered in unison, "Me too."

Kimmi looked at Sarge, "Well, Miss Sarge. Did you miss me too?"

"Of course sweetheart. Are you sure Scooter is gone?" answered Sarge.

Kimmi nodded her head and stated, "He told me he needed to get some peace and quiet so he was going to get me tape for my pie hole. I told him that I liked pie."

Interrupting the conversation Jess said, "We better get out of here before Scooter comes back?"

"Why?" asked Kimmi. "It's fun here. There's all sorts of things to do. "She paused and added, "But I do miss Mommy. Let me go inside and get my stuff. I'm just telling you - I'm taking Dinner home. He's my new bestest friend."

Marian asked, "What stuff could you possibly have?"

"Miss Marian Dander! I have stuff!" yelled Kimmi, tugging Dinner's leash and walking into the trailer.

"We got to follow her," I said, getting up from the ground.

I jumped two steps at a time to make sure I arrived directly behind Kimmi. Who is to say what might be in the trailer? Stuffed gophers wearing tutus? Boobie traps lined with peanut butter cookies? Whipped cream on a log of poo? But what I saw surprised me.

Except for the intermittent piles of chicken manure, the trailer looked like an interior decorator had tapped a magic wand and created a haven for the rich and famous. The interior of the trailer was bathed in rich beiges and golds. The blue leather couch and love seat in the living room made the earth tones pop. With the throw pillows, the furniture setting presented a variety of textures which looked poised for a magazine photo shoot.

"What the hell?" uttered Jess as he made his way into the trailer.

Julie added, "Never would have guessed this."

"Well, well," added Sarge.

Kimmi stared at the four of us and answered, "I know. Isn't he cute?"

I gave Kimmi a quizzical look and she answered, "Dinner! Isn't he cute? I just love the way he follows me and then pecks at the carpet like it's a worm."

Sarge walked past us and grabbed the roll of paper towels. She dipped her entire head under the kitchen faucet and washed the vomit from her face and neck. The rest of us followed her actions.

Then Sarge began searching through the kitchen cabinets. Periodically she shuffled through the cabinet contents and would then go to the next cabinet. She moved from the kitchen into a room set just off the kitchen.

"Hey, Sarge! Why are you going into Scooter's room? He really don't like no buddies going into his room. He's weal par- ticklar about his room," instructed Kimmi.

Sarge responded, "Why do you say that?"

"That's silly. Cause he says he's real par- tick-lar about his room. He must have told me a bazillion times to stay out of his room."

Sarge walked back to Kimmi and asked, "Did you ever find anything in his room that was interesting?"

Kimmi rolled her eyes. "Pleeeze. He don't have nothing interesting except books. Only he don't call them books he calls them 'windows into his soul.' Well, one time, I tried drawing Dinner in one of his windows and he got his panties into a real tight ball. One time he twisted so many times he got two balls."

"So you drew in his books?" asked Sarge.

Kimmi rolled her eyes, "Scooter called them his 'windows into his...'"

"soul," finished Sarge. "I wonder."

She paused. It was evident her brain activity warped into overdrive.

Sarge's eye went up and she asked, "Do you want to show me where he kept his journals - I mean windows into his soul?"

"Naw, better not," answered Kimmi. "Scooter would get mad."

"What if we play the hot and cold game?" Sarge asked.

"Oooooo! I love playing the hot and cold game!"

Sarge swirled around and walked to Scooter's room. Kimmi

hollered, "You are getting warmer. Ooo, Sarge, you are good at this game!"

We followed Sarge and Kimmi. Scooter's bedroom was as impeccable as the living area. Turquoise and a soft shade of gray accented the oak bookshelves that lined every wall except where the queen size bed graced the wall. A variety of pillows lined the headboard. Each pillow added enough color to make the turquoise wall color gently appear like an oasis for relaxation.

The sound of turning pages jerked me from my looking around the room. Sarge had pulled one of the books from the shelf.

Kimmi announced, "You found Scooter's windows! Good job, Sarge."

Sarge uttered a grunt and continued flipping through the soulful window journals. When she flipped through the second journal, a photo fluttered to the carpet. Marian retrieved it. I watched as she turned the photo right and left before she grimaced like someone round-housed her face.

"OH MY!!!" she yelled, allowing the photo to flutter back to the carpet.

Before I could grab the picture, Kimmi grabbed it, eyeballed it, and tossed it back to the carpet. She said lightly, "Oh, it's just mommy with a monkey. I've seen lots of these zoo pictures."

This time I grabbed the picture and gave it a once over, followed by a twice over, and finished my visual perusing with a violent gagging reaction.

"What's wrong? asked Julie.

"It's the picture. That monkey...well, it's not a monkey with Mrs. Dander. It's Scooter."

Julie responded, "Is he wearing a monkey costume?"

I closed my eyes and tried to erase the image with no avail. I responded, "No - um- it- well, it was Scooter with what looked like a tail doing arm curls."

"No way," said Jess. He scooped up the picture and turned it end over end. A range of emotions crossed his face starting with confusion and followed by concern.

He meekly asked, "Does THAT always look like a curled tail when a man gets older?"

"Let me see that," interrupted Sarge, barreling her way into the group. She looked at the picture and turned it right and left before turning it end over end.

"Well in all my days, I've never seen a man's part grip a can of hair spray...maybe a pencil but most certainly not hairspray. Jeeze, that's the hairspray we sell at Regina's Grocery. It has a really good price plus it has twenty more ounces that that other brand."

Chapter Twenty-Three

Explosion

A second later, an explosion rocked the trailer, and the five of us hit the carpet. Even Dinner covered her head with her wings.

"Intruders!" screamed Kimmi. "Someone didn't go around the brick. We gotta get in the bunker!"

I answered, "What?"

Kimmi responded in a voice eerily similar to Scooter's. "We got to get into the bunker,"

"Explain what you mean Kimmi," said Sarge.

"Intruders!" Kimmi said, pointing out the window to the smoke pluming into the sky. "They are coming. We gotta get in the bunker."

She tossed a rug away from the side of Scooter's bed revealing a metal hatch built into the floor. Kimmi gripped the latch and pulled.

"It's not moving!" she yelled. "Help me! They are coming!"

Jess moved Kimmi out of the way and yanked the hatch open, revealing stairs descending into what looked like a cellar.

"Why did you do that?" I asked.

Jess took two steps down, turned, and grabbed Julie's hand, pulling her into the cellar.

He answered, "Think about it. If Scooter rigged a brick to blow up, what did he do to this trailer?"

That was it. The six of us and Dinner herded down the stairs, and Sarge pulled the hatch closed. A metallic clink sounded, echoing through the bunker. A dim light suddenly cast long shadows into the room as a generator kicked into gear and instantly the light grew stronger, illuminating an area which appeared to be an underground footprint of the trailer.

"Now what?" asked Julie.

The question hung in the air. We craned our necks around the bunker. Canned food, bottled water and "windows into the soul" filled every bit of wall space except for a tiny kitchenette and a storage area. The six of us and Dinner surveyed the area, each in our own way. Kimmi skipped around the room, pulling Dinner behind her. At times, she pulled so hard an angry 'cluck cluck' reverberated through the room. Sarge fingered through Scooter's journals and periodically her finger stopped and read an interesting tidbit. Marian stood shell shocked and slowly turned in a jerky clockwise motion. Julie, Jess, and I made our way to a storage area. The area seemed more cave-like than storage. The odd shape of the area seemed curious. Stooping to enter the area, Jess moved mower blades and other mowing paraphernalia. Slowly, we made our way deeper and deeper into what we thought was a storage area, but I realized it was labyrinth of tunnels. The deeper we travelled, the lower and lower the ceiling. Finally, we resorted to crawling on our hands and knees to avoid smacking our heads.

Julie whispered, "I can't go any further. I'm getting claustrophobic. I'm going back."

"You okay babe?" asked Jess.

He slid his arm around her shoulder, giving her a quick squeeze and a smile. Julie began crawling back out. Jess followed her lead.

"No Jess. Stay with Raine - I'll be fine."

"Are you sure? Babe, you might need me."

The dialogue made me feel nauseated. "Cut it out! You two are grossing me out. Jess - either stay or get out. But I'm going to check out this area. This may be the way to get out of here without anything blowing up."

"I'll stay, but Julie," he responded.

221

"Really, Jess, I'll be okay. Take care of Raine," she answered.

"Okay, you two. No one will be taking care of me. I take care of myself. You, Jess, have already taken care of Julie and you see where that got you."

Julie huffed, "Raine that's not nice. You can be such a bi."

Jess snapped, "Julie! Don't say that! The babies will hear you. Remember, Dr. Spock says."

"Who the hell is Dr. Spock? Don't you mean Dr. Pooley?"

Answering in a fatherly manner, Jess responded, "Dr. Spock is a doctor who wrote a book on babies and child care. Julie and I have been reading the book so that we are good parents."

"Whatever," I answered.

Jess and I continued crawling forward until we had to position ourselves one in front of the other. Jess took the lead. Since light was limited, I felt very odd trying to stay close to him without sticking my nose in his butt crack.

I mused, "I wonder why Scooter added this space. He never did anything without a ..."

"Be quiet. I hear something coming at us," commanded Jess in a whisper.

I stopped talking.

He commanded again, "Raine, go and grab Dinner."

"What?" I whispered.

"Grab Dinner. We can put Dinner in the tunnel, and she will meet up with whoever or whatever is coming this way. Chickens don't like to be surprised."

I crawled backwards and made my way to the light and Dinner. As I entered the common area I asked, "Hey, Kimmi, could I take Dinner for a walk?"

Kimmi looked around and said, "Sure. I'll see you in a minute. This place is small."

"No worries," I responded. "I'll take her around several times."

With Dinner in tow, I made my way back. Dinner must have

sensed the tunnels lead to the outside because she began leading me. By the time we neared Jess, she was running into the hole. Jess tried to grab her but she slipped between his fingers before he was able to release the leash.

We could still hear the movement of someone or something coming toward us, but now, we could also hear the scraping of little nails and an occasional cluck, cluck. At that moment, all we could do was wait until the moment Dinner met the intruder.

Within several seconds a screech and cluck collided. This was followed by a feminine, "What the -" and a cluck, cluck!

It sounded like rolling and grabbing and pecking and perhaps biting. The intruder was definitely coming our way, and it sounded a lot like Mrs. Dander. Within seconds of the collision, we could see a small pen light shadowing a crawling, struggling person toward us. The light provided us with just enough illumination to show a green been shaped body - Mrs. Dander - and she did not look happy.

My heart triple tapped in my chest and I began backing up slightly faster than Jess. Apparently, he felt the same thumping within his chest. I don't think Mrs. Dander realized someone was near the tunnel's entrance. We heard her call in a whiney lovey-dovey voice, "Scoooootterrrr, Dinner got loose. Don't worry, I got him. Baby, I'm here just like we planned."

By the time she moved from the tunnel to the open area, six people stared at her grand entrance.

"Mommy!" yelled Kimmi, running and hugging her mother.

"Mother?" questioned Marian.

Sarge huffed, "Don't that beat all."

"Where's Scooter?" Mrs. Dander replied.

Kimmi just asked, "What do you mean? Where's Scooter? Mommy? How are we supposed to get out of here if Scooter isn't here? Mommy? Answer me!"

Mrs. Dander looked at Kimmi. I almost felt sorry for Mrs. Dander until she began to speak again. "You are not supposed to be here! You need to get out before Scooter finds you here...!"

Marian interrupted her tirade and yelled back, "And just what do you suppose we do? We are locked in here!"

"You will crawl out the same way I got in here!"

I think the seven of us had the same thought because we looked at Sarge and her oversized butt.

Kimmi provided the sentiments we all felt saying, "I don't think that will work. Sarge will get stuck like Winnie the Pooh did after he ate so much honey. We will have to starve her to get her out."

Marian added, "You are crazy if you think we are going to crawl out of here. Why aren't you acting like a mother instead of a horny slut?"

"Don't you ever talk to me like that!" Mrs. Dander belted back. As she responded to Marian, she took two steps forward and raised her hand to smack her. Jess went into his karate ninja mojo moves and laid Mrs. Dander out on the ground. Then he pinned her to the floor to discourage an attempt to plant another attempted smack down.

He may have been restricted her body, but her mouth verbally karate chopped the sound waves. She ripped loose an ear splitting scream.

"Julie, get back!" shouted Jess protectively.

Through the ruckus a metal pounding pierced the air. Mrs. Dander yelled, "Be quiet. They can't know we are here. It will ruin everything!"

Julie added, "Sort of a little too late for that."

At that moment, the metal hatch opened, and Officer Mahoney, holding a gun, slowly made his way down the stairs.

He shouted, "Put your hands up and don't move!"

His gaze swept the room and he uttered, "I am so tired of dealing with you folks. How the heck did you get down here?"

Kimmi answered for the group, "Someone runned over the brick and it blowed up. Scooter told me that when it blows up that I need to get in the bunker."

224

By the time Kimmi finished explaining, Officer Mahoney was joined by several other police officers, including Officer Matey.

"Raine, why is Jess holding down Mrs. Dander?" asked Officer Matey.

Julie answered for Raine, "Mrs. Dander was trying to hit Marian and Jess came to the rescue."

Officer Matey's eyebrow lifted and he asked, "Mrs. Dander is this true?"

She lifted her head slightly and asked, "Where's Scooter? This is not the way it was supposed to turn out."

Officer Mahoney asked, "What do you mean?"

"Scooter and I are supposed to get married. We were going to get married. Where's Scooter?"

"Mrs. Dander, did you know Scooter was going to get Kimmi from the park?"

"Don't be stupid. Of course, I knew."

Officer Mahoney said, "Officer Matey, would you take Kimmi outside to see the chickens. Marian and the rest of you, please go out too. I need a moment with Mrs. Dander."

Officer Matey extended his hand to Kimmi. She shot him an icy glare, twisted around, dashed into the storage area, and peeked out from around the mower blades.

I looked at Julie and she looked at me. We knew what was about the happen. The officer went after her. With each step forward he made, Kimmi went deeper into the storage area and finally began her descent into the tunnel. Officer Matey made a flying leap and grabbed Kimmi's foot just before she disappeared.

As the officer pulled Kimmi out of the tunnel, she screamed, "I'm not supposed to leave. Scooter is going to take Mommy and me to a new place to live. This will be a place where we can live like a real family."

Julie and I looked at each other again and waited for Marian to react. She squatted near her mother's face and asked, "What the hell does that mean, Mother?"

"Don't you dare talk to me like that!"

"I'll talk to you anyway I want. Were you going to leave me and go off with Scooter and Kimmi?"

Mrs. Dander's eyes cut away and then swiveled back to look directly into Marian's eyes. "Of course not. Kimmi doesn't know what she is talking about."

Julie and I looked at each other again. Jess maintained his restrictive hold on Mrs. Dander, and Sarge just leaned against Scooter's journals and watched. Marian was just about to respond when Officer Matey carried Kimmi out of the storage area.

Kimmi doused fuel on the verbal fire by announcing, "You know, Mommy, you should not lie. Scooter don't like when you don't tell the truth about him and you. Marian..." Kimmi paused and took a breath. "Marian - Scooter don't like you so he don't want you to go with us. He calls you a *wrongful spermizoid.*"

"Mother? Is this true? Does he really call me a *wrongful spermizoid*?"

Mrs. Dander remained unresponsive to the accusatory question. The pause in the dialogue added drama to the situation. I looked at Julie and she looked at me. We smiled slightly - I'm not sure why, but for some reason the circumstance was taking on a slightly sinister yet humorous slant. We took another step back until our backs hugged the journals. Mrs. Dander continued her silence, and Marian asked again, "Mother? Is this true?"

Still gripping Kimmi, Officer Matey said, "You know, Officer Mahoney and I would love to know why Scooter calls Marian a *wrongful spermizoid.*"

"I bet you would," grumbled Mrs. Dander.

"I'm waiting, Mother!"

Several other officers made their way into the bunker. One officer announced, "Okay folks, let's get out of here and make sense of the situation at the station."

"I'm not leaving until my mother gives me an answer."

Kimmi blasted, "He don't like you cause you're not his flesh

226

and blood. What does that mean anyway?"

"Mother. Answer me."

"Marian, I have nothing to say."

Julie and I gave each other another slight smile and watched Marian stomp her way up the metal bunker stairs. Officer Matey followed with Kimmi in tow.

"Um, Officers," began Jess. "Just what do you want me to do with her?"

Sarge snorted. Julie and I followed with laughter. Officer Mahoney tried to keep from laughing and failed. The more Sarge snorted, the more the rest of us laughed until finally Mrs. Dander hollered, "That's enough!"

Jess released Mrs. Dander, and she rolled away from Jess and straightened her clothes as she stood. Officer Mahoney tried to help her, but she wrenched away and began her ascent up the stairs.

The rest of us followed her out of the trailer. Police cars were haphazardly parked around the lawnmower graveyard. I watched as Mrs. Dander walked to the closest squad car and stood next to the backdoor of the car.

After a few seconds, she hollered, "I'm waiting! Anyone going to open the door for me?"

Officer Mahoney scrambled to the car and opened the door and said, "Oh, yes, Mrs. Dander."

Mrs. Dander extended her hand and patted the officer on the check saying, "Good boy. Your mother would be proud of your manners. Now, you want to put on my bracelets now or later?"

"Oh right," responded Officer Mahoney as he clicked the hand cuffs around Mrs. Dander's thin wrists.

As the officer tucked Mrs. Dander into the car she hollered, "Scooter, if you can hear me, you better make this right! If you don't…"

SLAM! The car door closed stifling Mrs. Dander's sentence.

Sarge started walking towards her car and the rest of us followed.

Officer Matey announced, "Now folks, we don't have an idea of what is really going on here, so you need to ride with us back to the station. It will only be until we can sort this out. We were funneled into the remaining police cars, and we arrived downtown in the caravan of cars.

Kimmi skipped from the police car and hopped up the police department steps. She moved to a small water fountain and balanced on its ledge. She looked down and spotted the wishing coins, and she squatted and began to fish out the money. I watched her and envied her oblivion to this warped situation. Granny would have called it canned fruit.

Chapter Twenty-Four

Family

"Kimmi, I am so glad you are okay," announced Dander who rounded the edge of the building.

Kimmi's head bounced up, and she asked, "Why wouldn't I be?"

"Well, when you disappeared from the park, I got scared."

"That's silly," responded Kimmi as she began walking towards Dander.

"Kimmi!" barked Scooter. "Geeet Awwway from that man!"

Dander responded, "No, you come to me."

Even though Scooter's hands were cuffed behind him, he motioned for Kimmi to come his way.

Kimmi looked from Dander to Scooter. About that time, a handcuffed Mrs. Dander walked into the scene. Kimmi stopped, turned to her mother, and asked, "Mommy? What do I do?"

"Go to your father," announced Mrs. Dander.

Kimmi started towards Dander but only took two steps before Mrs. Dander irritatedly stated, "Not him. Your real dad."

"Mommy?" questioned Kimmi, cocking her head in confusion. She continued, "What do you mean?"

"Go to Scooter – he's your real dad," answered Mrs. Dander, who looked at Dander with a deep rich satisfaction in knowing that she speared his heart with her words.

"Mommy?" questioned Kimmi, in more of a painful cry than question.

The police officer ushered Mrs. Dander into the booking area.

Mrs. Dander hollered one last directive before the door closed, "Kimmi, just remember, Scooter and I are your real parents."

Kimmi took in her words and crumpled to the ground. Scooter tried to go to her, but the officer dragged him into booking. Dander knelt beside Kimmi and rubbed her back until she launched into his arms.

"Daddy, what does that all mean? You are my real daddy, right?"

"Sweetheart, I am your daddy, now and forever."

He lifted and wrapped her in his arms. My mom rushed over and added her arms to the hug. Kimmi looked at my mom and asked, "Are you my real mom, too? I am so confused? Who are my real family, anyway?"

I felt Kimmi's pain. Not knowing my dad most of my life often left me wondering about my real family. In some ways, I was jealous of the love wrapped around Kimmi. My emotional side wanted to layer another hug around Kimmi, but my mind screamed there was no way I was going to become involved in the Dander hug sandwich.

The rest of the evening was a blur. We were questioned, and within a few hours, everyone except Mrs. Dander and Scooter, were allowed to leave the station. While Mrs. Dander enjoyed the finer things of jailhouse life, such as a cold cell, I figured Dander and my mom would return to Dander's house. I had hoped life would continue like before the principal's baby daddy reveal.

*****

"What are they doing now?" asked Granny after she had made herself a fresh cup of coffee. She sat in one of the four chairs positioned in front of a window facing the garage.

Kimmi cleared her throat and said newscaster like, "New Mommy pulled out some of that rusty treasure and is holding it up to Daddy. He likes it cause he put it in the back of the El Kaminnow.

What's a El Kaminnow anyway?"

"Yeah, what is an El Camino really? It looks like something between a car and a truck." asked Marian.

"You three don't know a classic truck when you see one. It may be small, but it's a statement vehicle. That's Grandpa Perth's muscle car. He spent hours juicing up the motor just so he could take me for a ride on the wild side."

"Couldn't be that wild if the truck barely holds one person or two small people," I added.

"Very funny," responded Granny. She paused and added, "What have those two found now? I have not seen that in years."

"What the heck is that?" I asked.

Granny chuckled and replied, "Oh that's Grandpa Perth's bedpan."

"Why would you need a pan in a bed?" asked Kimmi.

Marian snorted, "You don't know anything do you?"

"I know things," whined Kimmi. "...just cause I don't know what a bedpan is don't mean I don't know things."

"Kimmi, when people get sick, sometimes they can't make it to the bathroom, so they *GO* in the bedpan," explained Granny.

"Like pee?" giggled Kimmi.

I whispered, "And poo poo."

Kimmi began laughing. "But what happens if you fart a big one and the GO splats on the sheets?"

Granny interrupted the laughing, "Okay, Kimmi, that's enough. I don't like to remember Grandpa Perth's last few months."

"Oh," sadly stated Kimmi. "I'm sorry "

"That's okay. But I do wonder what those two are going to make out of it."

"Based on what we have been watching," I replied. "They will probably make the bedpan into a planter."

Marian snickered adding, "Planter – no way, it will probably be a hat or bottom of a guitar."

I added, "Or a potato soup server."

"Ya know, you two have good ideas. Maybe you should help Daddy and new Mommy with their rusty treasures," giggled Kimmi.

Granny added, "I would not want to touch that stuff. It's been out there a long time. Who would have ever thought someone could made something new out of the junk?"

Marian grunted in disgust. "I know. You would think we could have moved back into our old house, but nooooo, they want to make the house into a store to sell their repurposed stuff. Who would ever want to buy it?"

The four of us continued watching Dander and my mom dig through the Granny's hoarded trash. After several minutes, a rake, windmill blades, and a lawn mower were added to the pile of rusty treasure in the back of Mom's El Camino.

"Shhh. I didn't want to tell you this, but I gotta secret. I heared Daddy and new Mommy talking about our house being contam-men-ated," whispered Kimmi.

Granny's eyebrow raised and she whispered back, "By what?"

Kimmi leaned in and cupped her hands to her mouth, "New Mommy said Scooter and Mrs. Dander had something called monkey sex in the house which left eeveil growing on the walls. By the way, what is monkey sex?"

Granny snorted.

Marian covered her eyes and gagged.

I, on the other hand, laughed until I coughed.

Finally, Granny answered, "Monkey sex is when the things happen in a house which cause germs to grow."

"Germs on the walls? OHHH!" reacted Kimmi. "Germs are what grow on my hands when I don't wash after poopin'!"

A loud boom from the ceiling interrupted. We heard Julie call down, "Be quiet! I'm trying to take a nap."

Kimmi whispered, "I think Julie needs to put the bedpan over her head to block the noise. Then maybe she can sleep."

Granny smiled and walked to her recliner. She grabbed the

Daily News and said, "Let's be quiet and let her sleep. She needs her rest."

She leafed through several pages and then hovered over an article. Once again her mind flipped the track and she began yelling, "Just what the heck do they know?"

Granny flung the newspaper to the ground and left the house, slamming the front door in her wake. I grabbed the newspaper and read:

Couple Sets Fire - In More Ways than One

Runge, Texas finally has the answer to who set the fire at Runge High School. Grace Dander and Shelton Ramsey set the fire as part of an elaborate plan to cover their love affair. Grace Dander, Principal Dander's wife, and her lover, Shelton Ramsey, aka Scooter, were arrested for kidnapping Kimmi Dander from Crampton Park. According to Officer Matey, Mrs. Dander and Scooter spent years weaving an elaborate story to cover the long time affair between Grace Dander and Shelton Ramsey. As part of the plan, a fire was set at Runge High School causing a large amount of damage. Court date is two days after Mr. and Mrs. Dander will be legally declared divorced. More charges against Grace Dander and Shelton Ramsey will soon be filed.

One final note: This reporter discovered that another high school student has turned up pregnant – and that student lives in a home with Principal Dander, so who else wants to know who's the daddy?

I felt sucker punched. It is not that I truly believe that the town of Runge would believe the reporter's assertions, but people see things in black and white and words become truth and no future words clear the lies. How was I going to tell Julie? How would she take this news? Would anyone in Runge ever believe that Julie's twins were actually Jess's? For the rest of the twins' lives, 'who's the daddy?' rumors would surround them. It was at that moment I decided to tell Julie about the newspaper article before she could hear it from anyone else. Unfortunately, I did not get the chance.

Granny opened the front door. But it was then, I heard Julie's dad, "Where is my whore?"

The back door slammed and Dander barreled his way into the room. "Wayne, get out of Granny's house. You can't take Julie!"

"Why? You want to keep screwin' her? I saw the paper. You think you can pick any student you want just so you can have your way with them?"

Dander yelled, "Julie, *don't* come down here! And Marian, call the police."

"I'm only getting what belongs to me." He presented his gun and then shoved Granny to the side. He eyed the stairs and climbed them, two steps with each bound.

"Daddy! NO!" screamed Julie from upstairs. "You are going to hurt the babies."

Mr. Twain appeared, pulling Julie down the stairs by her hair. She struggled to keep her feet under her, but half the time her body slid across the floor.

I heard the car door slam and Julie left.

For months I heard nothing, until later, I received a slice of cheese in the mail with the attached note: 'Sister Friends, Julie'. I didn't know where she was, but I did know she was okay. Months later, Sarge announced she had adopted twins. She named one Robin and the other Jay.

My world continued with school, and my mom and Dander opened a junk business called Rusty Treasures.

*****

I closed the yearbook, and looked up at Julie.

She sniffed and wiped away a tear, "I think often about the day I added my babies to Sarge's circle."

"She has been quite a good momma to your kids," I added.

Nodding her head, Julie smiled, "It was the moment I placed the twins in Sarge's lap that I decided to become a teacher. I knew that it would allow me the opportunity to work with kids and guide them through tough patches in life."

"Speaking of tough patches – how is dear old Dad?" I asked Julie.

"From what mom says, he's loving his new cellmate."

"Really?"

"Apparently, it's Scooter."

"Are you kidding me?" I smiled thinking about Scooter's affection for monkey sex.

Julie laughed and commented, "I guess I could tell you about some of Scooter and my dad's issues living in a small area. Heck it might even help you with Granny's Wisdom."

"It might. You never know when I'll get a letter from someone requiring advice about a sexual deviant and anger management. You know all the strange events in my life made me want to write."

Julie laughed, "That's why you are such a great advice columnist. You have rolled in the gutter of life."

"No, Julie, I've have not rolled in the gutter of life. I've rolled in the rotten fruit of Runge. And speaking of rolling, let's talk about your date with Officer Matey."

"Raine, how did you know I have a date with him?"

"Sister-friends always know. Besides, your cell phone keeps ringing and a picture of Matey keeps popping up on the display."

Julie rolled her eyes and answered, "Okay, you got me. I have a date with him. Actually, I have been dating him."

"Wait, you and the Matey?" I peeled back my front teeth and laughed a mule-mouthed laugh fitting for only the best of friends. "So, you have kept this a secret from me."

"Yup," answered Julie. "And other things."

"What? What do you mean *other things*? Between you and Matey or other things?"

Julie snickered, "Oh, girl, what I have to tell you will give you three years of good advice columns."

We talked and laughed late into the night. Periodically, I did secretly jot down notes for my next advice column. It was at that moment I realized my sister-friendship was taking on a new life - one that transcends time, pimples, and morphs into a new zone - cellulite, and varicose veins.

Chapter Twenty-Five

Ronda and Pam

Although Unkept Promises is not a true story, my lifelong friendship with my best friend, Ronda, is real. Somehow, someway we made it through puberty – gosh I could tell you some stories when we learned about using monthly combat gear. Shhh! Don't tell Ronda I wrote that! Personally, I think she still needs therapy about the pictures on the box of tampons.

And now, we are in menopause. I've got a varicose map of Texas on each leg and some sort of growth indicating where I currently stand. Ronda has hormonal migraines with an accent of dry skin which I think looks like elephant feet. Don't tell her I wrote that either!

We don't live in the same city, but when we talk it's like we never left each other. She may not be related by blood, but I choose her for life as my sister-friend – and that is a kept promise.

Meet the Author

Pamela Edge

Growing up with two overgrown brothers, Darrell, 6'5", and Norman, 6'4", has made her develop a sense of humor and a fast 50-yard dash. Add the element of spending much of her childhood in a small town infused a unique perspective into her writing. Pamela Edge has written for a variety of magazines and educational books.

Made in the USA
Middletown, DE
29 October 2023

41415174R00136